The
BIG
DIG

The BIG DIG

NIMBUS
PUBLISHING
— NIMBUS.CA —

Lisa Harrington

Praise for
Lisa Harrington

The Goodbye Girls

"Harrington shines in this novel where two best friends—who couldn't be more different—navigate the struggles of high school drama, family, and friendships.... Refreshing and inspiring. The author offers a nuanced perspective on teen angst and relationships."

–School Library Journal

"A novel for any high-schooler who grew up loving the kids-on-a-mission tales of Andrew Clements, this fast read is filled with characters you can root for."

–Booklist

"There is a lot to like about *The Goodbye Girls*. It's topical, doesn't take any easy outs, and it's a fast, unsentimental read—whether you're in high school or just remember it well."

–Quill & Quire

"Funny the mess people can make of their love lives—or at least it is in *The Goodbye Girls*, Lisa Harrington's hilarious deep dive into the chaos of high school romance and revenge."

–Vicki Grant, award-winning author
of *36 Questions that Changed My Mind About You*

"Lisa Harrington is the Queen of Dialogue. Her words pull you into the teenage world with an effortless, snappy sense of humour, and realistic portrayal of the ups and downs of friendships and family. She makes writing look easy."

–Daphne Greer, Silver Birch–shortlisted
author of *Jacob's Landing* and *Finding Grace*

"Lisa Harrington's teen dialogue is always spot on and doesn't disappoint in her latest offering. Paired with a fast-paced plot that expertly weaves in deeper layers of family secrets and best-friend drama, *The Goodbye Girls* holds you in its grip until the end."

–Jo Ann Yhard, author of *Lost on Brier Island*

Live to Tell

*Winner: White Pine, Ann Connor Brimer,
and SYRCA Snow Willow Awards*

"Beautifully constructed.... Harrington does a confident job of balancing suspense and teenage angst."

–Toronto Star

"An intense, fast-paced, disquieting book."

–Atlantic Books Today

"As satisfying as it is for a reader to solve a mystery before the author provides the "reveal." even more satisfying is marvelling at the ability of an author to lead readers down the garden path while, at the same time, providing them with road signs telling them that they are not going in the right direction. A terrific read!"

–Canadian Review of Materials

Rattled

"[An] excellent debut novel."

–Canadian Review of Materials

Twisted

"Through convincing dialogue and well-paced scenes, Harrington captures the right balance of romance, self-discovery, and adolescent anxiety."

–National Reading Campaign

Nimbus Publishing Limited
3660 Strawberry Hill St, Halifax, NS, B3K 5A9
(902) 455-4286 nimbus.ca

Printed and bound in Canada
NB1425

This story is a work of fiction. Names characters, incidents, and places, including organizations and institutions, either are the product of the author's imagination or are used fictitiously.

Cover Design: Colin Smith, CS Design
Editor: Penelope Jackson
Editor for the press: Whitney Moran

Library and Archives Canada Cataloguing in Publication

Title: The big dig / Lisa Harrington.
Names: Harrington, Lisa, author.
Identifiers: Canadiana (print) 20189068574 | Canadiana (ebook) 20189068582 | ISBN 9781771087544 (softcover) ISBN 9781771087551 (HTML)
Classification: LCC PS8615.A7473 B54 2019 | DDC jC813/.6—dc23

Nimbus Publishing acknowledges the financial support for its publishing activities from the Government of Canada, the Canada Council for the Arts, and from the Province of Nova Scotia. We are pleased to work in partnership with the Province of Nova Scotia to develop and promote our creative industries for the benefit of all Nova Scotians.

Acknowledgements

The Big Dig was a long time in the making—the first version conceived over twelve years ago—therefore, there are many people to thank. From fiercely loyal friends, some whom typed up my manuscript from handwritten pages (I couldn't type; still can't, really) to the anonymous judges of the Atlantic Writing Competition who gave me positive, constructive feedback, to Norene Smiley, whose "Writing for Children" workshop changed my life.

My family—Ross, Lexi, and William: your constant support and encouragement means everything. And Hermione: sometimes you're stinky, but I wouldn't want anyone else to keep me company when I'm writing.

My editor—Penelope Jackson: this is our third project together, and it's like working with an old friend. To Whitney Moran, Emily MacKinnon, and the entire team at Nimbus: thank you for all that you do and for making me feel like family.

My writing group—Daphne Greer, Graham Bullock, Joann Yhard, Lexi Harrington, and Jennifer Thorne: I know you are bleary eyed from all the versions and read-throughs of this story, but I could not have done it without you guys. And an extra thank you to my daughter, Lexi, who had to talk me off the ledge more than once.

Lastly I would like to thank my mother, Donna, and my grandmother, Josie. They were the inspiration for this story and I am forever grateful for everything they taught me, and for the time we had together. I wish it could have been longer. I wonder what they would say if they could see me now....

PROLOGUE

May 1976

"UH-OH." LUCY CRINGED AS THE SCREEN DOOR slammed behind her.

"Lucy!" her mom shouted from the kitchen. "How many times do I have to remind you about that door?"

"Sorry!" She shrugged off her jacket, tossed it on the banister, and headed down the hall. When she saw her mom, she draped her arms around her and swooned dramatically. "Please, good mother. Don't throw me in the dungeon. I am but an innocent child." She pressed the back of her hand against her forehead.

Her mom raised her eyebrows. "Well, that's a bit much, I think. How about you just empty out the dishwasher and we'll call it even."

"Deal." Lucy pulled open the dishwasher and slid out the bottom rack.

"How was school?"

"Boring."

"You say that every day. How was babysitting, then?"

"Good." Lucy nodded. "Sadie just got two goldfish. She wants me to help her name them."

"How about Laverne and Shirley? You know, after the TV show?"

"Mom. She's four. She doesn't watch *Laverne and Shirley*," Lucy said, scraping something crusty off a fork with her fingernail. "Plus, she thinks they're both boys."

"Oh, okay. That won't work."

"And Mrs. Cooper wants to know if I'll be around this summer to babysit a few days a week."

Her mom made a face.

"What? I will be, won't I?"

"Well...I just don't want you to commit to any kind of schedule."

"Why?"

"You're too young for a summer job. You're only twelve, and I—"

"Almost thirteen."

"Okay, *almost* thirteen, and...I kind of wanted us to do a few things together this summer."

Lucy eyed her suspiciously. "Like what?"

"I haven't quite worked out all the details yet."

"But—"

"Look, I'll be away for at least a week in July, so why don't you just tell her you're good for July, but August is still up in the air."

Lucy scrunched up her nose, then sighed heavily. "Fine."

Her mom folded her arms. "You might actually have fun spending some time with your mother."

"What about Dad?"

"You know your father," she said, waving a hand dismissively through the air. "He says he's going to take time off, but he never does."

"Fine." Lucy sighed again.

"Could you try not to act like I'm punishing you?"

"I'm not," Lucy mumbled.

"Oh. I must have been imagining it." Her mom smiled, then

went over and cracked open the back door. "Linus! Here, Linus, *psss, psss, psss...*" A giant calico cat darted through the door, between her legs, and into the dining room.

"Why does he only come for you?" Lucy asked. "I think he hates me."

"Don't be silly. He hates your father too."

While putting the rest of the dishes away, Lucy noticed the lineup of stomach remedies on the counter—Pepto-Bismol, Mylanta, Tums, Alka-Seltzer. "Are you still feeling sick?"

Her mom unscrewed the top on the Tums and shook out a couple. "Who knew curry could wreak such havoc on my system?" She popped the Tums in her mouth. "I'm starting to think Helen didn't make it right. But then again, I've never had it before, so there's really no way to tell."

"Well, was anyone else from the dinner party sick?"

"No." Her mom chewed thoughtfully on the tablets, then shrugged. "It's probably an ulcer. That would make more sense.... I've rewritten the book ending twice and they're still not happy."

"Don't worry, Mom. Isn't it, like, three times lucky or something?"

"I think it's more like three strikes and you're out."

"Speaking of books." Lucy yanked open the junk drawer and dug out a pen. "They sent the Scholastic book orders home. There's a set of writing paper with butterflies on it."

"That sounds right up your alley."

"I know." Lucy pulled the leaflet from her book bag. "I can use my babysitting money."

"Or I can get it and keep it for your birthday."

"Oh." Lucy pinched her lips together. "Maybe...but I still want some Nancy Drew books, and that sundress we saw at Sears, and those butterfly barrettes."

"Yes." Her mom rolled her eyes. "I have your list."

"I put 'surprises' on there too, don't forget."

"I'm pretty sure I can come up with one or two surprises,"

her mom said. "Have you thought about what you want to do? It'll be here before you know it."

"The usual. Chocolate money-cake—with lots of quarters—and a sleepover."

"That's easy enough, I guess." Her mom filled the teapot and set it on the stove. "Now, before I forget. You have a dentist appointment tomorrow afternoon. I'll pick you up at three-thirty sharp, as soon as the bell rings."

Lucy dropped her chin to her chest. Ugh, the dentist. "Fine." She wrote her name on the book-order form.

"See if there's a thesaurus in there," her mom said, peeking over her shoulder. "You need some more options for *fine*."

LUCY STOOD IN THE SCHOOL'S basketball court checking her watch. *Mom's never late.* A minute later her dad's car pulled up to the curb. He reached over and pushed open the passenger door. "Hop in, pumpkin. I'm taking you to your appointment."

"But where's Mom?"

"She's still feeling a bit under the weather."

CHAPTER 1

April 1977

THE SERVICE WAS A QUIET AFFAIR. LUCY AND SADIE were the only two in attendance. They stood like statues in the empty yard as a biting wind swirled decayed, leftover winter leaves in and around their feet. It felt more like February than April.

Lucy reached down for Sadie's hand and gave it a squeeze. "Ready?"

Sadie sniffed loudly and dragged her arm under her nose, leaving a wet streak on the sleeve of her purple jacket. "I guess so," she whispered.

They both crouched down, gathered up a handful of gravelly dirt, and took a step closer to the tiny grave.

"You go first," Sadie said.

Lucy nodded. "Goodbye, Bert. Happy travels." There was a tinkling sound as the dirt hit the lid of the metal Sucrets tin.

"You were a good fish, Bert," Sadie said hoarsely. "Everyone liked Ernie best because they thought he was the funny one, but you were funny too. And smart. I'm gonna miss you." She sprinkled her handful of dirt over the tin.

Lucy knelt on the grass and shoved the rest of the earth into the grave. It only took a second. The ground was still partly frozen, so she'd only been able to manage the shallowest of holes, barely more than an indent. When it was filled, she patted the top and smoothed out the grapefruit-sized mound.

"Let's go in and warm up," Lucy said, wiping her hands on her pants and collecting the soup spoon she'd used as a shovel. "I'll make you some hot chocolate."

"Beep, please," Sadie said. "It was Bert's favourite."

Lucy raised her eyebrows. "Sure," she said slowly. "Beep it is."

HICCUPPING BACK A SOB, SADIE scrambled up onto a kitchen stool. "He was still alive when I went in to get my Barbies."

"It was just his time," Lucy said gently as she tugged open the fridge door, shuffled some stuff around, and pulled out the carton of Beep.

Sadie tilted her head and frowned. She seemed to be thinking hard. "Was it your mommy's time too?"

Lucy felt the carton slip a bit between her fingers. She licked her lips and swallowed. "Um...yeah. I guess it was."

"Mommy told me your mommy got sick and now she's an angel in heaven. She said it was really sad and—oh no, I forgot."

Lucy's eyes started to sting. She turned away and poured some Beep into a pink cup. Taking a deep breath, she set it in front of Sadie. "Forgot what?"

"I'm not supposed to ask about your mommy," she said, staring down at her lap.

"It's okay, Sadie. I don't mind."

The little girl looked up. "Phew." She reached for her cup and took a noisy slurp. "How come your mommy died? My Aunt Jeannie got sick, but *she* didn't die. She had penonya."

"My mom was a different kind of sick. She was really, *really* sick."

"Do you think Bert was really, *really* sick?"

2

Lucy glanced over at the carton of Beep. "Maybe?"

Sadie sighed loudly. "I wanted to take him for show and tell next week."

"Hmm, let me think. Do you have a picture of Bert?"

Sadie shook her head.

"Well, you could *draw* a picture of him. Show your class, talk about how special he was, how much fun you had together, how much you're going to miss him."

"Is that what you did for show and tell when your mommy died?"

Something caught in Lucy's throat. "No," she said, turning away again. "We don't have show and tell anymore."

There was a commotion in the front hall. Sadie's mom bustled into the kitchen, loaded down with a bunch of paper grocery bags.

"Mommy!" Sadie wailed as she hopped off her stool, ran to her mother, and wrapped her arms around her waist. "Bert's dead! He *died*!"

Sadie's mom shot Lucy a questioning look over the grocery bags. Lucy nodded.

Her face fell. "Oh," she mouthed.

"Here, Mrs. Cooper. I can take those," Lucy said, helping her transfer the bags to the counter.

Mrs. Cooper smiled gratefully, then leaned down to Sadie's level. "I'm so sorry, honey. He lived a long life though, for a goldfish. Way longer than Ernie."

Sadie bobbed her head bravely, unshed tears clinging to her long eyelashes.

"And sorry all this fell on you, Lucy." Mrs. Cooper straightened and dug her wallet out of her purse. "Bad timing."

"Oh, that's all right." Lucy shrugged. "But just so you know, we had a funeral. He's buried in the yard. She wouldn't let me flush him."

Mrs. Cooper rolled her eyes and pressed a five-dollar bill into

3

Lucy's hand. "Yes. I flushed Ernie," she said out the corner of her mouth. "Needless to say, it didn't go over too well."

Lucy grinned as she jammed the money into the back pocket of her cords. "Bye, Sadie. See you Saturday."

"Will you help me draw a picture of Bert for show and tell?"

"Definitely. And you get to stay up until it's perfect."

Sadie smiled wide.

Mrs. Cooper followed Lucy to the door. "So, Lucy. I know it's still a couple months away, and, well, you've had a lot going on, but I'm looking for some part-time childcare again for Sadie through the summer. Do you think you might be available?"

Lucy's brain immediately kicked into overdrive. She'd seen a pamphlet in her dad's office about the All City Band Summer Camp. And last she heard, icky Jean Pierre from her clarinet class was going. "You're way too flat, *Lucy*. You're using the wrong size reed, *Lucy*." She wanted to smash her clarinet over his head every time he opened his mouth. Then there was always this huge puddle of spit on the floor in front of his chair. A whole summer of that? No. Way. "Yeah, I'll do it. I have no plans."

"Wonderful!" Mrs. Cooper said. "But you talk to your dad first and get back to me when you can."

"Sure."

LUCY STOPPED THE SCREEN DOOR with her butt so it wouldn't slam. She shook off her jacket, hung it in the hall closet, and made her way to the kitchen. As she dumped her book bag on the table, she noticed steam shooting out of the kettle simmering on the stove—a mug and teabag waited on the counter. Smiling and shaking her head, Lucy tossed the bag into the kettle and turned off the burner. She gave the tea a couple of minutes to steep, then filled the mug and headed off in search of her dad. She wouldn't have to look hard. She knew he'd be in his study. He'd been trying to work from home most afternoons so Lucy wouldn't be alone so much.

"Hi, Dad," Lucy said from the doorway.

He looked up from his desk. "Hi, pumpkin. Did I forget the kettle again?"

Lucy grinned and passed him his mug. "Like you do every day."

He set it on a stack of file folders. "How was babysitting?"

"Good. Well, Sadie's fish died, so not so good for her. Or Bert, the fish, for that matter."

"That's unfortunate."

"For Sadie or the fish?"

"Both, I guess."

Out of habit, Lucy began straightening up her dad's desk. The two of them had fallen into a kind of routine, and so far it had been...okay. The flow of casseroles and baked goods had ended a long time ago. Luckily, Lucy had started the cooking part of Home Ec this term and was managing to recreate the recipes at home. And they usually turned out...okay. They hadn't starved yet. Her dad was a better cook, but even though he was often home, he worked late hours and just forgot a lot of the time. As far as Lucy's laundry and housekeeping skills, they too were...okay. This was her life now. Okay. Dad kept saying things would get better in time, but she wasn't sure she believed him.

She gathered up some crumpled napkins and swept random crumbs off his desk onto a piece of paper. "Did you remember to eat lunch?"

"Toast." He gestured to the paper. "Hence the crumbs."

As she shook the crumbs into the garbage can, she glanced over at him. He looked tired. The corners of his mouth drooped downwards, like he hadn't smiled, really smiled, in a long time.

"Dad. Why don't you take a break for a while? Go lie down or watch golf or something, and I'll start supper."

"No, no. I'm fine. It's just been a long day." He sighed and raked a hand through his hair. "Listen, pumpkin. I should let you know, I had a call this morning. A bit of bad news."

Lisa Harrington

Oddly, Lucy felt no alarm. How bad could the news be? She'd already had the worst news possible. She didn't say anything.

"Gran Irene passed away."

Lucy digested this for a moment. "Oh. That's too bad." She said it because she figured she should. She hadn't known her mom's mom very well and wasn't sure how she should feel about it, or express herself.

"I know it was expected any day, so no great shock, but still." It was like her dad wasn't sure how he should feel about it either.

Right after her mom's death, Lucy's grandmother had suffered another stroke. She'd already had a few over the years, but this one was bad. Lucy and her dad had gone to visit her numerous times in the nursing home. She was pretty sure her grandmother hadn't even been aware they were there, but they'd done it for Mom—it seemed like something she might have wanted them to do.

"The visitation is the day after tomorrow," he said, then a pained look crossed his face. "But it's at the same place we had your mom's, so you don't have to go if you don't want to. It might be a little too soon."

"I'll go." She shrugged. "She was my grandmother, after all."

He frowned. "Are you sure it won't be too much for you?"

Lucy thought about his question. That room. That stuffy room with the blue velvet wingback chairs, the sickening smell from all the flower arrangements, the sad, sympathetic looks from all those people she didn't know...but she'd survived it. And the months since. *Go ahead, world; do your worst. I can take it.* So yeah, she could handle walking back into that room where her mom's casket had been on display. It had been closed, but Lucy had still spent the entire time avoiding it. That was also the room where she had said goodbye for the last time before they took the body away to burn it up in a furnace, leaving only a pile of ashes in a marble box.

"Don't worry, Dad. I'll be fine."

6

CHAPTER 2

"**M**ISS TAPPER?"

Lucy looked up from her math worksheet.

"It's two-thirty," Mrs. Kelly announced. "You're free to go."

Quietly, Lucy cleared off her desk and left the classroom.

Today was her grandmother's visitation at the funeral home.

Halfway down the hall, she stopped at the bathroom and pushed open the door with her shoulder. There was a musty, gross odour mixed with the smell of bleach. Water dripped from some unknown source, echoing loudly in the empty space. She edged along the length of the counter, searching for a part of the mirror that wasn't smeared in foamy pink soap from the dispenser. *Why do people have to write their name on everything? "Cathy was here." I know you were here, Cathy. You're in my class.* The last sink offered the clearest view. She'd had gym right after lunch, which explained the tinge of red still on her cheeks and the escaped strands of hair from her ponytail. Her eyes fell on a forgotten yellow pocket comb with sparkles on the handle lying on top of the paper towel holder. She debated for a moment, then pulled out her elastic and redid her ponytail, leaving the comb and everything else in the bathroom undisturbed. She took a final look in the mirror. Her fingers lightly touched the butterfly resting at her throat, the necklace her mom had given her on her last birthday. She sniffed and blinked a few times. Maybe going back to that funeral home wasn't going to be as easy as she thought.

But she was determined to go. Her mom was gone. Lucy had to go in her place. Her mom would have expected her to.

Two teachers were standing in the hallway by the front office. "Such a shame," one whispered to the other as Lucy walked past. "That family's been through so much."

Lucy looked at them briefly as she pressed her back against the crossbar of the front door. They tilted their heads and smiled at her sympathetically. Lucy didn't smile back.

The wind was out of the north. Bone-chilling. In Nova Scotia, spring was just a cold, damp shiver between winter and summer. A fresh gust of wind made her eyes water. She pulled her coat up tighter around her ears and picked up her pace.

Lucy's father was going to be busy in court most of the day and had wanted her to go to the evening visitation with him after work.

"But Dad, I have a Social Studies project due tomorrow," Lucy had said. "Can't I just go to the afternoon one?"

"No. I don't want you to go alone."

Lucy had tugged on her lip, thinking. "Why can't we just skip the visitation and go to the funeral instead?" That was something Lucy had noticed when her mom died. Acquaintances, people they didn't know that well, had attended one or the other, not both. So it must be an okay thing to do.

"There's no funeral," Dad had said.

"Oh?" Lucy didn't know much about her grandmother, but she *did* know that she had been super religious.

Dad had nodded. "Do you remember Josie? You may have seen her at your mom's funeral."

"Yeah. I met her when I was little. Gran Irene's sister. Deaf.

Kinda wacky. Mom always talked about her."

"That's Josie. Anyhow, it was her idea. Your grandmother's being cremated and Josie wanted the urn for her mantle. Assuming no one objected."

Lucy had raised her eyebrows.

"No one did," Dad had added.

So after Lucy had assured her dad over and over again that she would be perfectly okay to go alone, he had reluctantly agreed to let her attend the afternoon session. *Missing French class doesn't have anything to do with it at all*, Lucy thought slyly to herself as she waited at the crosswalk, but then immediately felt guilty. Guilty because she didn't really feel that sad about her grandmother dying. She did a little, sort of. It was always sad when someone died. But after her mom, Lucy couldn't imagine feeling anything close to that kind of sadness again.

The whine of a siren startled her as an ambulance sped through the intersection. She'd forgotten she had to pass by the hospital to get to the funeral home. *I wonder if they're close together on purpose?*

Her steps slowed as she neared the hospital. She came to a full stop when she was directly across the street. Staring up at the looming brick building, she quickly counted eight windows across the bottom, then six up. The window was empty. When it had been her mom's room, it had been filled with yellow butterflies suspended from a mobile. Lucy had been able to see it from outside every time she came and went. It had made her feel better. She wasn't really sure why.

She couldn't seem to drag her eyes away from that empty window. Who was in there now? Did their kids decorate the room for them? Were they going to die too? Lucy felt that familiar burning, the tears collecting in the rims of her eyes. She had been so good lately, hadn't cried in almost a month. Now she'd have to start keeping track all over again.

As if the sky knew what Lucy was feeling, it started to rain.

Hurrying down the street, she was almost relieved to see the funeral home on the next block.

A blast of warm air hit her in the face as she swung open the heavy wooden door. It took a moment for her eyes to adjust to the dim lighting. She hung up her coat and made her way to the reception room. It looked different than she remembered. Did the carpet always have that dot pattern? Weren't those wingback chairs blue? She frowned, looking around. Shouldn't every detail of that day be tattooed onto her brain? Now that she thought about it, maybe she didn't remember much about that day...or the funeral... or the weeks that followed.

Brushing the damp hair off her forehead, Lucy moved deeper into the room. The suffocating heat and stuffiness was definitely still the same. A sea of grey heads attached to elderly, hunched bodies stretched out before her. She'd only been there for a minute and she'd already counted three walkers and five canes. She guessed the average age to be about a hundred.

She paused in front of a framed picture of her grandmother. It was propped up on an easel surrounded by a wreath of flowers. Lucy studied it, trying to find a family resemblance. There was none that she could see. The ribbon banner read, "Irene Marion Mosher, 1896–1977." Marion. That was her mom's middle name too.

Some kind of ruckus broke out on the other side of the room and caught her attention. It looked like a few old ladies fighting.

Nope. Not fighting. Their walkers just got hooked together.

She found a spot against the wall and let her eyes sweep the room. Not surprisingly, there was no one she recognized. She checked her watch.

When she looked up she saw two old ladies engaged in a conversation. Slowly her eyes widened. One of them had triggered a memory, and Lucy recognized her right away. There was no mistaking that hair, deep reddish-purple. That eyeshadow, robin's-egg blue.

It was Josie, keeper of the urn.

She watched them as they spoke to each other. *You really can't tell she's deaf.*

Her mom had told her Josie had been hit in the head with a baseball bat when she was just a teenager. Lucy still recalled the shudder that travelled through her whole body when she'd heard the story, even though Mom had assured her it had been an accident.

Lucy continued to watch the exchange. She was fascinated by the idea of lip-reading and wondered if Josie was picking up everything the other lady was saying. She remembered her mom telling her how Josie often didn't like to admit when she didn't understand or catch something, so she'd just fake it and never let on. Throw in the fact that she already knew how to speak before she lost her hearing, her speech was pretty much like everyone else's. You'd have to be a detective to ever figure it out.

At that moment, Josie's eyes met Lucy's over the other lady's shoulder. Her face broke into a huge smile as she made her way over to Lucy's spot against the wall.

She stopped short, arms open. Faced with no other option, Lucy leaned forward and gave her a hug. There was a strong smell of menthol, like Vicks VapoRub, that stung Lucy's nose as she was crushed against Josie's woolly cardigan.

At last Josie released her. She stepped back and held her by the shoulders. "I swear you've grown a foot. You look so mature and grown up."

"Thank you," Lucy said, hoping she said it carefully enough for Josie to read her lips.

"Here, come with me and I'll introduce you to everyone. They'd all love to meet Irene's grandbaby."

Lucy shook her head and pressed her back flatly against the wall. "No, thank you." She couldn't think of anything she'd rather do less.

Josie looked at her for a moment. "That's fine, honey." She pulled Lucy snugly against her and began pointing out people around the room—some cousins, some of her grandmother's friends and neighbours. Some names sounded familiar, but most didn't. Lucy just bobbed her head after each name. It was easier than speaking and worrying whether or not Josie could understand her. Plus, she was finding it hard to stay focused. She was paying more attention to Josie's brilliant red lipstick and how it bled into the million tiny wrinkles around her mouth than who Josie was pointing to. That was until Josie said, "Now, there's Ellen over there."

Instantly Lucy snapped to attention. Ellen was her mom's older sister. A long time ago, something big had happened between them and they had never spoken again. *Ever.* Lucy always wondered what could have been so bad. Whatever it was, it must have been Ellen's fault; Lucy couldn't imagine her mom ever doing anything awful enough to make someone *that* mad. But her mom wouldn't talk about it. The odd time it was brought up, she'd change the subject. After a while, no one brought it up anymore.

"Such nasty business," Josie continued, shaking her head. "Never saw two girls more stubborn. What they both needed was a good kick in the arse."

Lucy's eyebrows shot up.

"Sorry," Josie said. "I should probably watch my language, being in the house of the Lord and everything." She frowned and looked around. "Well, I don't know. Is this considered a house of the Lord?"

"I'm not sure," Lucy admitted. She wanted to steer Josie back on track. Though she wasn't keen on meeting Ellen, she definitely wanted at good look at her. "So where did you say Ellen was?"

Craning her neck, she tried to see where Josie had pointed. Josie would know what had happened, know the whole story. Maybe this was her chance to get an answer.

"Say it again, honey."

"Oh, sorry." Lucy made sure she looked directly at Josie. "Where is Ellen?" She tried to follow Josie's finger again but suddenly they were engulfed in what could only be described as a gang of grannies. They turned out to be Josie's bridge club.

Slapping her arms to her sides to make herself as small as possible, Lucy squeezed her way out of the huddle. *So much for that plan.* She moved back to her spot against the wall and waited. But how long should she wait? She still had to stop at the library on the way home. She needed one more book for her Social Studies project. Mrs. Moore was a real stickler for having at least three sources.

All the old ladies were still grouped around Josie. It didn't look like she would be untangled anytime soon. Lucy sighed and made her way out to the front foyer. She pulled on her coat, signed the guestbook, and slipped quietly out the front doors.

The rain turned to drizzle as she walked towards the library. The church clock began to sound. It was four. She stood there for a moment, staring at the massive hands, listening to the booming chimes. It was the same melody as their doorbell at home.

The day her mom died, the doorbell had rung at 6:13 in the morning. Lucy knew right away what had happened. Why else would someone be at the door that early? The voices were muffled, but she was still able to tell it was Mrs. Gardiner. All the ladies in the neighbourhood had set up shifts at the hospital so that Lucy's mom was never alone, day or night.

"She just drifted off, Mike. No pain or anything." Mrs. Gardiner paused and blew her nose. "It was around five o'clock. I figured there was no point waking you. It wasn't like there was anything you could do."

After Lucy had heard the door close, a slow, airy breath leaked out through her mouth. Relief. She couldn't help it. Her heart would no longer skid to a stop every time the phone or doorbell rang, or when she walked into her mom's hospital room. But then that feeling quickly disappeared, replaced with panic.

Instead of stopping, her heart had begun to beat so fast there was a moment when she thought it might explode right out of her chest.

Cold and wet, she jammed her hands into her pockets and ran the rest of the way to the library.

HER DAD'S CAR WAS ALREADY in the driveway by the time she got home. Good. She was starving. Thursday night was hot-dog pizza night. She hoped he had already made up the dough. That was the deal. Whoever got home first made up the dough.

The Kraft Pizza box sat unopened on the counter.

Darn!

As usual, the kettle was simmering away on the stove. Lucy plopped in a teabag, waited, poured a mug of steaming tea, and headed down the hall to her dad's study.

His door was slightly ajar. She heard his voice; he was talking to someone. The mug was burning her hand, but when she tried to switch it to the other hand, some tea dribbled onto the floor. As she was mopping up the spill with her sock, bits of conversation drifted out through the opening. And then her own name oozed around the edge of the door. She inched closer to listen.

"I told you, Scotty, I don't know. Part of me wants to forget the whole thing." Her dad sounded kind of angry.

Pause.

He must be on the phone.

"How do you *think* she's going to react?" There was sarcasm in his voice. "Not to mention, how do you think *he's* going to react?"

Pause.

"Look, I'm just not sure I see the point of—"

Pause.

"Yes, yes, I know. I don't have a better idea, but I need some time to think about it."

Pause.

"No, we'll do it together. I just don't know if I'm ready yet. I'll be in touch."

The hairs on the back of Lucy's neck were standing straight up. When she finally let out the breath she was holding, she noticed a throbbing in her hand. She'd been concentrating so hard on trying to make sense of what her dad was saying, she hadn't noticed that her fingers had practically fused to the hot mug. He was talking about her. Why? Who was Scotty? And who was "he"? And what wasn't her dad ready for?

An eternity passed. Or at least that's what it felt like. *Well, I can't stand here forever.* Good chance she was making a big deal of nothing. She'd just ask him. Whatever it was, he was probably planning on telling her anyway.

She knocked lightly on the door and pushed it open.

Her dad glanced up. Though the conversation had ended ages ago, he was still holding the receiver. A strange look flashed across his face. "Hey. Didn't hear you come home," he said. But his tone was off, like he was trying too hard to sound normal.

Lucy squinted at him, then announced, "Tea," and placed the mug on his desk.

He smiled weakly and set the receiver back in the cradle. "How was the funeral home?"

"Fine, I guess." Her eyes shifted to the phone. "I didn't interrupt, did I?"

"Oh...um...." His Adam's apple bobbed up and down as he swallowed. "No, no. Just work stuff."

She tried again. "New case or something?"

"Yes. No." He made a production of blowing on his tea. "I mean, not mine...Jonathan's...from the office. He wanted to meet me tonight, get my opinion." His eyes stayed on the rim of his mug. "But I don't have time. I've got to go to the visitation."

"Oh." Lucy didn't ask any more questions. She didn't want him to keep lying. "Okay. I'm gonna go work on my project." She backed out of the room, leaving him shuffling and reshuffling a pile of papers.

Her dad never lied to her. Even when her mom was sick and everyone else had avoided giving her a straight answer, he hadn't. He hadn't tried to shelter her or protect her feelings. He had put it all out there and told her the truth.

So why was he lying to her now?

CHAPTER 3

A S THE DAYS PASSED, LUCY KEPT WAITING FOR HER dad to say something like, "Listen, pumpkin, about the other day. That phone call wasn't from Jonathan..." But it didn't happen. And for some reason, she couldn't bring herself to ask him.

She should just forget about it. He was a grownup, after all. He had a right to have his own secrets, things he didn't feel the need to share with her. That was fine; she could live with that. Plus, there was no proof it had anything to do with her. Even as she was telling herself all this, she was shaking her head. *Of course it has something to do with me. I heard my name.*

Three nights in a row, she lay in bed trying to list off every person she'd ever met. Neighbours new and old, people from her dad's work, guys from his basketball team, guys he golfed with, couples he and Mom had played bridge with, relatives, anyone she could remember from her mom's funeral. There was no Scotty.

She began to study her dad every chance she got, in spite of the fact she had no idea what was she looking for. The only thing she noticed was that he seemed distracted, a little on edge. Did it have something to do with that phone call? She knew *she* was distracted by that phone call.

Or maybe he just missed Mom. She knew *she* missed Mom.

It took almost three weeks, but then it finally happened.

Dad stuck his head in her bedroom door. "Hey, pumpkin. Pop down to my study when you're finished, would you? I want to talk to you about something."

He was trying to sound normal, casual, just like he had after that phone call, so she tried too. "Sure, Dad," she said, not looking up from her textbook.

Once he left she sat on the bed tapping her pencil against her scribbler. What was she waiting for? Wasn't this what she wanted?

She stood outside the study door, off to one side and out of her dad's sightline. Why couldn't she shake the feeling that whatever he was going to tell her, she wasn't going to like? After a moment of rocking back and forth on her heels, she squared her shoulders and walked in.

He looked up from the folder in his hand as she plopped herself in the chair that faced his desk.

"That was quick," he said.

Lucy shrugged.

"So, pumpkin, that was some great macaroni casserole you—"

"Dad." She stopped him. "What did you want me for?"

"Well, uh...." He scratched at the stubble on his chin. "I've been meaning to discuss something with you. I've been making some plans."

Lucy scrunched her eyebrows together. "Plans?" Who would have thought that word could sound so ominous?

He nodded slowly, then continued: "School's going to be out soon, so I've been giving some thought as to what I'm going to do with you for the summer."

"What do you mean, *do* with me?"

He held up a hand. "Now, just hear me out. You might be pleasantly surprised."

I doubt it. "Dad, you don't need to make any plans for me. Mrs. Cooper wants me to babysit Sadie for the summer. And I really want to because I'm saving for a new cassette player," Lucy blurted as fast as she could. "And I know what you're going to say: 'Don't you already have one?' But no, I don't. That's a tape recorder. It's not the same thing."

Dad smiled, but only with one side of his mouth. "Luce, honey. This summer I have two huge cases. They're going to take up all my time, involve a lot of travel. I don't want you to be alone."

"But I won't be. I'll be looking after Sadie."

"I think you'll have to tell Mrs. Cooper no."

"*Why?*"

"I told you. I don't want to leave you alone all summer."

And then the brochure about band camp flashed in her head. *Oh god, no. This better not be about that. Maybe Scotty is the camp director or something.*

She crossed her arms. "Is this about band camp?"

He frowned, a confused expression on his face. "No. Not band camp." He paused and leaned back in his chair. "You know, after last summer, your mom in the hospital all those months, both of us in a kind of fog, and well...everything that went with that...."

Lucy felt a glob of something lodge in her throat. He was right. They had been in a kind of fog. It was the sadness—so heavy, so dense.

"I thought it would be good for you to do something completely different," he said. "Like having a kind of do-over."

Do-over? Now it was her turn to look confused.

He sighed. "Every time summer comes around, I don't want you to associate it with your mom getting sick."

"I won't, Dad," she said quietly. Though she didn't know if that was true.

Shifting uncomfortably, he said, "I got a letter from Josie, and she's offered to have you come stay with her for the summer. In Cape John."

What? Once band camp was taken off the table, she'd had no clue what he was going to throw at her, and she certainly hadn't been expecting this. "What?!"

"I know, I know, you're probably not that big on the idea right now."

"*What*?!" It was like she couldn't process his words.

"Just think about it. A change of scenery, getting out of the city for the summer."

Lucy's mouth fell open. He was serious. "Why are you trying to get rid of me?"

"I'm not!" He looked stung. "Don't *ever* think that. It's—"

"But I don't even *know* Josie. I've met her like four times in my whole life!"

"All the more reason to spend some time with her," Dad said reasonably.

"Dad!" She felt an overwhelming urge to stomp her foot, but she was sitting down.

"Lucy." Leaning forward, he suddenly looked extra serious. "I think this summer could be...." It was like he was searching for the right word. "Life altering for you."

"Life altering?" Her chest tightened. "I already had a life-altering summer," she snapped.

For a minute, neither of them said anything.

She felt kind of bad for saying that, and for saying it that way, but she wasn't going down without a fight.

"It's in the middle of nowhere, Dad," she said. "Nothing to do. No mall, no rec centre, no theatre, no friends, no nothing."

He came out from behind his desk, sat on the corner, and placed his hand on her shoulder. "You're overreacting. Cape John is beautiful. It's quiet and peaceful, great beaches, you know how you love to swim. Most people would be jealous."

She jerked her shoulder away. "You said you didn't want me to be alone, but that's exactly what I'll be. Alone."

"No, you won't. You have family there—your mom's family. You should get to know them."

"But I want to go to band camp! Just send me to band camp!"

His eyes narrowed. "I always got the distinct impression you weren't interested in band camp. Are you now telling me you want to go?"

Lucy thought about saying yes, but ended up looking down at her hands clenched in her lap. "But who's going to look after *you*? You know, do the cooking and cleaning?"

"I'm a big boy. You don't need to worry about me."

"But what about Linus? Who's going to look after him?"

"I think I can manage to look after the cat. Remember, you are talking about a cat who hates us and spends ninety-nine percent of his time outside and as far away from us as possible."

Okay, he was right about the cat. "But, but—" She frantically searched for more excuses. She was out. "Please don't make me go," she pleaded. "I'll be homesick, I know it. *Pleeease*, Dad."

"Pumpkin," he said softly. "You'll be with Josie. Remember all those stories your mom told us about her? Now you'll be able to see if they're true."

"I don't care about the stories!"

"Lucy—"

"You know she's deaf, right? How am I supposed to even talk to her?"

"You'll manage. She's an excellent lip—"

"And she swears. Did you know that? She swears a lot. I heard her!"

He tilted his head. "I don't think a few bad words ever killed anyone."

"Wow! That's the kind of role model you want for me?"

"Your mom seemed to turn out okay." He smiled. "*More* than okay."

Throwing her mom into it was a low blow. Lucy lifted her chin. "Well, I'm not going. I'm just not going. You can't make me."

He got that serious look again. "I know this might be hard, but in the end, I think it will be a good thing."

She stubbornly held his gaze even though she felt the prick of tears. "Why are you punishing me?"

"I am *not* punishing you. Just give yourself some time to get used to the idea."

"And if I don't get used to idea?"

Silence.

She mashed her lips together. "If I go and don't like it, can I come home?"

More silence.

"Yeah! I didn't think so!" She shot him an angry glare and stomped out of the study.

When she reached her room, she slammed the door and kicked her garbage can. It smacked into the wall beside her dresser and flipped upside down. Unfortunately, she had emptied her pencil sharpener yesterday, and now that part of her room was covered with a fine film of lead dust and pencil shavings. Kneeling on the floor to clean it up, she started to cry. Frustrated tears mixed with the black mess, making everything even worse.

CHAPTER 4

LUCY KNEW SHE COULD HAVE PUT UP MORE OF A stink—kicked and screamed, maybe erupted into a number of cleverly timed crying fits—but in the end, it would have been a waste of energy. She had seen that look on her dad's face before, the way he had set his jaw. He wasn't changing his mind.

Standing in front of the calendar hanging on the back of her door, she drew an X in black marker, crossing off the days. As each day passed, she felt the life slowly being sucked out of her.

In a kind of zombie state, she made her way back and forth to school. When home, she would barricade herself in her room, determined to avoid any contact with her dad. There was no way she was going to cave and talk to him. Cherry on the sundae was that he didn't seem to notice, which made Lucy think maybe they didn't speak to each other that much.

She stubbornly maintained her silent treatment right through the school's June fun fair, in spite of the fact that her dad volunteered to work the cake walk and they ended up having to spend the entire morning together. And continued it right

Lisa Harrington

through her fourteenth birthday, when she had shaken her head, crossed her arms, and refused to celebrate.

HER BEST FRIEND, SARAH, SAT on Lucy's bed after school one afternoon. "I'm really gonna miss you, Luce. How many days left?"

"Thirteen. I'm gonna miss you, too."

"The rec centre is going to be dead boring without you. And Mom's still making me take swimming lessons." Sarah stuck her finger in her mouth and made a gagging sound. "You know how I hate them."

"I hate them too." Lucy sniffed. "Wish I was taking them with you."

They hugged, resting their heads on each other's shoulders for a bit. Sarah pulled away first. "I finally have your birthday gift." She got up and went to her book bag. "Sorry it's late. I had to wait for the Donovans to pay me. God. They never have the cash. They always book me at least a week ahead. I don't know why they act all confused and caught off guard when they have to pay me. Jeez."

Momentarily pulled out of her funk, Lucy smiled. She really was going to miss Sarah. A *lot*.

Sarah placed a small, brightly wrapped gift in Lucy's lap. Lucy excitedly ripped away the paper. It was the butterfly-shaped stickpin from the jewellery store in the mall that she had had her eye on for ages. *Yes!* But then her dad appeared in her bedroom doorway, causing her smile to immediately straighten into a thin line.

"Why don't you let me take you girls out to the House of Mei Mei for supper?" he asked.

Lucy didn't answer and began tearing up a scrap of wrapping paper into tinier pieces.

"We could even catch a movie first," he added, trying to sound all chipper. "I tell ya, I'd love to see that *Star Wars*."

Lucy rolled her eyes. Who was he kidding? He'd already seen it with the neighbours and had talked non-stop for days about the special effects. She'd already seen it with her friends. Three times. He knew that.

He sighed and leaned against the door frame.

"Oh, come on." Sarah nudged her. "Let's at least do dinner. It's the buffet on Friday nights."

Lucy kept on shredding the wrapping paper.

Her dad sighed again then turned to Sarah. "Tell her we have to do *something* for her birthday. I haven't even given her a gift yet."

"All the egg rolls and honey-garlic spareribs you can eat," Sarah sang.

Lucy's eyes shifted back and forth between Sarah and her dad. "Fine. I'll go, but I'm not talking."

"Great!" Her dad beamed and made a loud clap with his hands.

At the restaurant, they slid into the booth, Lucy and Sarah on one side, her dad on the other. For Sarah's sake, Lucy did manage to grunt out a few words, but they were mostly about her legs sticking to the vinyl bench and the blobs of plum sauce crusted on the table. Her dad presented her with a card containing twenty-five dollars along with the new Bee Gees album. She mumbled a thank you without making eye contact. He paid the cheque and the drive home was even more silent than the dinner. In the privacy of the back seat, Lucy pressed her hands against her cheeks. They felt hot. *God, I'm being such a brat.* But she couldn't seem to stop herself.

LUCY SNAPPED THE CAP BACK on the marker after drawing the last X through Wednesday. Tomorrow. Thursday. Thursday was the day. Though she had been praying for some kind of reprieve, it obviously wasn't coming. She couldn't put it off any longer. It was time to pack. She started lining up things on her bed, things she knew she couldn't leave behind—her giant root beer Lip Smacker, her new stickpin from Sarah, her silver sparkly belt, her sequined butterfly T-shirt, and her super-wide-leg jeans. Two months of allowance had gone to pay for those jeans. In junior high your popularity was measured by the width of your pant leg. That's what she used to think, anyway. It took her a while to realize they hadn't really made a difference one way or the other. She stared at the denim blue against her pale green bedspread. *It'll probably be too hot for jeans.* She put them back in her drawer.

There was a knock on her door. "Lucy?" It was her dad. "Why don't you come out and watch some TV? We'll watch whatever you want. *Bionic Woman's* on soon."

She didn't answer.

"Come on, pumpkin. It's our last night together for a while."

Whose fault is that? She pushed in the lock button on the doorknob. Pressing her ear against the door, she listened. After a moment, she heard a loud sigh and the flip of his slippers as he retreated down the hall.

She turned and faced her closet, hands on her hips, as if waiting for something to happen. Nothing did. She started pulling clothes off hangers, scooping stuff off shelves. Folding was too time consuming, so she just tossed them across the room, forming a heap on the floor.

Goggles, goggles...where are my swim goggles? She knelt down and dug through the rubble at the back of her closet, feeling for the rubbery strap. Her hand came in contact with something unfamiliar, square, cardboard. She slid it out. *Oh, right. The Box.*

It was all get-well cards that had come first, then all the sympathy cards had followed. Lucy had saved every one and kept them in a shoebox. She'd even saved all the cards from the Cancer Society that said, "A donation has been made in Laura's name from...." There were a million of those.

Her eyes fell on some torn papers sticking out at one end of the box—handwritten notes. She had saved those, too. The ones her mom had written to her or her dad when it had become too hard to talk with the oxygen mask on. Lucy pulled out a couple. The one on top was to her, reminding her to pick the tomatoes before they rotted on the vine. The writing was shaky and uneven, like it'd been done by a child. The next one was written on the back of a torn yellow envelope. *Promise me you'll talk to Scotty. Figure out what to do together. Not the way I planned it. Sorry. Forgive me.* Lucy reread the words, more slowly this time. There was that name, Scotty, again. Who was this guy? What did they have to do? She rubbed the paper between her fingers and thought hard. *He must be a lawyer or something.* Maybe having to do with her mom's will. Her eyes were drawn back to the last line. What was she sorry about? Lucy hoped it wasn't about getting sick; it wasn't her mom's fault. She bit down on her shaking bottom lip, then returned the papers to the box and pushed it to the back of her closet.

Jumping to her feet, Lucy stepped away from the closet as if trying to separate herself from the brush with memories. She hauled her suitcase out from under her bed, filled it with the heap of clothes on her floor, and threw in a few more odds and ends. After surveying her room for anything she might have forgotten, she slowly zipped up her suitcase, leaving only a small opening at the top to jam in her toothbrush the next morning.

Lucy went to bed that night already feeling homesick. Despite all her wishing, tomorrow was coming. She curled up on her side and stared at the pale blue numbers on her clock radio. She still couldn't believe that her dad was actually going through with it, that he was sending her away knowing how miserable it was making her.

I'm never going to forgive him.

"BEAUTIFUL DAY FOR A DRIVE!" Lucy's dad declared enthusiastically as he held open the car door.

God. Lucy scowled at his back as he walked around to the driver's side. Sitting in the car, she kept her hand on the door handle, as if she were contemplating making a last-minute break for it. The engine turned over. The car started to back out of the driveway. She moved her hand to her lap. Too late.

She rolled down the window and said a mental goodbye to the street, to the neighbourhood, and then, as they crossed the MacKay Bridge, to Halifax. Her dad was right: the day was beautiful, warm, sunny, and bright—the exact opposite of how she felt.

The drive to Cape John would take about two hours. She wasn't sure how she was going to survive it without pummelling the dashboard or bursting into tears.

Numerous times her dad made a stab at conversation. He finally gave up and turned on the radio.

About an hour in, Lucy saw a sign ahead on the left. A giant wooden cut-out of an ice cream cone. She remembered this place. The Fundy Dairy Bar. Her mom had taken her when she was little, way back when they used to occasionally visit her grandmother.

"Wanna stop?" her dad asked.

"Yeah!" Then she slapped her hand over her mouth. She'd forgotten and answered without thinking.

The blinker ticked and her dad pulled into the dirt parking lot.

It took Lucy forever to decide. They had over two-dozen flavours. In the end, she picked chocolate chip. She always picked chocolate chip.

Her dad picked orange pineapple. He always picked orange pineapple.

The elbow rest dug into her back as Lucy leaned against the door and looked at him between licks of ice cream. Even though she was never going to speak to him again, she was still going to miss him. Ever since Mom died, it had just been him and her. What was it going to be like not seeing him every day? It didn't mean she forgave him or anything, but the next time he spoke to her, maybe she would answer. It was a lot of work keeping up the silent treatment.

As if sensing her change in attitude, her dad said, "Hey. Look at all those cows lined up along the fence. Bet it's going to rain."

"Great." Without her meaning it to, it came out sarcastic.

Her dad ignored her tone, pointing out numerous passing attractions. The massive cornfields, the sheep farm, the Sausage House—the sign said "Homemade Sausages." *Gross.*

"Now, this place up here." He gestured with his head to a farm on her side. "I think they keep a llama there. Do you want to check it out?"

She made a face and shook her head. "No." *Isn't that like a camel-sheep or something?* "No thanks."

"Suit yourself." He shrugged. "Could be really neat, though. Are you sure?"

She rolled her eyes and nodded, "Yup." *Okay, that's enough. I've spoken five words. That's all you're getting for now.*

"Now, look at that!" he said. "Those rolls of hay are taller than you."

God, Dad. Why do you think I'd be interested in some rolls of hay? They were kind of cool, though. Enormous. Like Shredded Wheat for giants.

After what felt like forever, they drove through the village of River John. A church, a fire hall, the Co-op, a post office, a river, a bridge, another church, another church, a drugstore—blink once and you'd miss it all. *No great loss, really.*

At the Shell station, they turned onto a bumpy road that ran along the ocean. "This is the Cape John Road," her dad said. "If you looked at the Cape from above, it would look long and pointy, kind of like a witch's hat, with this road running through it."

"Great," she said. It didn't sound so sarcastic this time.

"If I remember correctly," her dad continued, "there's a fishing wharf at the very end." He leaned forward and peered through the windshield. "Josie's is about halfway down this road."

Lucy could tell they must be getting closer; things were starting to look kind of familiar. She felt the ice cream inch its way back up her throat.

"I have one last thing to talk to you about." His tone was serious. She looked at him sideways. "It's a well-known fact that Josie, uh, can't cook to save her life. Your mother mentioned that often. I mean, *often*."

"O...kay."

"I'm just saying, there's always peanut butter and jam. Or cereal."

Serves you right if I die of malnutrition. "Great," Lucy said. Definitely back to sarcastic.

He pulled onto a kind of grassy driveway. Lucy recognized the two-storey farmhouse with the huge front porch. Though it was Josie's now, it used to be Gran Irene's—this was where her mom grew up. This was also where they had stayed whenever they'd come to visit Gran Irene. It hadn't changed much since the last time she'd been here, almost nine years ago. A missing shutter, a bit of peeling paint.

Josie came rushing out of the house, wiping her hands on a tea towel. She wrapped her fleshy arms around Lucy before Lucy had even gotten her whole self out of the car. "I've been going out of my mind waiting for you!" Josie said. "Did you have a good drive?"

Lucy couldn't answer because her face was mashed against Josie's chest, breathing in that weird mentholly smell again.

She wiggled free as Josie turned to her dad. "Mike, you'll stay to eat? You need some food before you drive back."

His eyes widened slightly and he coughed. "No—no, Josie, really, I'm fine. We stopped for ice cream."

Lucy saw that Josie looked confused. *Dad! She's deaf. You have to look right at her and speak clearly.*

But then he realized his mistake. "Ice cream," he repeated, mimicking holding a cone and licking.

Josie's face cleared and she nodded.

"I had a large." He patted his stomach. "Full."

Lucy's eyes narrowed. *Coward.*

"Plus," he said, looking at Lucy, "The longer I stay, the harder it'll be to say goodbye."

He took Lucy in his arms and held her tight. "I know you're still mad at me," he whispered into her hair, "but *always* remember I love you." He stepped back and looked at her, studied her, as if he knew that this was the last time he would see her like she was at this very moment. Like the next time he saw her, she would be somehow different.

Not trusting herself to speak, Lucy could only stare back at him.

"I have to go out of town for a few days for work," he said, tucking a strand of hair behind her ear. "I'll call and check in when I get back."

He handed Josie a piece of paper with what looked like phone numbers scribbled on it. *Shouldn't I be in charge of those?* Lucy thought. There was definitely a phone here—her mom used to call Gran Irene on Sunday nights—but she couldn't guess how Josie would use it. He gave Josie a hug, and then just like that, he left.

Lucy stood in the driveway watching the back of her dad's station wagon get smaller and smaller. Standing on her tiptoes, she shaded her eyes with her hand, hoping to see the brake lights go on, when he realized what a terrible mistake he'd made.

No lights came on. The car kept driving away. She stayed there long after it disappeared.

CHAPTER 5

LUCY FELT JOSIE'S ARM ENCIRCLE HER SHOULDERS as she sniffed back some tears. She was thankful Josie didn't try to talk to her. She didn't think she could manage any words right now. After a moment, Josie gave her a squeeze and said, "When you're ready, top of the stairs, the blue room."

Lucy nodded. She waited for Josie to go inside first, then she picked up her suitcase and dragged it up onto the porch, bouncing it off each step as she went.

Just like the outside, nothing had changed much on the inside. She was surprised at how well she remembered it. The worn wood floors, the faded floral wallpaper, the equally faded, floral, lumpy sofa. Everything looked so old. It had looked old even back then—the last time she had visited. Maybe things get to a certain point when they just hit a wall and can't look any older. Then her eyes landed on something that didn't look so old. On the mantle was what appeared to be a shiny copper vase. But it had a lid. *Gran Irene?* Lucy had no intention of checking to see if she was right. She continued through the house, bouncing and bumping her suitcase up the stairs covered in frayed carpet.

At the top, she paused to catch her breath. One, two, three, four, five. Five doors. Two on one side of the dark hallway, three on the other. She remembered the blue room was the second on the right, across from the bathroom. Her hand lingered on the clear, cut-glass doorknob. She remembered how when she was five, she'd thought they all looked like giant jewels, and she'd devoted an entire afternoon to twisting and turning one, trying to get it off so she could take it home. That was until her grandmother found her and whacked her on the butt with the back of a hairbrush. Not very hard, but hard enough that she still remembered.

Lucy took only one step inside the room, letting the stillness settle over her. It felt like no one had been in here for a long time. The late-afternoon sun poured in through the windows, making a pattern of slanted rectangles on the carpet. She walked to the bed and sat down on the edge. Her movements stirred up the dust, and she watched the particles catch in the light as they floated back down onto the furniture and floor. It was hypnotizing.

She let her body flop back on the bed. As she lay there, she studied the sprawling cracks on the ceiling. Some were short. Some were long. Most met up at a point in the middle. They reminded her of the road map of Nova Scotia her dad kept in the glovebox.

Her nose started to tingle. Determined not to cry, she rolled over onto her side and looked around the room that was to be hers for the next two months. It was her mom's old room. She couldn't remember if she'd ever even been in here before, except maybe to take a quick peek. The bed was only a twin, so when they had visited together, they had stayed in the green room—Ellen's old room—that had a double. The walls in here were pale blue. A grey rug with a swirly pattern of pink roses covered the floor. There was a tall chest of drawers and a matching mirrored dresser cluttered with her mom's old stuff—a bunch of mostly empty perfume bottles, a jar of marbles, and a collection of porcelain bunnies. Lucy remembered those from when she was little. She had asked her mom if she could play with them, but her mom had said no. There was also a giant...Humpty Dumpty? Lucy lifted her head slightly. She could see a slot. *Must be a piggy bank.* Under the window there was a faded blue upholstered armchair with a spring poking through.

Though there was still daylight, Lucy reached out and turned on the lamp on the nightstand. It had a blue plastic shade, pleated all around like an accordion and gathered in the middle with a white lace ribbon. She ran her fingers along the pointy edges of the pleats. It would make a good tutu for a doll.

Her arm dropped. She was so tired. She couldn't remember the last time she'd had a decent night's sleep. Staring at the lamp, her eyelids began to feel heavy, and she finally fell asleep.

LUCY WAS FLAT ON HER stomach when she opened one eye. The flimsy cotton curtains were fighting a losing battle against the brightness of morning. It took her a moment to register where she was, and that she had slept all through the evening and right on through the night.

There was a quilt draped over her. She didn't remember covering herself up. Josie must have done it. Scratching the back of her head and yawning, she stumbled to the dresser and leaned forward to look in the mirror. One long sleep wasn't enough to erase the dark circles under her eyes and she was suffering a bad case of pillow face. The overall effect was...ouch. A light tap on the door dragged her gaze from the mirror.

"Come in," she called. No response. *Right. Deaf.* Lucy hurried over to open the door.

"Good morning, dear," Josie said cheerfully but then frowned. "Oh my. Who does your hair? The northwest wind?" She patted her chest and laughed loudly at her own joke.

It was Lucy's turn to frown. *You're one to talk.* Lucy was

35

pretty sure she'd coloured her hair since yesterday, because there was no way she wouldn't have noticed that blinding cherry red. Fresh dye stains were visible on the skin along Josie's hairline, confirming Lucy's suspicions. Josie could be the poster girl for dye jobs gone bad. Not to mention the cigarette jammed in the corner of her mouth. *It's eight o'clock in the morning!*

"I'm just foolin' with ya, honey," Josie said.

Not really knowing what to say, Lucy just stood there scraping her lower lip with her thumbnail.

"You can come down for breakfast anytime, but I hope you don't have big expectations. Not many people know this," Josie said, lowering her voice to a whisper, "but I'm not that great a cook."

Ya don't say.... "Don't worry, I can look after myself," Lucy mumbled.

"Say that again?"

Right. "I can look after myself," Lucy repeated, looking up.

"I'm sure you can. Coffee's on, though. Get it while it's hot."

Who offers a fourteen-year-old coffee? "I don't really like coffee, so, uh, don't keep any for me."

"Suit yourself, but you may change your mind. It's one of the few things I make that doesn't have...after-effects." She laughed to herself again, shaking her head as she walked down the hall.

Leaning against the closed door, Lucy let her head drop forward. *Good God, what's going to happen to me?* Mentally she flashed ahead to the end of the summer, grey and sickly from breathing in cigarette smoke for two months, nothing but skin and bones from near starvation, hands shaking from too much caffeine. She crawled back into bed and pulled the quilt over her head. The pillow made a crunchy sound—feathers. Why hadn't she brought her own? And the pillowcase was stiff and scratchy against her skin. Everything smelled of mothballs. She must have been too tired last night to notice. *I want to go home.*

As she lay buried under the quilt, determined to stay there

for the next sixty days, she thought about Josie. Her mom always said she was the greatest thing since sliced bread. *She seems like a complete kook to me!*

Her stomach grumbled. She hadn't eaten since her ice cream cone. She sat up and looked at her suitcase lying on the floor. Unpack or breakfast? Her stomach growled again—angrier this time. She padded down the stairs to the kitchen.

Josie had her back turned, doing something at the kitchen counter. Lucy went and stood beside her. But then Josie made a strange squeak and jumped. Which made Lucy make the same strange squeak and jump too.

"You scared the bejesus out of me!" Josie raised her hand to her throat. "Next time just flick the lights or stomp your foot."

Nodding, Lucy sat down on the closest chair and waited for her heartbeat to return to normal. The kitchen smelled like coffee, and it smelled good.

Josie went to the freezer. "Here. I think you kids like this kind of garbage." She pulled out a box of Eggos and tossed them onto the table in front of Lucy.

Lucy sat up straight. *We do, we do like this kind of garbage.* She opened the box and slid two in the toaster while Josie dug out the butter and syrup. The waffles seemed to take ages to toast. Probably because the toaster was ancient. Or maybe it was because she was way hungrier than she thought. Finally, they popped.

She screwed up her face as she picked up the syrup. The bottle said "Pure." At home it said "Maple Flavoured." This might mess up the results.

Her goal was to carefully fill each square of the waffle with syrup, one by one, before moving on to the next. It took patience and a steady hand. If you poured too fast or too much, it would overflow, and there wasn't allowed to be any runoff over the edge. There were many factors that affected the outcome—the thickness of the syrup, whether the syrup had been refrigerated or kept at room temperature, atmospheric conditions, humidity, stuff like that. And now, Lucy suspected, "Pure" was going to be added to the list.

She sat back and judged her effort. She was pleased. A perfectly smooth coating of syrup—like amber glass. She almost didn't want to eat it. Sometimes if she cut in the exact right place, in the very middle of the ridge, the syrup would stay put. She slowly cut into her waffle, then swore under her breath as the syrup flowed into a puddle on her plate.

"I'll be in the garden," Josie announced, rinsing out her coffee mug and setting it in the sink.

Lucy was about to say "Okay," but decided to nod instead. It was easier and more effective. As a taste test, she stuck her finger in the syrup and gave it a lick. It was super sweet, caramelly, different, but *yum*. After finishing her waffles, she stayed at the table for a while. She was surprised that Josie hadn't asked her anything, like how she was settling in, what she would like to do, if she needed anything. Josie was kind of leaving her alone. *Good. That's what I want.*

She wandered out to the front porch. What was she was supposed to do for the next two months that didn't involve dying of boredom? Sarah was probably at the rec centre this very second, swimming, sailing, playing tennis with whoever her *new* best friend was. Who else was there? Everybody. Everybody except her. She plunked herself down on the porch swing and sulked. This was all too brutal, too unfair. She couldn't wait for her dad to call so she could *not* to talk to him. He'd get the message pretty fast that she was still mad and that the silent treatment was totally back on.

She looked around, trying to suss out where Josie's garden might be. Her eyes fell on a wicker table by the railing. On top a book was open, upside down. She reached for it and flipped it over. *Summer of Forbidden Love*, a Harlequin Romance. Her mom had told her that Josie had read every single Harlequin Romance ever published. That she would plough through them like someone ploughed through a bag of chips. "Brain candy. Strictly for entertainment." That's what her mom had said. Lucy smiled and placed the book back on the table.

The sun was shining, but the morning hadn't quite warmed up yet. She shivered. Time to get dressed. As she pulled open the screen door, she glanced over at the Harlequin. *Hmm.* She let the door go and went back for a closer look. The guy on the cover was shirtless. He had bulgy muscles and long hair—long enough to put into a ponytail. And the girl in his arms...Lucy would have given anything for her hair to feather like that. Actually, the guy's hair was feathered even nicer. She picked up the book and quickly read the back. The books her mom had kept around the house all seemed to be about history, and super boring. She memorized Josie's page number and tucked it under her arm. This didn't look boring at all.

It was as she was brushing her hair a few minutes later that Lucy first heard the noise. It sounded like shovelling. She went to the window and peered out over the yard. There, in the field across the lane, a boy was digging a hole.

Lucy watched for a moment. The boy dropped his shovel, took a swig of something from a plastic jug, and spat it out. Then he spat a couple more times. *Gross.* Obviously a bumpkin.

He tossed the jug onto the grass, wiped his mouth on the bottom of his T-shirt, and then looked up. Right at Lucy. Mortified she'd been caught spying, she froze. To make matters worse, the boy pointed to his eye and then to her—the universal sign for "I see you" or "I know you see me." *Crap!* She gasped and flung herself away from the window, mashing her back up against the wall.

Her heart thumped in her ears as she waited for the shovelling sound to start up again. It didn't. *He better not still be staring at my window.* She kept waiting, listening. Nothing. And then finally, there it was. The noise. Like music to her ears. He'd gone back to his shovelling. She laughed to herself. *What do I have to be embarrassed about? I'm allowed to look out my own window.*

He's the one who should be embarrassed.

After she'd calmed down and shoved the encounter to the back of her mind, she got dressed, went back down to the porch, sat on the top step, and examined her toenails. She debated giving them another coat of bubblegum pink polish. It would kill a good twenty minutes. That only left 59 days, 22 hours, and 40 minutes.

There was humming as Josie came around the corner of the house, cigarette hanging out of her mouth. She was wearing gardening gloves and a zip-up smock covered with bright green leprechauns and four-leaf clovers.

Lucy's eyes widened.

"Got the material seventy-five percent off," Josie explained.

Gee. Wonder why.

"Thought it was kind of snazzy," she continued.

Lucy nodded as if in agreement.

"Finished my weeding." Josie peeled off her gloves and smacked them together to loosen the caked-on dirt, creating a huge cloud of dust. "My neighbour Muriel's heading to the village later today. Thought I might give her a note to drop off to your Aunt Ellen. I want to set something up. She just lives up the road, on the other side, you know."

Lucy didn't react. She began picking at a piece of chipped toenail polish. The more she thought about it, the more she realized her feelings were mixed. Curiosity was killing her, but she didn't want to actually come face to face with the enemy. What she really wanted was for Josie to just *tell* her what happened between Ellen and her mom. She wanted to ask, but something held her back. Maybe it was because she knew, for whatever reason, her mom hadn't wanted to share it with her, so in a way it sort of felt like she was going behind her mom's back.

"She has a daughter," Josie said after taking a couple drags of her cigarette. "I think she's at some kind of summer camp right now. Might be nice for you to have a chum. She'd be around your age."

Lucy felt her insides instantly fill with dread. She shrugged. "Maybe." She had zero interest in meeting any kid of Ellen's.

Josie snorted. "I've seen *that* look before."

Lucy frowned back at her.

"On your mother," Josie said. "Every time I made my Chicken Surprise Casserole. She'd get a look just like that—all wishy-washy and nervous-like."

Oh no. I hope she's not planning to make Chicken Surprise Casserole for me.

Josie took another drag of her cigarette and studied Lucy through a haze of smoke. "You think about it." She huffed past Lucy on the stairs and went inside, letting the screen door smack shut behind her.

A few seconds later, it squeaked open again. "I think you and me should go for a walk on the beach," she announced, now sporting a straw hat with multicoloured pompoms hanging from its wide brim. It definitely did nothing to tone down her leprechaun ensemble.

Is that a sombrero? Lucy realized she was staring. Worried her expression might give her away, she said, "Very unique look."

"Fairy you need a look?"

"No. No." Lucy shook her head. "Very. *Unique*. Look," she corrected, enunciating carefully.

"Oh, that's all right, then. Come on." Josie started down the stairs then stopped, glanced back at Lucy, and waited.

Lucy let out a huge sigh. *Fine. Nothing better to do.* And she got up and followed.

Suddenly a thought occurred to her. To get to the beach, they would have to pass the field where that boy was digging. As she traipsed along the lane behind Josie, she strained her ears. She didn't *think* she heard any shovelling. *Please let him be gone, please let him be gone.* Lucy had her fingers crossed on both hands as they came around the corner of a giant hedge. The shovel was there, stuck in a pile of dirt, but the boy was nowhere to be seen. She almost fainted with relief.

"Murray Wilson passed on last year," Josie said, pointing to a house through the trees at the far end of the field with the shovel. "Broke Millie's heart to sell, but she was just too old to keep up the place all by herself. And of course that Deenie...well, *she* wouldn't lift a finger!"

Lucy didn't have the faintest idea who these people were, but that didn't seem to matter to Josie.

"And Ricky! That lazy, good-for-nothin' husband of hers. They *both* need a good kick in the arse."

In spite of herself, Lucy smiled. Wanting to hear more about the people whose arses needed to be kicked, she picked up her pace so she was walking a little more beside Josie, instead of behind. She had a funny feeling there were a lot of people whose arses Josie thought needed kicking. But Josie had finished with that topic and was now talking about the different wildflowers native to the area. Boring.

The morning had warmed up nicely and the sun beat down on the back of Lucy's neck. There wasn't a breath of wind as they walked along the lane. Just ahead she could see the top of the stair rails that led down to the beach. She had a vague memory of digging with her mom on the sandbars, and hunting for beach glass.

When the lane came to an end, the earth just seemed to drop away. Lucy stood on the edge of the clay-coloured cliff enjoying the breeze from the ocean as it lifted the stickiness off her body. She scanned the beach from one end to the other. The tide was almost all the way out and the crests of the sandbars were just beginning to break through the surface of the water.

After they carefully made their way down the rickety wooden steps, Josie positioned herself on a large flat rock about the size of a kitchen table.

"What about our walk?" Lucy asked, making walking motions with her first two fingers.

"I thought I might let you poke around on your own for a bit while I finish the last chapter of my book." She pulled a Harlequin out of the pocket of her smock.

Lucy nodded. She had meant to tell Josie she'd swiped the one from the porch, but they were littered all over the house. Lucy got the impression she had a half dozen on the go at once.

Lucy stepped towards the water, avoiding the mounds of seaweed. She didn't mind the black stringy grass so much, but didn't like the long, flat, brown stuff. It felt slimy and slippery, though it did have neat ruffled edges. Lucy remembered asking her mom if they were giant lasagne noodles. There was a tiny squeeze on her heart. From behind her she heard the strike of a match, smelled cigarette smoke.

"The tide's good for finding beach glass," Josie called.

Beach glass basically came in four colours—blue, green, brown, and white. Broken pieces of jars and bottles tossed around in the ocean, edges worn smooth over time from the salt and the sand, finally washed ashore waiting to be added to someone's collection. With every turn of the tide, like magic, new ones appeared.

Spotting a piece of green a few feet away, Lucy picked it up. She felt the smoothness of the edges with her fingers. As she slipped it in her pocket, she tried to imagine where it had come from, to whom it had belonged.

A half hour of walking on the beach doubled over started to make her back ache. Stopping to stretch, she was surprised at how little a distance she'd covered. Hunting for beach glass was slow going. She turned and headed back.

Josie was lying on the rock with the straw hat covering her face. Gurgling snores sporadically erupted from her body. Lucy sat on a patch of sand next to her and emptied her pockets. She lined up all her finds, examining each piece one at a time. She was excited she'd found a piece of blue. Blue was the prettiest, and the most elusive. Not a lot of things came in blue glass bottles. At home, her mom had kept a jam jar on the kitchen windowsill of blue beach glass—her favourite. It was still there.

She sat quietly, waiting for Josie to wake up. Shading her eyes, she looked out across the ocean. There was a cluster of brightly coloured fishing boats tied to a wharf off on the horizon. It would have made the perfect postcard.

The morning had gone from warm to hot, and the wind had completely disappeared as the tide reached dead low. She could see the skin on her arms starting to turn pink. Gently she prodded Josie.

Josie lifted her hat and blinked a few times. "Just resting my eyes."

Lucy motioned her head towards the stairs and gathered up her pieces of glass as Josie hoisted herself off the rock.

On the walk back to the house, Lucy kept patting her pocket with satisfaction. She couldn't wait to rinse the salt and sand off and look at all the pieces again. Maybe Josie had something she could keep them in. Something big enough that she could add more, like if she found some tomorrow, or even the next day.

Any blue pieces she'd add to her mom's jar, back home on the kitchen windowsill.

CHAPTER 6

FOR THE FOURTH MORNING IN A ROW, LUCY TOSSED two waffles onto her plate. It didn't seem to bother Josie. She didn't say one word about it. Maybe she was trying out some kind of reverse psychology—the old "She thinks she wants waffles every day, but when she actually has waffles every day, she'll get sick of them and choose my homemade porridge instead" strategy.

On her way to the table, Lucy looked in the sink at the pot filled with globs of lumpy grey goo and shook her head. *Never gonna happen.*

After she wolfed down her waffles, using her finger to squee-gee up every last drop of syrup, she poured herself a half a cup of coffee. It wasn't so bad once you added five teaspoons of sugar and a squirt of canned whipped cream—that was Josie's idea—to help ease her into a morning routine of coffee drinking.

Up in her bedroom, Lucy closed the door, stood perfectly still, and listened. Nothing. She checked out the window. Where was he? He'd been there earlier. Just like every morning. And every morning, in spite of the fact that he'd already caught her, she watched him. She couldn't help it. It was like a car accident she couldn't look away from. Every morning she would press herself against the wall and carefully slide one eyeball past the window frame until he came into view. And every morning, though she was perfectly hidden, he would stop and look up. It was as if he could tell. Which there was no way he could. Lucy figured he was doing it on purpose, trying to catch her. It was weird. He was weird.

And yucky. Even from her window, she could see the ginormous pit stains under his arms. Not to mention his greasy hair—well, she *assumed* it was greasy, it *had* to be. It was plastered flat against his head with sweat. Also she was pretty sure he wore the same clothes every day.

And what exactly was he digging? The hole kept getting bigger and bigger, but what was it for? A pool? A pond? A bomb shelter? Lucy scratched her head. *Or is he looking for something? Does he think something's buried out there?* It was making her crazy.

Whatever. Luckily, at this moment, he was nowhere to be seen. Her plan was to go hunt for beach glass, and now she didn't have to wait till after lunch. That's when he usually seemed to finish his...work?

Lucy went in search of Josie. She didn't want to leave without letting her know where she was going. She paused on the landing, stuck her nose in the air, and sniffed—*Just follow the smell of smoke.* Lucy found her outside sitting on the porch swing, reading. There was a cigarette hanging loosely from her mouth and she was wearing what looked like some kind of Hawaiian muumuu. *Wow, those colours clash. What do you call someone who designs fabric? Well, whoever it was, bet they were fired on the spot.*

She waved her fingers across Josie's open book.

A gust of smoke filled the air as Josie looked up and exhaled.

Lucy scrunched up her nose and stepped back. "I'm going to the beach."

Josie nodded. "You should take a hat and some Coppertone. It's gonna be a hot one. My thermometer is close to ninety already."

Lucy grabbed her Red Sox hat from her room and did another check out the window. Still all clear. She stopped by the kitchen and slathered on some suntan lotion, knowing she was probably missing a ton of spots. But there was no time to lose. She had to get while the gettin' was good.

There wasn't a cloud in the sky as she headed for the beach. The only noise came from the clicking and buzzing of insects hiding in the grass and flowers. It made her think of when she and Sarah had had to do that stupid project on bugs. They had to catch a bunch, pin them on a board, and label them. It was disgusting.

She missed Sarah, and wished she were here. This might not be so bad if she had someone to hang out with. She still had no clue what was she going to do with herself all summer. The beach glass thing was okay, but every day? And Josie didn't even have TV. Well, she *had* one, but it only got channels 3 and 5, and they were fuzzy at the best of times. Josie told Lucy she might get better reception if she wrapped tinfoil around the rabbit ears and stood on a certain spot in the living room. It sounded like a lot of work. And not very comfortable for watching an entire show.

Lucy was halfway down the lane and lost in her thoughts, and by the time she realized what was happening, it was too late. Stopping dead in her tracks, she felt her feet turn to cement blocks. She felt her throat squeezing shut, like someone tightening a twist tie.

There, less than ten feet away, was the boy. The Digger. He'd tricked her. There hadn't been *any* shovelling sounds. She wildly looked around for some tree or shrub to dive behind. None! He'd already seen her, anyway. She prayed for something to happen, the earth to swallow her up, a volcano to erupt, spontaneous combustion, *anything*!

He stood there, leaning on his shovel, watching her. He was smirking but he didn't say anything. He just did that thing again—pointed to his eye, then to her. She knew he knew. It was obvious. She knew he knew that it was her eyeball every morning. Her face was on fire and it had nothing to do with the ninety-degree heat. So, because she couldn't think of anything else to do, she started speed walking towards the beach, forcing herself not to break into a run. His eyes were on her back the entire time, she could feel them, and it wasn't until she scurried down the rickety steps and was safely out of sight that she finally let herself take a breath.

"Idiot!" But who was she was calling an idiot, him or her? And how long was he going to be there? How was she ever going to get back home?

Okay, Lucy, calm down. It's not like you're stranded on a desert island and you're going to die lost and alone. You're a five-minute walk from the house.

Pulling off her hat, she wiped her sweaty forehead with her arm and took a deep breath. *You might as well do what you came here to do.*

She didn't find much on the beach that morning: six pieces, and only one was blue. She was too busy pacing and worrying about what was going on up in the field just above her. As though she had a nervous tic, her eyes constantly darted to the stairs, terrified at the thought of him at some point following her.

The tide was close to low and there was no breeze off the water, no shade—the heat was starting to get uncomfortable. *So maybe I won't die lost and alone, but there's a good chance thirst or heatstroke will do me in.* She checked her watch, gnawed on the corner of her lip. *Almost noon. Maybe he's gone by now.*

Slowly, she crept up the stairs until she was able to inch her head over the top step. She couldn't see or hear anyone. Scrambling up the last couple of steps, Lucy ran like she was being chased by the boogieman until she was safely back on Josie's front porch. The Digger may have been somewhere in the field for all she knew, but she hadn't bothered to slow down long enough to check.

She threw herself onto the closest chair and waited for her heart to stop smacking against her ribcage.

Josie came out and handed her a glass of lemonade. "How was the beach?"

"Okay."

"Anything interesting?"

"No."

"Did you meet Colin?"

Lucy squinted. "Who?"

"Colin. I'm sure I saw him down the lane."

The Digger had a name. "Uh, I didn't notice anyone," Lucy lied into her lemonade.

"Hmm?"

"Sorry." She looked back up so Josie could read her lips. "No. I didn't see him."

"He just moved here," Josie said. "He's older, but not by much. You need a chum."

What is with her obsession with me having a "chum"? And has she seen the sweat on him?!

"I don't think I need a *chum*," Lucy said, pressing the ice-cold glass against her temple.

"Don't talk so crazy!" Josie jammed her hands into her hips. "You think I'm going to let you hide out in the house all summer?"

Lucy slumped down deeper in her chair and didn't reply.

"And I haven't forgotten about taking you to visit Ellen," Josie added. "It's time you got to know your family."

Lucy glared into her lemonade. Who was this person giving her all these orders? What happened to the Josie of the last few days, the one who let her do anything she wanted, no questions asked? It was like *Invasion of the Body Snatchers. Man, I can't wait for Dad to call.*

That very night Lucy's dad *did* call. The original plan to give him the silent treatment took a back seat to her annoyance with Josie and all her threats.

"But Dad," Lucy whined. "I don't want to meet Ellen! What would Mom think?"

She heard her dad sigh on the other end. "Mom would think it was good, Lucy. It was what she was planning last summer— well, you know...before she got sick."

Lucy sniffed a couple times. "What do you mean, 'what she was planning'?"

"She was going to take you to Cape John for a vacation. Take you to meet Ellen, let you get to know your aunt and uncle and cousin."

"Why?" She wasn't sure she believed him. "They hadn't spoken in years."

"She wanted to fix that."

Lucy twisted the curly phone cord around her finger. "Dad, do you know what happened between them? Can you just tell me?"

He didn't respond right away. "Your mom never liked to talk about it."

That doesn't mean you don't know. "Well, can Josie tell me?"

"She may not know."

Lucy huffed in disbelief. "How could she not know?"

"Like I said, your mom didn't like to talk about it."

She kept wrapping and twisting the cord and didn't say anything.

"I know you think Ellen is the enemy, Luce, but she's not," her dad continued. "Give her a break. Get to know her. Trust me, your mom would want this."

Drawing in a giant breath, she slowly leaked it out. "Promise?"

"Promise."

"Do you think she'll tell me about the fight or whatever happened?"

"Maybe."

What could it be? And why did Mom want to make nice after all this time? A thought dawned on Lucy. *What if it's because it was really all Mom's fault? What if Ellen tells me something terrible about her?* That was something she was only just now considering.

Lucy had the sudden urge to change the subject. "Yeah, well, Josie wants me to meet *other* people too," she blurted. "To like, make *friends*."

"No!" Her dad fake gasped, seemingly eager for a subject change as well. "She sounds like a complete monster! Should I call the police?"

"Dad. It's not funny," she said stiffly.

"I know, pumpkin," he said, but she could tell he still thought it was.

They continued to argue back and forth for a few more minutes and ended with her agreeing to keep an open mind about Ellen. But she had her fingers crossed when she made the agreement. *Maybe Mom had wanted this meeting to happen, but I'm still not a hundred percent convinced.*

Josie was old. Maybe she'd just forget about the whole Ellen thing anyway.

To be on the safe side, Lucy spent the next couple days trying to stay under the radar. She lived in constant fear Josie was on the verge of making some kind of proclamation concerning a get-together or family reunion dinner. She mostly hid out at the beach, planning each trip with military precision, never again wanting to run into The Digger.

So far, so good.

WHEN LUCY WENT DOWN TO make her breakfast, Josie was standing at the kitchen counter. Lucy stopped in the doorway and stomped her foot. She was getting better at remembering. The other day she'd forgotten. "You can't sneak up on me like that!" Josie had said, knocking over her mug, both hands fluttering in the air.

"I *didn't*," Lucy had insisted, kneeling down to sponge up the spilled coffee. "I just forgot to let you know I was here."

As Lucy put her waffles in the toaster, she glanced sideways at Josie. What was she doing? Lucy edged her way along the counter to get a better look. There was an open bag of marshmallows and a bowl filled with some brown flaky stuff...*wheat?* She watched as Josie sliced a marshmallow into thin discs, then dipped them in the bowl. The brown stuff stuck to both the sticky cut sides. She popped a slice in her mouth and chewed thoughtfully, looking out the window. Then she popped in another.

Lucy tapped her on the shoulder. "What are you eating?"

"This? It's bran."

Lucy raised her eyebrows and pointed to the marshmallows.

"The doctor says I need more fibre in my diet. The bran's supposed to be good for my bowels, but it tastes like cardboard."

Bowels. Lucy shuddered.

"I tried sprinkling the stuff on my food like he told me," she went on. "But it just made me gag. Came up with this on my own. Seems to work fine."

"Oh. That's smart thinking." Lucy was pretty sure this wasn't what the doctor had in mind at all.

Josie returned to chewing and staring out the window. Then, "I have an idea," she announced.

Uh-oh. Lucy's body instantly went rigid. What had she been thinking? She'd let her guard down, struck up a conversation. She braced herself.

"It's hotter than the hinges of hell out there. Colin's probably in that field again. You should take him a cold drink. Introduce yourself." Josie's tone was firm.

Lucy's jaw dropped to the floor. She thought it would have something to do with Ellen, or even Ellen's kid, but this was way worse. A mental image of The Digger leaning on his shovel materialized in her head. His sweaty T-shirt, him pointing to his eye, her face burning with embarrassment. "No." She shook her head. "No way. Nuh-uh."

Josie squinted at her. "You've got two choices. I can drag

you over there kicking and screaming, or you can act like a lovely young lady and go on your own," she said, dredging another marshmallow.

Josie may as well have tilted Lucy's head back and poured that entire box of bran in her mouth—same results. She couldn't breathe. She couldn't swallow. And there was a pain in her chest. *Am I old enough to have a heart attack?*

"It won't be that bad," Josie said. "Finish your breakfast and go get dressed."

After forcing down only half her waffles, Lucy slowly dragged herself up the stairs, jaw still open and shaking her head the whole way. *This can't be happening.* How was she supposed to even do this? She made a silent wish for one of those transporter things from *Star Trek*, or some kind of time-travel machine. Unfortunately, there was no high-pitched hum, nor did her body dissolve into a million tiny particles. *Crap.*

That's it. When Dad calls again, the silent treatment is back on for real.

She slammed her bedroom door and began violently pulling things from the dresser. *Stupid T-shirt, stupid shorts, stupid, stupid, stupid.*

"You can't make me do this," she muttered. *Why am I whispering?* "You can't make me do this, you know!" she hollered. "You're not the boss of me!" Wow. That felt good.

"Get the lead out!" Josie yelled from below.

Lucy slapped a hand over her mouth. *She couldn't hear me, could she?!*

THERE WERE TWO ICY COLD glasses of red Kool-Aid on the table when Lucy got back to the kitchen.

"Thought you should take one for yourself. More social that way; you two could have a chit-chat," Josie said.

A chit-chat? Was she serious? "I'm not going," Lucy said, folding her arms.

Josie sighed. "You're a bit of a sourpuss, aren't you?"

Hey!

"When you were little, you had your mother's sweet and sunny disposition," she continued, pulling a cigarette from beneath her bra strap and lighting it—she kept an entire day's supply tucked all over her body. Smoke filled the air, creating a hazy wall between them.

Lucy waited. For what, she wasn't sure.

Josie looked at her through the curls of smoke, puffing away. "Oh, well. Kind of a shame, though," she finally said.

Against her better judgement Lucy asked, "What's a shame?"

"Colin's mom. She was your mom's best friend."

"*What?*"

Josie nodded. "Right from kindergarten. She and your mom, joined at the hip. Of course, Irene, your gran, wasn't too happy about it. Esther was a bit of a wild thing." Josie smiled at the memory.

Lucy digested this information. Except for stories about Josie, it was like her dad had said—her mom had never talked much about her past, including her childhood. She'd certainly never mentioned anyone named Esther, let alone *wild* Esther. Lucy would have definitely remembered that.

Josie plucked a piece of tobacco off the tip of her tongue and flicked it across the room. "So there. You and Colin would have something in common."

"Wait. You said Colin just moved here."

"He did. Esther left home right after high school. Now she's back."

"Oh."

"But." Josie sighed again, more heavily this time, and picked up the glasses. "If you're dead set against it, I'll put all this back. I just can't help think how your mom would have gotten such a kick—"

"Fine," Lucy said tightly. She wasn't born yesterday. She knew what Josie was doing. She reached out to stop her. "Give me the drink. *One*." She held up one finger.

Josie grinned a satisfied grin and handed her a glass.

Lucy marched out of the house and down the steps. She couldn't help feel that maybe she'd just been emotionally black-mailed. That aside, she had to admit she was more than a little intrigued. Not so much about Colin, but about his mom. Maybe she didn't have to make nice with Ellen after all. Colin's mom, this Esther person, probably knew everything there was to know about her mom, *and* Ellen.

Jackpot!

CHAPTER 7

L UCY'S PACE SLOWED AS THE SHOVELLING GOT louder. *Why did I ever agree to this? What was I thinking?* Beads of sweat prickled along her hairline. She switched the glass of Kool-Aid to the other hand so she could hold the cold one to her forehead. *I know what I was thinking. I was thinking about The Digger's mom.*

The hamster in Lucy's head had been going around and around on its little wheel ever since she'd found out The Digger's mom had been her mom's best friend. Maybe she could get him to take her to meet his mom. But then she shook her head. *No. How would that happen?* That would mean she would have to have some kind of conversation. *Ick.* No way she was going to do anything more than she had to. All Josie said was to take him a drink. So that's just what she was going to do, take him this drink. Because then Josie would have to do something for *her,* right? She'd owe her. Lucy would get Josie to take her to meet The Digger's mom. *Might almost be worth it.*

Feeling a little more confident now that she knew how it was all going to play out, she took a deep breath and rounded the corner of the lane. There he was, in the middle of the field, digging away.... Who was she kidding? *Dump the glass and run! Dump the glass and run!*

He stopped shovelling when he saw her and waved—a wide, sweeping wave over his head.

She jerked to a stop. *Did he just wave? Like all friendly? Who does he think he is?* She clenched her teeth and continued towards the hole. *I'm getting this over with as fast as possible.*

She stood next to a pile of dirt, the condensation from the glass dripping down her arm. They studied each other, sizing each other up. She noticed he had the same grey T-shirt on as always. It looked about ten sizes too big. So did his jean shorts. He looked like a hobo clown. She wondered who would speak first. *Well, it's not gonna be me. I don't plan on speaking at all.*

"Hey," he said.

"Hey," she said back. She couldn't help it—automatic reflex.

His eyes went to the glass in her hand. "It would be really cool if that was for me."

She frowned. She expected him to have some kind of hick accent, but he didn't.

His eyebrows shot up in surprise when she extended her arm and offered him the glass. "Thanks. I was sort of joking." He chugged it all at once, and handed it back to her. "I needed that," he said, wiping his mouth with the back of his hand.

Ick.

A few seconds passed.

Okay, Lucy. Deed done. Free to go. But her feet stayed firmly on the spot. "Nice hole," she said, then immediately winced. *Nice hole? What?*

She could tell he was trying not to laugh.

Attempting to hide her face, she focused on the empty glass in her hand. "Josie, my aunt, uh, great-aunt, made me bring this so, yeah, it was her idea. Just so you know...."

"That it wasn't your idea?"

She stuck out her chin. "Yeah. Because it wasn't."

"Okay." He shrugged.

"So...um...what are you digging?"

He shook his head. "You wouldn't get it."

"Try me."

"I'm not digging anything in particular."

"Oh. Then why are you doing it?"

"It's more of a protest type thing."

"Protest for what?"

"Against my mom. I'm really, really...." He paused and screwed up his mouth. "Mad at her."

"I see," Lucy said, nodding. Maybe he was right about her not getting it.

He stabbed his shovel into a pile of dirt dangerously close to where she was standing. "She drags us here. Moves us without even discussing it first. Just up and moves us! I didn't even get a vote. No one did. I had to leave everything—my friends, my school, my baseball team, my *boat*!" He yanked out the shovel and jammed it in the pile again.

Lucy kept nodding; she wasn't sure if she was supposed to comment.

"And then! She left my suitcase in some hotel in New Brunswick," he went on. "She says it's my fault for not keeping track of it. But she's the mom. She's supposed to check that I have all my stuff, right?"

Lucy played it safe. "Sure."

"Now I have to wait for the moving truck to get here with the rest of my clothes." He hiked up his baggy shorts. "Lucky for me, I found these in the barn with this shirt. Came with the house."

"And your mom won't buy you any clothes to tide you over?"

"She offered, but I said no. I don't want anything from her." He gave his waistband another tug. "These will do just fine."

Lucy rolled her eyes. "You still didn't explain the hole."

"It's to symbolize my need to escape," he said importantly,

like he was addressing a crowd. "I'm tunnelling my way to freedom."

Freak show. "Wow. That's...deep."

"Ha! Good one. Clever. Deep. Like the hole."

"Yup. That's me. Clever." Lucy forced a smile—the pun had been pure coincidence. "Does your mom get it? Is it working?"

"No." He moved towards the edge of the hole and started digging. "She thinks it's great that I'm spending so much time outdoors getting exercise."

This time it was Lucy who tried not to laugh.

"Now I think I'm just doing it more to wreck the field," he continued. "I know she's planning on making it into a garden. I'll trash the whole friggin' thing if I have to."

Lucy looked around at the field. "Going to be a lot of work. Plus the heat's wicked."

"I feel better when I dig. And it keeps me away from her. I don't have to worry about saying something I might regret." The blade of the shovel hit a rock and he made a face. "She needs to say sorry. Because something big like this—like moving halfway across the country—isn't all up to her. I mean, shouldn't I get a say?"

She knew how he felt. But at least at the end of the summer she got to go home and back to her friends. "Yeah. Something like this, you should get a say."

Blasting out a giant sigh, he looked past her, up the lane. "You're staying with Josie, huh? My mom told me about her, back in the old days, when we were speaking. She's supposed to be a riot."

"Yup. A real barrel of laughs."

"Mom's been threatening to drag me over to meet you," he said.

"I was kind of threatened too. It wasn't my idea to...you know...." She held up the glass.

"Yeah, you mentioned that."

Right.

"It's Lucy, isn't it?"

She nodded.

"Colin," he said.

She nodded again.

He tilted his head. "Lucy. Don't think I know a Lucy. Is it short for anything? Lucille?"

"Ew. No."

"Lucy from Charlie Brown? 'Cause that'd be kind of cool."

"No." At least she didn't think so.

"I have this thing about names, how people got theirs. Weird, huh?"

"Not really," she lied.

"Like, I was named after my mom's favourite soap opera character. I don't spread that around, though."

"Oh." *General Hospital? Another World?* She tried to remember which one had a Colin.

"Maybe you're named after a soap star too," he said. "Bet there's a Lucy on one of them."

She couldn't think of any. "Maybe my mom just liked the name."

"You should ask her. Might be a story there."

I should have. Why didn't I? "I can't. She, uh, died."

Red crept up his neck. "Right." He looked down and kicked at some loose rocks. "I knew that. I'm really sorry."

"It's okay."

"I guess I forgot for a sec."

"Really, it's okay. Umm...." She chewed on the inside of her cheek. She wanted to ask him how he knew. *Must have been his mom.* "I should probably go."

"Well, thanks for the drink," he said.

"It was—"

"Not your idea. Yeah, I know."

She started towards the lane.

"I'm here pretty much every morning!" he called after her. "You could come and hang out you know, if you're bored. I know I am."

"Uh, yeah, maybe," she answered, not very loudly, and without turning around.

"Okay! Maybe I'll see you later then!" he shouted.

She started walking faster.

That did not go at all the way I planned it.

FOR THE FIRST MORNING SINCE she'd arrived, Lucy didn't wake to the sound of shovelling. She woke to a completely different sound. A sound she couldn't identify. It was mechanical, and it seemed to be right next to her head. Tossing back her covers, she thumped down the hall to the room next door. There was Josie, sitting at a sewing machine, foot pressed to the pedal, running a long length of fabric under the needle. She was totally unaware of how much noise she was making or that Lucy was standing in the doorway. The machine was against the same wall as Lucy's bed, which explained all the racket.

A cigarette was hanging out of Josie's mouth, the curve of the ash bending straight downwards. Lucy couldn't take her eyes off it, waiting for it to fall onto the material at any second. She was afraid to stomp her foot in case the vibration caused it to break off.

Josie paused, squinting through the smoke as she cut a strand of thread. But that curve of ash was still hanging on for dear life.

Lucy held her breath. *Flick the ash!* She was about to rush over and cup her hands under the cigarette when Josie finally transferred the cigarette to an ashtray.

Lucy's breath gushed out and she stomped her foot.

Josie looked up. "Did I wake you?"

"A bit." Lucy said. "I'm going down for breakfast."

"Put the coffee on."

Lucy measured out the coffee and plugged in the percolator. After a minute, the smell filled the kitchen, and she drummed her fingers impatiently on the counter as she listened to the hissing and gurgling.

Josie came in just as the coffee finished perking.

The sugar bowl was empty. Lucy held it out, turning it on its side so Josie could see. "Sugar?"

"Here." Josie opened the cupboard and pulled out a large plastic ice cream container. Inside were hundreds of sugar packets, the kind from restaurants and coffee shops. "Anytime I'm out somewhere, I just throw a few extra in my purse."

A few? "Isn't that like stealing?" Lucy asked.

"Last word again?"

"Stealing," Lucy repeated carefully.

"*Pfft*. That's what I thought you said."

"Well, isn't it?"

"Do you have rocks in your head?" She flicked her hand. "They factor all that into the price. Some people use no sugar, I only put in one, and then there's people like you, who use four or five sugars. It all evens out."

"I guess...." But she wasn't so sure as she watched Josie tear the tops off a bunch of packets and pour them into the bowl.

Lucy sipped her coffee sweetened with sugar of questionable origins and curled up on the porch swing with another of Josie's Harlequins. She'd finished the last one in a day and a half, and it had been pretty good. More than pretty good. She hadn't been able to put it down. This one was called *A New Nanny for the King*, and she could tell from the cover that it was going to be even better. A girl in a green velvet ball gown was dancing with a gorgeous, shirtless guy. *Who goes to a ball with no shirt?* And the King—he was wearing a crown—was in the background, arms folded, glaring at them. *Oooh.* There was definitely going to be a love triangle. *Perfect!*

She glanced towards the lane. It bordered one end of Colin's field. He wasn't there this morning. It was weird. It was also weird that Josie hadn't asked how their meeting went. She'd just looked very pleased with herself when Lucy brought back the empty glass. How did she know Lucy had even gone through with it? How did she know Lucy hadn't pretended to go and then just poured out the glass? Because that *had* crossed her mind. Probably another one of her reverse-psychology tricks—she didn't want to make a fuss about it.

Opening her book, she tried to concentrate on the first page, but her eyes kept drifting back to the lane. She strained her ears. Still no shovelling. Hmm...he'd told her he was there every morning. Maybe this was his way of letting her know he'd changed his mind, that he didn't want any company.

Fine by me. I wasn't planning on going over anyway.

CHAPTER 8

L UCY LAY IN BED, ONE ARM THROWN ACROSS HER eyes to block the sun. The shovelling—it was back. She got up and checked out her window. *Yup, there he is.*

He looked up and waved, that same giant sweep of a wave. Maybe he hadn't been sending a message that he'd changed his mind after all. He could have just been sick or something.

She supposed it wouldn't kill her to go talk to him for a few minutes. She could take pity on him, do him a huge favour. He had mentioned how bored he was. And he'd sure appreciated the drink. It's not like she had anything better to do, which was quickly becoming the theme of her summer.

Josie was sitting on the sewing machine stool, winding thread onto a bobbin. Lucy stomped her foot and waited for Josie to look up. "Do you have any more Kool-Aid?" She held an imaginary glass to her mouth and tilted her head back.

"There should be some packets on the freezer door."

"Thanks." Lucy wasn't surprised. Josie froze everything. In the kitchen, she swung open the freezer door. The first thing she saw was two jars of Miracle Whip. The mixture had separated, white on the bottom, yellowy oil on the top. Lucy shuddered and moved a package of Kraft cheese singles to get to the Kool-Aid packets underneath.

After she'd finished her breakfast, Lucy mixed some cherry Kool-Aid. It took a lot of stirring because the powder had turned a bit chunky from being frozen, but it tasted fine.

"Did you ask him what he was doing out there?" Josie asked, coming into the kitchen.

Lucy shrugged. "It's like a protest or something."

Josie pulled a cigarette from behind her ear, stuck it in her mouth.

"He's trying to make a point," Lucy added, pouring a glass of Kool-Aid.

Josie frowned. "Say it again."

Lucy looked up. "A protest." She shook her fists in the air. "He's trying to make a point."

Smoke filled the air. Josie still looked confused.

"Something to do with having to move here. He didn't want to," Lucy explained. "But his mom didn't care. The hole is supposed to represent his"—she began running on the spot—"escape."

Josie raised her eyebrows. "Escape from *what*?"

"I dunno." Lucy shrugged again. "His parents' control? I'm not sure. I only talked to him for like, five minutes."

"That's the trouble with you kids today," Josie said, taking a drag off her cigarette. "You think the whole world revolves around you. What you really need is a good kick in the arse."

Lucy rolled her eyes and picked up the glass. Josie thought everyone needed a good kick in the arse.

"Tell Colin to let his mom know we'll bring over a basket of homemade goodies once she's had a bit of time to settle in."

Don't you mean warn *him?* Josie had made cookies the other day. When Lucy took a bite, her tooth had hit something—she still didn't know what—and she had had to take an aspirin for the pain, as well as a Tums for her upset stomach.

66

"Um, yeah, okay."

At least she would get the introduction to Esther she wanted.

Hopefully no one would break a tooth or be struck down with food poisoning as a result.

LUCY KEPT HER EYES ON the rim of the glass, trying to keep the juice from sloshing as she walked down the lane. She couldn't believe she was actually doing this. And all on her own. *Guess boredom can make you desperate.*

Colin looked up when he saw her. "Hey." He jammed his shovel into a mound of dirt.

"Hey." She passed him the Kool-Aid and crawled up to sit on a flat rock. He still had on the same grody T-shirt and shorts. *Guess the moving truck hasn't shown up yet.*

The girls in the Harlequins got all swoony whenever they saw a sweaty guy.

Lucy sat perfectly still for a second, checking to see if she felt any different. Nope. Must only work in romance novels.

"Did Josie make you come?"

"No. Didn't have anything better to do."

"Gee, thanks," he said, then he downed his drink all at once, just like before, and passed it back to her. "But I hear ya."

Lucy set the glass down on the grass and tried to think of something to say. "You weren't here yesterday."

"No. Thursday's Mom's grocery day. I had to babysit my brother and sister."

"Oh, you have a brother and sister?"

"Yup. They're five. Twins."

Colin had to be about...fifteen or sixteen? Lucy did some mental math. *That's a big age difference.*

"Yeah, we're almost eleven years apart," he said as if reading her mind. "I keep telling them they were an accident."

"No." Lucy looked horrified. "You do *not* tell them that."

"I do when they tick me off. It's okay. They don't even know what it means." He smiled mischievously. "But they keep going to Mom and asking, so...."

Lucy laughed out loud.

He picked up his shovel. "I'm going to start over there and see how long it takes me to make it back over to the big hole."

"Okay." Lucy frowned. "Want me to time you or something?"

His eyes lit up. "Yeah! Time me."

Holding up a finger, she looked at her watch. "And...go!"

As she watched him dig, she couldn't help thinking he reminded her of someone. Who? She thought for moment while she kept track of the time. Jean Pierre! From clarinet class. Jean Pierre, who she wanted to punch on a regular basis. They were both tall and thin, with the same stringy hair. *Please don't let Colin have the same personality.*

He was almost to the hole's edge when she remembered Josie's message. "I'm supposed to tell you to tell your mom that we're bringing over some homemade treats later, after you guys are settled, I guess."

Colin immediately stopped and straightened. "Really?"

So much for the timing. "Yeah."

"Should I be scared?"

Lucy was about to ask why when it dawned on her. "Oh. You're aware of Josie's—"

"Cooking skills? Yeah. Mom's got loads of stories."

Lucy nodded. "She's legendary."

"How are you even surviving, anyway?"

"It's not so bad. She doesn't make me eat anything I don't want or can't recognize. And thankfully—I'm not saying she's lazy or anything—but she doesn't cook that much. I don't think she likes it. So...I eat a lot of frozen waffles. And bread. She makes amazing bread." Lucy paused and scratched her forehead. "You'd think if you could master bread, you could master other things. But nope."

"Keep crackers and a jar of peanut butter under your bed, that's what I do. And cereal's a good backup too."

"Your mom can't cook either?"

"No, she can. I'm just always hungry." He started digging again. "It's all the fresh air and exercise I'm getting."

Lucy smiled. "Actually, I already thought of cereal. But it's the milk. Josie has powdered milk. I can't even explain how gross it looks. The lumps." She cringed. "I can't bring myself to even try it."

"Man. I'm sorry," Colin said, flinging a load of dirt to his side.

"I'll be okay. I forgot to say she loves bananas, so they're always around. And marshmallows. She always has marshmallows."

Colin drove his shovel under a big rock and tried to pry it up. "Well, when it comes to our welcome basket, maybe you could get her to stick to bread. Like, tell her it's our favourite thing."

"Yeah. I'll see what I can do."

That night Lucy's dad called, and she was surprised how good it felt to hear his voice. He talked about the Bennets next door having their sprinkler on all day even though they were supposed to be conserving water because there'd been no rain. He told her he'd run into Sadie and her mom at the IGA and they said to say hi and that they missed her. It made Lucy sad to think of her dad going to the grocery store by himself, then going home and cooking his dinner alone. She had planned on giving him the silent treatment for the first half of the conversation and then causing a stink over how Josie was still making her do stuff she didn't want to do, but the moment passed. It just didn't seem that important anymore.

IT WAS OFFICIAL. LUCY WAS actually getting sick of waffles. She'd be willing to trade almost anything for a bowl of Rice Krispies with real milk. She hung on the freezer door and scanned the contents. Sighing, she pushed aside a giant bone wrapped in plastic wrap—*Please don't be human*—then pulled out a new box of waffles and tossed two in the toaster.

With zero enthusiasm, she plunked herself down at the table and carefully filled the waffle holes with syrup. Some habits were hard to break.

"The tide's finally starting to switch around," Josie announced, sitting down across from her. "Should have enough water for a swim today."

For almost a week the tide had been low during the daytime. Lucy had tried to go for a swim a couple times but she would wade straight out for what seemed like a mile and the water never got past her knees.

Josie leaned back in her chair. "What do you got going on today, missy?"

Lucy shrugged and poked at her waffles. She didn't feel much like eating them.

"You've got a pout on about something," Josie said, snapping back the lid on her lighter.

Here it was, her moment. *Say something.* "Your milk. It's not like my milk at home."

Josie looked confused.

"Milk," Lucy repeated, doing her holding-a-glass-and-drinking move. "Yours is different. I like *store* milk. In a carton. And I have money," she added quickly, rubbing her fingers together. "I'll pay, next time at the grocery store."

"You're off your rocker," Josie said.

She got up, took the jug from the fridge, shook it, poured a glass, and set it in front of Lucy. "Drink that and tell me it's not the best milk you've ever tasted."

Lucy rolled her lips inward over her teeth and shook her head.

Josie sighed loudly. "Just try it."

Lucy stared at the glass. Okay, she could do this. If she drank it and still didn't like it, what could Josie say? At least she could say she tried, right? She lowered her head, eye level with the glass. It was so...beige. And there they were. Tiny, chunky, yellow floaties. Like boogers. Even if she did manage to swallow a mouthful, there's no way it would stay down. She shook her head again and, using one finger, she pushed the glass back across the table, away from her, as if it was an unexploded grenade.

There was complete silence as their eyes locked.

"Oh, for Christ's sake," Josie said. "Don't get your knickers in a twist. You want fancy store milk? I'll get you fancy store milk. Muriel will take me this week."

"Thank you," Lucy said, blowing out a sigh of relief.

"You done with that?" Josie pointed her cigarette at the waffles.

"Yup." Lucy slid the plate over and watched Josie drown the waffles in more syrup till every hole overflowed.

COLIN WAS SO BUSY DIGGING, he didn't notice Lucy until she was standing right beside him.

"Hey," he said, wiping the sweat from his forehead. "Good timing. I need a break."

The hole was so deep now that Lucy could sit and dangle her feet over the edge with still a few inches to spare. She pulled a handful of suckers from her back pocket and held them up.

Colin dropped his shovel and sat down next to her. "*Sweet.* Thanks."

"I found a whole drawer of them in the kitchen."

"Wow."

"Yeah. She's not what you'd call a health nut."

"Lucky for us."

"They were probably giving them out free somewhere, and she kept going back until her purse was full."

Colin laughed and crunched on his sucker. She threw him another one. They sat quietly for a few minutes enjoying the breeze coming up over the bank from the water.

"So what's it like?" he asked. "Living with her. Her being deaf and all that."

Lucy moved her sucker to one side and jammed it into her cheek. "Not that different, actually. Like sometimes she talks loud, I guess. But she's really good at lip-reading, so as long as you don't mumble and you look right at her, it's fine. And I act things out a lot too, without even realizing it." She shrugged. "But yeah, other than that, it's pretty normal."

They went back to enjoying the breeze. She felt him looking at her.

"I saw you before, you know," he said. "Before you came to the hole."

"Yeah. The window. I know. Thanks for pointing it out, though."

"No. I mean like a long time ago."

She moved her sucker to the other cheek. "What?"

"The funeral. I was at your mom's funeral."

Some of the lemon goo went down the wrong way and she coughed. "*What*? How come you never said?"

"I dunno. I just didn't."

"You were there?" She said it slowly, like she was trying to understand the words as she spoke them.

He nodded. "It was really weird. Just Mom and me. We came all that way and then when we got there, it was like she didn't want to see anybody, like she didn't want anyone to know we'd come."

"What do you mean?" Lucy watched him bend his sucker stick in half, back and forth till it broke.

"Well. We came. We went to the funeral. She talked to your dad. Then we left. I pretended not to notice, you know, how quick it all was, how weird she was acting. But like I said. It was weird."

Lucy thought for a minute. "Did you ask her about it?"

"No. She was so upset. I sort of didn't want to bring it up."

"Why would she even take you?"

"Dad had to stay home and look after the twins. Maybe she didn't want to go alone."

"Yeah. I guess that makes sense."

Colin jumped off the edge into the hole and picked up his shovel. "Could just be she was so upset that she got weird."

Lucy slid her butt back and leaned against a tree. She needed some time to let Colin's words sink in. She let her mind drift back to that day of the funeral, something she almost never did. Most of it was a blur. What she did remember about that day was the fear of not being able to make it through. She knew she couldn't let herself fall apart; she was the only thing holding her dad together. The memory made her nose sting and her eyes get watery.

The church had been completely full, standing-room only. Lucy had stared straight ahead at the altar, focusing on anything except what was actually happening around her. She had counted. Counted the members in the choir, the candles, the chain links in the chandelier. Whenever she'd felt like crying, she looked up and counted the ceiling tiles. That way, the tears collected in her eyes and didn't spill out. The worst had been when she felt her dad shaking beside her, sobbing. She had wanted to reach out, comfort him, touch his hand, but she couldn't. So she had stood there, still as a statue, and had kept counting the ceiling tiles until it was over.

Those were the moments that were crystal clear. She had no memory of things like what the minister had said, who had been there, or who she'd talked to. Colin could have easily been there and she didn't remember. She just may not have seen him. There had been so many people....

"Damnit!" Colin swore loudly and snapped her back.

"What's wrong?"

"Rock. Ginormous!" he said in disgust, pointing to the floor of the hole.

She got up, peeked over, and tried to look sympathetic. "Oh yeah, I see."

He let his shovel drop. "Got any suckers left?"

"Yeah, just a sec." She weeded through the debris of empty wrappers in her pocket. "Should be one—wait. Do you hear that?"

They both tilted their heads, straining their ears. There was something—a sound—off in the distance.

"What *is* that?" Lucy asked.

"If I didn't know better, I'd swear it was...the theme from *Star Wars*?" Colin scrunched up his eyebrows and looked around.

Lucy listened. He was right. Someone was whistling, loudly. And it was definitely the theme from *Star Wars*. She squinted off into the distance. It was a girl. And she was walking across the field towards them.

"Do you see what I see?" he said.

Lucy nodded, and kept nodding as the girl got closer. The girl had her hair done up in two buns, one over each ear, and she had what looked to be a white sheet draped around her, toga style. It was tied at her waist with a pink skipping rope.

"Who *is* that?" Lucy whispered.

"Isn't it obvious? It's Princess Leia."

CHAPTER 9

LUCY WAS WAITING FOR THE GIRL TO VEER OFF IN another direction, but she didn't. She kept coming towards them, weaving her way through the tall grass, her whistling getting louder and louder.

The girl stopped a few feet from them and blew a giant pink bubble out of a mouth bulging with gum. It popped then wilted, momentarily hanging and sticking to her chin, before she noisily sucked it back in.

"Hey," she said brightly.

Lucy and Colin shot each other a sideways look.

"Whatcha doin'?" she asked.

"Uh..." Colin started.

"Not much," Lucy finished. She tried to guess the girl's age. Twelve? Thirteen? Would a thirteen-year-old dress up like Princess Leia? In public? Would a twelve-year-old?

The girl stood there, chomping on her gum. "I saw you guys from the road. Thought I'd check you out."

Colin and Lucy nodded in unison. There was a stretch of

silence as they watched her blow, pop, and suck, over and over. It was hypnotic.

Lucy came out of the trance first. The stretch of silence was getting longer. "I'm Lucy. This is Colin," she said, half expecting the girl to introduce herself as Princess Leia.

The girl's eyes narrowed, like she knew what Lucy was thinking. "Kit. The name's Kit."

"Kit, huh?" Colin repeated thoughtfully. "Like Kit Kat? You know, the chocolate bar?"

Lucy jerked her head and glared at him. Was he out of his mind? What was he doing starting a conversation?

"Yeah. I know what a Kit Kat is," the girl replied. "And no, I'm not named after a chocolate bar."

"Oh. Okay." Colin looked disappointed.

"If you must know," the girl said, putting her hands on her hips, "as an infant, I was left on the front steps of the county orphanage. When they found me, I was in a giant knapsack—you know, like a kit bag? You *do* know what a kit bag is, don't you?" She waited for them to answer. Speechless, all they could do was nod. "Anyhow, the people there named me Kit, which is much nicer than Knap, don't you think?"

Lucy could only stare back with her mouth open.

Colin seemed to be searching for the right words. "Sure, yeah, sorry, I guess?"

"No biggie," the girl said casually. She smiled and blew another bubble.

Colin frowned. "Wait a second...that's not a true story, is it?"

"Nah," she said. "I'm just messin' with ya. But it's a good one, isn't it? Shock value and all that?" She didn't wait for them to answer this time. "Well, I'm off to the coop. Things to do."

"You're going to the store? Dressed like that?" Colin asked.

"Yeah." Kit shrugged. "Most of the locals think I'm a bit out there. Might as well not let them down."

Lucy nodded again, because she still couldn't think of anything to say.

"I don't care what they think," Kit continued. "I'm going to be a famous actress someday. I'm blowin' this popsicle stand as soon as I get the chance. Well. See ya!" She tightened her skipping rope, and off she went.

Lucy and Colin watched her go, her white sheet billowing behind her.

"'Popsicle stand'?" Lucy echoed. They looked at each other and burst out laughing.

Colin finally pulled himself together. "Welcome to Crazytown. Population: one."

"Oh my gosh," Lucy gasped, running her fingers under her eyes.

"Do you think that was even her name?"

"No idea. You've never seen her before?"

Colin shook his head. "Uh-uh."

"And what's the coop?" Lucy asked, picturing a cage full of chickens. Maybe she was going to get eggs?

"The Co-op. Mom calls it that too."

Lucy thought for a second. "Ha. I like that. That's funny." She sat back down at the edge of the hole and unwrapped another sucker. "Guess my dad didn't think it was important to mention there was a looney bin up here."

LUCY CLIMBED THE STAIRS FROM the beach, clutching a handful of glass. She had woken up early that morning and couldn't get back to sleep. Yesterday afternoon she'd stayed in the water too long, stretched across the air mattress, using her goggles to spy on a family of hermit crabs—at least they'd looked like a family to her. She'd had no suntan lotion on and now she was paying for it, her stinging shoulders and back making it impossible to lie in bed.

When she got to the hole, she knelt down on the grass and lined up her eleven pieces of glass on a flat rock. Two were blue.

She was happy about that. *What now?* She sighed and looked off in the direction of Colin's house. He was going to be late today. His mom was on his case. She'd told him he could dig his way to China for all she cared, but he still had to do his chores. She wanted the place unpacked and in tiptop shape before his dad arrived.

Mistakenly, Lucy had assumed Colin's dad was here—just off working. But apparently he was a chef at some big resort out west. The move had happened so fast, he'd stayed behind to wrap things up with the sale of the house and train his work replacement.

Lucy still hadn't met Colin's mom. She kept hoping Colin would invite her over, she'd even hinted at it a couple times, but considering he and his mom were barely speaking, it probably wasn't going to happen any time soon. She'd just have to wait for Josie and the dreaded "basket of homemade goodies" drop-off.

Something landed on the ground not far from her leg. She frowned. A rock. She jumped up and looked across the field. Colin. "Did you just throw a rock at me?" she shouted.

"I didn't *aim* for you!"

"Yeah, right!"

"If I had," he said as he reached the hole, "you'd be screaming in pain by now."

"Hmph." Lucy doubted he was as great an aim as he thought he was. "Get all your stuff done?"

"Done enough," he replied. "Dad called and all hell broke loose, everyone grabbing for the phone so they could talk to him. Teddy pushed Hannah off the kitchen stool and she smacked her head on the door frame."

"Ouch. Was she hurt?"

"Well, you'd think by the way she was screaming she'd been decapitated."

"She'd hardly be able to scream if she'd been decapitated."

Colin gave her a fake smile as he pulled his shovel from a pile of dirt. "Thanks, detective. Anyhow, made a break for it while everyone was crying. Oh, and all this happening while Dad's on the phone—long distance. Cha-ching. I wouldn't blame him if he put off coming for as long as possible."

She could hear it in his voice. He missed his dad.

"We should have all just stayed until the house sold," he said. "I mean, I don't know what Mom's big rush to get here was all about. If this place is so great, why'd she boot it out of here five minutes after she finished high school?"

Not sure if she was supposed to answer, Lucy swatted at some imaginary flies.

"And why am I the only one who's pissed off?" he went on. "No one else seems bothered at all. They just let her off the hook, happy as clams."

"Things will probably be better once your dad gets here," Lucy said. "Things will start to feel more normal then."

"Maybe." He sounded doubtful and gazed off at something over her shoulder. "Hey. Get a load of that."

"What?" Her first thought was it was that Princess Leia kid again. She spun around then laughed with relief. "It's just Josie."

"But what's she got on?"

"Oh. That." Josie had obviously finished her black-and-white optical illusion dress and couldn't wait to wear it. The pattern was all swirls and zig-zags. "I wouldn't stare at it too long; you might get a headache."

Josie reached them, panting, a cigarette nestled in the corner of her mouth. "I want you to finish up here soon," she told Lucy, then she turned to Colin. "Hello, Colin. Nice to meet you. I'm Josie. A friend of your mom's. Known her since she was a little hellion." She nudged him with her elbow and winked. "Whoops. I mean since she was a little girl."

"Hello," he said, looking a little awestruck.

"How's your mom making out?" Josie asked. "She must be dead on her feet. Hope you're being a good boy and helping her out."

He nodded.

"Yeah right," Lucy mouthed at Colin just out of Josie's view.

"Tell her we'll pop by sometime next week. I'll bring a batch of my famous muffins," Josie said with another wink.

Lucy touched Josie's arm. "Do I have to leave right now?"

"Yup."

"Why?"

"Your Aunt Ellen came by. She's invited us over."

"Oh." Lucy felt her stomach twist into a knot.

"You've got a bunch of relatives you couldn't pick out of a police lineup," Josie said sternly, as if it were all Lucy's fault.

"Fine." Lucy sighed and held up a finger. "I'll be up in one minute."

"Don't dilly-dally." Josie turned and headed back to the house.

Colin shook his head. "It's really something, isn't it? The way she reads lips. I'd never know she was deaf."

"I still forget sometimes."

"And how does she get that cigarette to stay like that even when she's talking? Did you see it bouncing around there? It's like it's glued on or something."

"Yes. She's very talented."

"And I thought you were going to push for homemade bread. How come we're getting *muffins*?"

Lucy spread her hands. "I tried! She insists on muffins. She says they're famous!"

"For *what*?"

"I don't know. But unfortunately, I think you're about to find out."

Colin made a face like he had indigestion.

"I'll try again," Lucy offered. "But I can't make any promises."

"Try *hard*," he said, sounding super serious. Then, "So, who's Ellen?"

"Oh. My aunt. My mom's sister."

"What's the big deal? How come you don't know her?"

"There was some kind of dustup between her and my mom." Lucy shrugged. "It was before I was born. They didn't speak. Whenever I asked her what happened, she said she didn't want to talk about it."

"Weird. What does Josie say?"

"I tried asking her once, but we got interrupted." Lucy remembered Josie's mob of bridge ladies and how they almost crushed her at the funeral home. "She did manage to say that they both needed a good kick in the arse, but that's all I got."

The corner of Colin's mouth twitched, probably at the arse comment.

"And I didn't want to ask her again," she continued, "because I didn't want to remind her about Ellen, because she's all hell bent on me meeting her and I don't want to. But as you can see that didn't work. If only," Lucy looked thoughtfully up at the sky, "there was someone else to ask."

Colin seemed to be thinking. She crossed her fingers on one hand and waited for him to connect the dots, say something like, "Hey, your mom and my mom were friends. She might know what happened."

But instead he asked, "What about your dad?"

"He said he didn't know." She bit down on her lower lip. She used to think her dad would never lie to her, but then she'd caught him in that lie on the phone. "Maybe he was just going along with Mom, though."

Colin nodded.

Kneeling down, she gathered up her beach glass. "I'd better go."

"Yeah." Colin stared into the hole. "At least now I can get serious. I got no digging done this morning."

Lucy rolled her eyes. "Would it really have made a difference?"

"Hey! It's the principle."

"If you say so."

"Tomorrow, I want all the details of the family reunion."

"How bored are you?"

"Don't ask."

Lucy turned around, walking backwards. "There'll probably be nothing to tell."

"You might find out what happened."

She shook her head. "Doubt it."

As she made her way back to the house she gave herself a mental head slap. Why was she being such a weenie? Why hadn't she just suggested they ask Colin's mom? But then she remembered something he had said—his mom had "booted it out of here five minutes after she finished high school." She may not have been around for the fight with Ellen. Lucy felt her shoulders sag. It looked like Ellen might be her only option after all.

Josie was waiting for her on the front porch. She had changed her clothes and was now wearing a bright yellow dress with a matching yellow hat and sandals. She looked like a banana. A short, wide banana. "Go put a face on," she ordered. "Then we'll hit the road."

Put a face on. What does that even mean? Lucy schlepped up the stairs to her room. She pulled on a clean shirt, brushed her hair and looped it into a ponytail, then gave her lips a good coating of root beer Lip Smacker. *There. Is this a face?*

ELLEN LIVED ON THE OTHER side of the Cape. It wasn't a long walk, but the whole way Lucy felt all clenched up inside. What was Ellen going to be like? What should Lucy say to her? Should she pretend she was happy to meet her? Should she just act like everything was easy-peasy? That she was in the dark about everything?

On Ellen's front step, Lucy hovered behind Josie. She listened to the doorbell ring inside the house. What if Ellen hadn't even invited them over and this was some plan Josie had cooked up? What if Ellen didn't want to meet her either? Or what if Ellen was nasty, or all snooty and looked down her nose at her? *I bet that's what she's like. Cruella de Vil.*

All those thoughts fell away as soon as Ellen opened the door. She looked so much like Lucy's mom. A complete stranger, but not. It took Lucy's breath away.

"Josie. Lucy. Come in." She sounded eager and nervous at the same time. "I can't believe you're finally here." Her voice cracked on the last word, and she hugged them both. Lucy longer. As Ellen pulled away, she touched Lucy's cheek. "You look just like your mother."

"So do you," Lucy whispered.

"You've grown so much," Ellen said.

Lucy nodded. *Grown so much...since when?* Lucy was pretty sure they hadn't seen each other at Gran Irene's visitation. *When's the last time you saw me?* Maybe no matter how mad you are, you still go to your sister's funeral.

"Come on in." Ellen gestured with her head. "I want you to meet someone."

They followed her into the kitchen. Ellen even walked like her mom.

There was a girl standing at the counter with a spatula in her hand, frosting a cake.

"Lucy, this is your cousin, Kathleen."

The girl looked up.

Lucy felt her eyes stretch so wide she was pretty sure her forehead disappeared.

It was Princess Leia. Again.

CHAPTER 10

"**K**ATHLEEN." ELLEN MOVED HER HAND THROUGH the air like she was presenting a side-by-side refrigerator-freezer on *The Price is Right*. "This is Lucy."

"Hey." Princess Leia barely looked up. She was focused on licking the icing off the spatula. "And I go by Kit."

Lucy smirked. *You don't say.*

Ellen sighed loudly and grabbed the spatula from Kit just as she was about to stick it back into the bowl, then she turned and smiled. "Hope you like chocolate cake, Lucy."

Lucy nodded.

"Um...." Ellen seemed to be searching for something to say as she smoothed the top of the cake with a clean spatula. "How are you enjoying your stay so far? You've had a beautiful stretch of weather."

"Yeah, fine, good," Lucy said hoarsely. Her voice didn't seem to be working right.

Ellen stepped away from the cake and said to Lucy, "I can't tell you how happy I am that you're here."

Lucy couldn't help but notice her eyes were the same as her mom's—same colour, same shape. She shifted uncomfortably beneath Ellen's gaze.

Josie cleared her throat, pulled out a cigarette that she'd tucked in her hat band, and held it up.

"Kathleen," Ellen said. "Go get Josie an ashtray."

Kit disappeared and after a second returned with a heavy crystal ashtray that she placed on the kitchen table. Then she looked at Lucy. "Wanna go to my room?"

"Uh...." Lucy waited for some direction from the adults. None came. "Sure," she said, and followed Kit upstairs.

Once behind the closed bedroom door, Lucy said, "So *you're* Kit?"

"Yup."

"Unbelievable." Lucy shook her head. "And in the field. Did you know who I was?"

"Yup. Well...I suspected. And then once you told me your name...."

"You could have *said* something!"

Kit laughed. "And miss the look on your face when you got here? No way."

"*Nice.*"

Kit bellyflopped across her frilly, lace-trimmed canopy bed and reached for something on the floor underneath. Sliding out a plastic bin heaped with candy, she rooted around and tossed something at Lucy. "Peace offering?"

Lucy instinctively grabbed for it then looked in her hand. A Kit Kat bar. "Real funny." It was her favourite, but she wasn't about to tell Kit that.

Kit chose a Coffee Crisp, and as they ate their chocolate in silence, Lucy's eyes did a sweep of the room. First thing she noticed was that it was very pink—pinks walls, pink curtains, pink shag carpet. There were feather boas, strings of beads and baubles, a couple tiaras, assorted straw and floppy hats, numerous pairs of oversized sunglasses, all hanging off every bed post, dresser knob, anything that could serve as a hook. *It looks like a dress-up trunk threw up in here.* She did a double take when her eyes landed on a massive pile of Barbies. There must have been at least thirty, stacked like a cord of wood.

"How old are you again?" Lucy asked.

"Thirteen," she said. "Pretty much, anyway."

Lucy raised her eyebrows.

"Okay, I'm twelve. But almost twelve and a half, so then you just round up, right?" Kit picked a chunk of Coffee Crisp off her T-shirt and popped it in her mouth. "How 'bout you?"

"Fourteen."

"Well, I'm very mature for my age, like, if you're worried we won't be intellectually compatible or something."

"Uh, okay. Good to know." Lucy snapped another finger off her Kit Kat.

"So," Kit started, balling up her wrapper, "are you going to give me the scoop?"

Lucy was nibbling a ridge of chocolate off the side of her bar. She always ate the chocolate edge first and saved the wafer for last. "Sorry?"

"You know. The scoop."

"What?"

Kit sighed dramatically. "*Your* mom? *My* mom? The big family secret nobody talks about?"

Lucy lowered her finger of chocolate. "You mean their fight?"

"Duh."

"Me? I know nothing."

Aiming for the garbage can, Kit tossed her wrapper. It hit the rim and tumbled to the floor. "There goes *that* plan."

"Sorry," Lucy said again.

Kit sighed. "When I asked Mom why she didn't speak to her sister, why had I never met her, all she said was that they had a disagreement. Then she clammed right up. I could tell just by lookin' at her, she felt bad about it." Kit reached into her candy bin and pulled out an Aero bar this time. "And probably even more now, what with your mom being dead and all, because there's no way they can ever make up."

Lucy looked at her Kit Kat bar. Suddenly she didn't feel like finishing it.

"I think the fight had something to do with a desk," Kit said.

Lucy frowned. "A desk?"

"Yeah. Some desk that belonged to our grandfather."

"They stopped talking because of a piece of furniture? No way." Lucy shook her head. That didn't sound like her mom at all.

"All I heard," whispered Kit as if on guard for eavesdroppers, "was there was some antique desk that my mom loved, came all the way from Scotland, always said she wanted it. You can fill in the blanks."

Lucy nervously picked at a hangnail on her thumb. *From Scotland? Uh-oh.* She knew that desk. They had that desk. It was in their living room. "So how did my mom end up with it?"

"Gran gave it to her."

"Shouldn't your mom be mad at Gran Irene, then?"

"Maybe she thinks your mom shouldn't have taken it. You know, since she knew how much *my* mom wanted it," Kit added.

Lucy wasn't sure if she detected a tone there or not. She felt a twinge of guilt anyway.

They lay on their stomachs across Kit's bed, arms hanging over one side, feet dangling over the other. They didn't say anything for a while.

Lucy thought about the desk. And how when she was little, she had used it as an apartment building for her Fisher Price people—made them little Kleenex beds in all the cubbies. It was a nice desk, but not nice enough to cause a family war. Lucy wasn't buying it.

Kit rolled onto her side, resting her head on her hand. "So, Colin. What's his deal?"

"No deal, really."

"A bit odd, isn't he?"

Lucy swallowed the wrong way and had to sit up. *Talk about the pot calling the kettle black.* "No." She coughed and pounded on her chest. "He seems normal, I guess."

"If you say so." Kit sounded doubtful. "He looked kinda sweaty. You like him?"

"You mean *like*, like?"

Kit nodded.

"No," Lucy said, wrinkling her nose. "Plus, he's older. Maybe even high school." And she'd had a mad crush on their paperboy for almost two years now. But that was definitely none of Kit's business. "We're just friends. The boredom brought us together."

"Okay. I guess that's cool then."

"Why? You interested?" Lucy joked.

"No siree." Kit shook her head. "I'm looking for someone a bit more...posh."

"Of course you are," Lucy said dryly. *How old are you again?*

"What do you guys do? Just hang out around that hole?"

"Pretty much." There was another moment of quiet. It seemed to go on and on. "You could...umm...come by sometime, you know, if you wanted to," Lucy offered. *Shut up! What am I doing? Stop talking!*

"Hmmmm." Kit rocked her head from side to side like she was thinking it over. "Maybe."

"Girls!" Ellen called from downstairs. "Cake!"

They sat on the back deck for the rest of their visit and had iced tea and chocolate cake. Lucy wasn't sure how she should act around Ellen. She didn't think she should be too friendly, but she knew she couldn't be rude either.

Ellen asked Lucy a thousand questions—stuff about what she liked to do, friends, school. She really seemed interested. Maybe she was just being nice. Or maybe she was just nervous. Lucy knew *she* definitely was.

Trying not to be obvious, Lucy studied Ellen from beneath her lashes. She couldn't help it. It was like being in a parallel universe—her facial expressions, her voice, the way her hands moved. Lucy was finding it hard to follow the conversation. She was relieved when Josie announced it was time to go.

BACK ON JOSIE'S PORCH, LUCY fluttered her fingers across Josie's open Harlequin to get her attention. "What was Mom and Ellen's fight about?"

Josie frowned and blinked at her a few times.

Lucy tried again, carefully enunciating her words and even throwing in some boxing moves.

Josie's expression remained unchanged. "Again?"

Faker. There's no way you don't know what I'm saying. Lucy reached for the notepad and pen that were on the wicker table. They were still out from when Muriel had stopped by for a visit. Apparently, Muriel didn't like to wear her dentures, and no dentures made lip-reading impossible, so she just wrote to Josie instead.

Flipping to a blank page Lucy printed, in big letters, WHAT DID MOM AND ELLEN FIGHT ABOUT?

Josie's frown deepened as she puckered and unpuckered her lips over and over. After a moment she said, "Honey, that's not my story to tell."

Huh? She didn't know what she'd thought Josie's answer was going to be, but it wasn't that. She obviously knew. But if she wasn't going to tell her, who was? Her mom wasn't an option. It *had* to be Ellen. "Will Ellen tell me?"

"When the time is right, you'll know everything you need to know."

What the heck does that mean? "So...from Ellen?"

"I'm sure Ellen will have a talk with you at some point."

"But—"

Josie held up her hand. "That's all I'm going to say about it for now." Her voice was firm.

Why? Why won't you just tell me? "But, but...." Lucy's mind frantically raced ahead, not wanting to lose her chance to learn something, anything. "Was it over a desk?"

Josie looked at her blankly.

Lucy ripped the used pages off the notepad and quickly wrote the word *desk* in giant letters. She held it up, jabbing the paper with the pencil. "A desk. Was it about a desk?"

Josie's whole body did a little jerk. "A desk? Gawd! Who told you that?"

"Kit. Kathleen," Lucy corrected.

"Kathleen?" Josie shook her head. "Don't get me wrong, she's a precious little thing, but she's nuttier than a fruitcake. I'd take anything that comes out of *her* mouth with a grain of salt."

With a heavy sigh, Lucy closed the notebook and placed it back on the table.

Josie pulled a cigarette from behind her ear. "I'm going out to the garden to pick some green beans for our dinner." She said it as if their previous conversation had never happened, like everything was normal.

There was a flip in Lucy's stomach. Josie had cooked green beans a few nights ago. She'd boiled them for so long, they were no longer green beans; they were drab, grey-brown beans.

Lucy watched her huff and puff her way across the yard.

Mentally exhausted, Lucy headed for the quiet of her room. Once upstairs, she sank into the chair by the window and tried to weed through the tangle of thoughts in her head. Everything that had happened today only ended up creating more questions and no answers. It was like the cosmos was playing some joke that everyone was in on except her. And Kit. Whatever happened, it had to have been pretty epic to make everyone refuse to talk about it. Either that, or it was so stupid everyone was too embarrassed to talk about it. She dug her palms into her eye sockets and pressed hard. *It shouldn't be this difficult to find out the truth.*

Lisa Harrington

She slouched even deeper into the chair, feeling frustrated and sulky. The tag on her T-shirt was rubbing against her sunburnt neck and she kept scratching at it. Every time she did, she winced. But she still kept doing it. The last scratch made her yelp out loud. "I need Noxzema," she muttered. Josie would have Noxzema. Everybody had Noxzema. At least, that's what her mom said.

She tried the medicine cabinet in the bathroom first. Nail polish remover, hand lotion, a compact of robin's-egg blue eyeshadow, a compact of blush, three lipsticks, a giant fluffy powder puff, Polident, a tube of something called Minard's Liniment. She unscrewed the cap and took a whiff. *Ick*. It made her eyes water. She'd smelled it before—on Josie. There was a roll-on deodorant, a bottle of Tums, but no familiar blue jar. She looked down the hall at the yellow room that used to be Gran Irene's, now Josie's. Lucy knew Josie hadn't come back yet. Because Josie couldn't hear herself, she tended to make more noise than the average person—a lot of banging and crashing around, doors slamming, that kind of thing. There was no way she could ever sneak up on anyone.

Josie's dresser was tidy. A comb and brush, some bottles of perfume, the biggest can of hairspray Lucy had ever seen, and that was it. She yanked open the first drawer. Underwear and bras, or *brassieres* as Josie called them. Drawer two: nighties. Drawer three: about a hundred pairs of pantyhose in varying shades of beige. So far, no blue jar. She was about to close the drawer when something caught her eye. Peeking out from beneath a clump of particularly light beige pantyhose, a patch of pink. She shoved the hosiery to one side. It was a bunny. A pink ceramic bunny.

92

CHAPTER 11

LUCY HELD THE FIGURINE IN HER HAND AND stared at it for a second. Was she losing it? Scrambling to her feet, she stuck her head out the doorway and glanced down the hall. All clear. She crossed over to her own room and stood there, frowning at the dresser.

Her eyes went back and forth from the bunny to the dresser top. *Yup*, she nodded to herself. She was sure it had been there, part of the collection. She thought could even see the space where it used to be. So why did Josie remove it? Did she think Lucy would take it? Break it?

Hmph. Lucy tried not to feel offended. *But why just this one?*

Back in Josie's room, she knelt down in front of drawer number three and pushed aside the mound of pantyhose. As she placed the bunny back in its spot, it snagged on some nylon. The actual figurine didn't, but a tiny metal hinge on the back of the bunny's neck, barely noticeable. The head opened—a bunny-shaped box.

There was something inside.

She pulled out a small pouch.

It was shaped like an envelope, made of blue velvet, a single gold snap holding it closed. She undid the snap and slid the contents onto the floor. There were six tiny plastic bags with a kind of blue circle design stamped on them. In each one, a gold chain with a green stone. An emerald? She took one out and examined it closely. There was a 10K stamp on the clasp—the chain was real gold. She let the necklace dangle from her finger. The stone sparkled in the afternoon sun. It looked real, too. Puzzled, Lucy lined the other bags up in a row. Why would her mom have six identical necklaces? At least, she assumed they were her mom's. They'd been in her mom's room, inside one of her bunnies.

Lucy heard the smack of the screen door. Josie was back. She quickly jammed the bags back in the pouch, put the pouch back in the bunny, and shoved the bunny under the pantyhose, plumping up the heap so it looked as it had. Running back to her room, she perched herself on the edge of the bed and tried not to look guilty as she listened to the *thump, thump* of Josie making her way up the stairs.

She appeared at Lucy's door, an unlit cigarette dangling out of her mouth. "Thought you might want to go for a swim, wash off the day."

Lucy shook her head. "Maybe later?" Her head was too jumbled—she'd probably forget how to float and drown.

Josie scratched her chin. "Mabel Lauther? Honey, she's been dead for years."

What? "No." Lucy shook her head again. "Maybe *swim* later," she repeated, making breaststroke motions with her arms.

"Ha!" Josie laughed. "That makes more sense. Because how would you know Mabel? Mabel. Now she was a piece of work." Josie wagged her finger at Lucy. "A bigger cheater at bridge there never was. And let me just say, if it hadn't been for her prize-winning strawberry jam, I wouldn't have ever let her step foot in my house."

Lucy nodded, as though she totally knew what Josie was talking about.

"Ha!" Josie laughed again. "Mabel Lauther. Haven't thought of her in ages." She continued to mutter and chuckle to herself all the way back down the stairs.

"HI, DAD."

"Hi, pumpkin. How's it going up there?"

"Okay, I guess."

"You don't sound like yourself. You all right?"

Lucy hadn't slept well. Her brain wouldn't turn off. "Yup. Just a little tired."

"All that fun can be exhausting, huh?"

"Yeah." She felt her eyes start to get hot. "That must be it." She wanted to change the subject. "Dad. Am I named after Lucy from Charlie Brown?"

He laughed. "That's a funny question. I guess I don't really know. Your mom had the name picked and ready to go. Though now that I think about it, we do have a cat named Linus."

"And remember how we could never miss any of the Charlie Brown specials?"

"Yeah. She made us all sit together on the couch."

They were both silent for a moment. "How are things in town?" Lucy asked.

"It's pretty quiet around here without you."

"I can come home," she sniffed. "You can come get me."

"No, no. I'm hardly here anyhow. You'd be bored out of your tree."

Doubt it.

"Your meeting with Ellen," he said. "How was it?"

Lucy made a face into the phone. "Okay. Sort of weird. She looks a lot like Mom."

She heard him swallow. "She does, doesn't she?"

"But she didn't have horns or anything, so that was nice."

95

He laughed. "See? I told you it wouldn't be so bad. And even though you didn't want to, you're actually meeting people. Ellen, Gordon...."

"Is Gordon the dad?" Lucy interrupted. "I think he must have been at work or something."

"Okay, but you met Kathleen, right?"

"Yup." Lucy rolled her eyes. "She's a bit of a trip."

"Well, between her and Colin, at least you have some kids to play with."

"No, Dad. You don't understand. Kathleen, Kit, whoever, is living on another planet. She's a total space cadet." She thought of Kit's room, all the crazy stuff she'd said. It gave her an idea. "Are you sure you don't know what Mom and Ellen fought about? It wasn't about a desk, was it?" If he said it *wasn't* about a desk, wouldn't that mean he knew what it *was* about?

There was a pause.

"Dad?"

"Sorry. I thought I heard something." Another pause. "Look. Roberto is at the door. He's looking for his paper money. I missed him last week when I was out of town. Coming!" he yelled away from the phone.

"But Dad—"

"Gotta go, pumpkin. We'll talk soon, okay? Love you."

And the line went dead.

Lucy held the receiver in her hand and glared at it, willing it to be her dad's face. Roberto was the paperboy she'd been in love with forever. He was also in her class and she pretty well knew all there was to know about him. Like that his dad had a job with a fancy name—the Italian Consulate—and that the whole family had gone to Italy for the summer, returning September 3. She still remembered Sarah rubbing her back sympathetically when Roberto showed up the last day of school for all of five minutes to collect his report card and say *arrivederci* to the class.

Kind of impossible for him to be at the door, Dad!

About to slam down the phone, she paused in mid-air. *Wait. How did you know I met Colin? I haven't mentioned him. I know I haven't.* Slowly, she placed the receiver back in the cradle. *It's not like Josie called for a chat.*

She leaned her head back against the fridge and closed her eyes. Okay. Her dad was definitely lying. Josie knew stuff but refused to tell her. No one would answer any of her questions. Not to mention the bunny full of necklaces that for some reason had been removed from her room. What was going on here?

Lucy poured herself a glass of water and took an aspirin from the bottle Josie kept on the kitchen windowsill, right next to a green can of Export A tobacco, a chipped teacup containing assorted buttons, and a jar of powdery peppermints. Josie was always pushing peppermints at her. "You have to keep your swallow wet," she'd say. Why? Why did she have to keep her swallow wet? Just add it to the list of things she didn't know.

"PRINCESS LEIA IS YOUR COUSIN?!" Colin's mouth hung open. "Wow! Never saw that one comin'."

Lucy had just finished telling him about her visit to Ellen's. He was still shaking his head as he picked up his shovel and drove it into the dirt. She watched him for a while and tried to organize her thoughts. She wanted to tell him everything that was in her head, if only to spread the confusion to someone else and take some of the load off her.

"Hey," she said. "You've only been digging for five minutes and you already look like you need a break." The sun wasn't out, but the air was thick and heavy, not a breath of wind. Colin's hair was stuck flat to his head and his T-shirt was damp with sweat. "Let's go down to the beach and splash some water on us."

Colin wiped the side of face on his sleeve, then turned his head to spit. "Okay. Just for a few minutes, though."

Lucy rolled her eyes. *Ew.*

They cut across the field to the lane. The *swish, swish* of the tall grass sounded extra loud in the stillness. After what felt like forever they made it to the top of the stairs. Lucy had been hoping that a rush of sea breeze would billow up over the cliff, but no such luck. The tide was as far out as it could go, with not a single ripple breaking the water's surface.

Wading through what water there was, they headed out to the giant sandbars. Colin wrote, *Colin was here* with a stick then handed it to Lucy. She flashed back to the soap-smeared mirrors in the school bathroom. *Oh, you're one of those.* As she finished drawing a daisy, she said, "Do you ever sometimes wonder if—?" She was going to tell him, but then stopped. Could be she didn't feel like sharing the fact that her dad was a liar, or that she had been snooping in Josie's drawers, and that maybe Josie didn't trust her enough to leave gold jewellery in her room. That idea had popped into her head overnight and she was still kind of iffy about it. It just didn't seem like Josie.

Colin seemed not to notice she hadn't finished her sentence. He was staring up at the sky. It had turned a steely grey. "Uh-oh."

A huge plop of rain landed with a *splat* on Lucy's bare arm. A loud rumble of thunder sounded out over the water. The heavens opened and the rain came pelting down in sheets, immediately soaking them to the skin.

"Come on!" Colin shouted over the pounding. "My house is closer!"

Lucy nodded and took off after him. It was hard to run in flip-flops; the ground kept trying to suck them off her feet. She slipped more than once and punched Colin hard in the arm when she caught him laughing.

When they arrived on Colin's front porch, he opened the door and shoved her through into the front hall. "I'll get you a towel," he said, trying to catch his breath.

Lucy stood on tiptoes, as if that was somehow going to keep her from dripping on the wood floor. Her hair hung in long strings, water trickling from the tips down her arms and back. She craned her neck, trying to get a look into the closest room. It was mostly filled with boxes, ones that still needed to be unpacked and others that had been flattened and stacked into piles. The moving truck had obviously made it, so why did Colin insist on still wearing those disgusting barn clothes?

He returned wearing a dry, finally different, T-shirt and handed her a fluffy blue towel. She quickly patted herself off before mopping up the puddle on the floor that had formed around her feet.

"This works out, actually," Colin said. "Mom's been bugging me to bring you over."

"Oh?" She ran her fingers through her drenched hair, trying to fix it up a bit.

"Yeah. She freaked when she found out I'd already met you," Colin said, rolling his eyes. "Prepare yourself. She can be kind of dramatic."

Lucy followed him down the hallway to the kitchen. The radio was blasting KC and the Sunshine Band's "Boogie Shoes." She felt a twinge of homesickness. Her dad loved that song and sang it all the time. Badly.

Colin's mom was standing on the counter, paintbrush in hand, painting the cupboard doors.

"Mom!" Colin shouted as he turned down the radio.

She carefully turned around, taking tiny steps so as not to lose her balance. When she saw Lucy, a huge smile spread across her face.

"Mom, Lucy. Lucy, Mom," Colin said flatly as he yanked open the fridge door.

Colin's mom shot him a look. "Thanks for that heartfelt introduction, Colin." She climbed down from the counter and wiped her hands on the back of her jean shorts. Her eyes got all watery. "Gosh, Lucy! Is that really you?"

"Um...yup."

She smiled again. "Call me Esther."

Lucy nodded.

"I'm sorry I haven't been over to see you at Josie's. First Teddy had a double ear infection, then the moving truck broke down...." She rubbed her forehead. "My plan was for us to all go over together to meet you, but nothing's been going right."

"That's okay," Lucy said. "Josie was planning for us to come over anyway. So yeah, we can come to you instead."

"And I can't believe this kid met you ages ago and never bothered to mention it till the other day."

"It hasn't really been ages, Mom," Colin said.

"It's fine. All is forgiven," Esther said. "You're here now, that's all that matters." She took a step back and gave Lucy a good once-over. "Your colouring's a bit darker, but I see a lot of your mom in you. I hope you don't mind me saying that."

Lucy shook her head. She knew right away that she liked Esther. She didn't seem dramatic at all. There was definitely something about her. It could have been her bare feet and ankle bracelet, the paint smeared across her cheek and streaked through her mass of red curls, or the silver hoop earrings the size of a bread-and-butter plates. All together, it made Lucy smile.

"Oh, you have your mom's mouth, her exact smile," Esther said. "Perfect lips for bright red lipstick—which your mom loved, of course."

Lucy raised her fingers to her mouth. She couldn't remember ever seeing red lipstick on her mom. Cherry Chapstick was about it.

Colin was still hanging off the fridge door.

Esther sighed. "For God's sake, Colin. Are you having a conversation with something in there?"

"I'm looking for something to drink!" he said.

"I just made some Tang for the twins. It's in the door."

He lifted out the pitcher and poured two glasses. As he handed Lucy a glass, he said, "We don't have to stay in here."

But she didn't want to leave Esther. "That's okay," she said, pulling out a stool.

Colin made a face and sat down.

Esther leaned against the sink. "I'm guessing Josie told you that your mom and I were best friends growing up."

Lucy sipped her juice. "Yup."

"She was like a sister to me. It was one of the worst days of my life when she passed away. I don't mean to upset you, but I just really wanted you to know that."

Lucy's chest tightened. "Thanks."

"The very first day of school, I dropped my sandwich on the classroom floor. Your mom gave me half of hers—strawberry jam and bologna. I remember it like it was yesterday."

"That's when you met?" Lucy asked, wanting to hear more.

"Yes. We were best friends from that minute on. Much to your grandmother's horror," she added with a smile.

"I think Josie said you were a little, uh...."

"Untamed?" Esther said. "Wild?"

Lucy nodded. "Yeah. That."

Esther smirked and scraped some dried paint off her arm.

"So were you?" Lucy pressed. "Wild?"

"I guess it depends on your definition."

"Come on, Mom, just spill," Colin demanded, looking bored with the conversation.

"You'd love that, wouldn't you?" Esther said then looked at Lucy. "I don't know if Josie mentioned, but I grew up with a foster family in the village."

Lucy shook her head. "No."

"They were lovely people. But I was one of six, not a lot of supervision. Needless to say, plenty of opportunities to get up to no good."

Lucy tried to imagine what she meant by "no good," and whether or not her mom had gotten "up to" it with her.

"We definitely got ourselves into some messes," Esther continued. "It was always my fault though, my idea." She laughed to herself. "Your mom, I could talk her into anything."

My mom? "Really?"

"I think I said that wrong. I just meant she was a good head, game for adventure. Plus she was super smart. Because of her, we hardly ever got caught. She was queen of the cover-up." Esther poured herself a glass of Tang. "Probably shouldn't be telling you all this."

"All of what?" Colin said. "You haven't told her anything. The story would be better if you said what you guys actually *did*."

"Oh, settle down," Esther said. "Silly stuff—graffiti, pranks at school, playing hooky. We didn't knock over a bank or anything. I think the most scandalous thing we ever did was pierce each other's ears. We were in grade...six, maybe? What made it worse was we both got infections." She shook her head and laughed to herself again.

Lucy frowned and touched her unpunctured earlobe. She had begged her mom a hundred times to get her ears pierced.

"Wow," Colin said disappointedly. "Basically, you were just a small-time hood."

Esther ignored him and topped up Lucy's glass. "I'm sure your grandmother had a panic attack every time she saw me at the front door. No, she did not like me. Not one little bit."

A faraway look settled on Esther's face as she turned to the window and stared outside. She fiddled with the chain around her neck. It made Lucy remember the pouch of necklaces. And then everything else. A wave of tiredness washed over her, and she suddenly felt a need to leave.

Lucy jumped up off her stool. "I should go."

The abrupt movement brought Esther back. "Yes. I guess you don't want to worry Josie." She leaned closer to the window. "At least it seems to have stopped raining. Colin can walk you back."

"No," Lucy answered, maybe a little too quickly, but she just wanted to be alone. "Um. I'm fine to walk back. Thanks, though."

Colin shrugged and walked her to the door.

"I want you to know you can come back anytime," Esther said, following them down the hall. "I want you to feel comfortable and know that you're always welcome here."

Lucy awkwardly handed her the wet towel. "Thanks."

"See ya tomorrow?" Colin said.

Lucy nodded, hurried down the steps, and didn't look back. Once hidden in a cluster of trees, she stopped and leaned against the closest one. It was like she couldn't catch her breath. In the last couple of days too much had happened, too many new people. She'd been dying to meet Esther, but hearing her talk about her mom, about when she was young, what she was like, it was as if she was talking about someone Lucy didn't know. A complete stranger.

She couldn't help but feel a little betrayed by her mom.

CHAPTER 12

DEEP IN THOUGHT, LUCY DIDN'T NOTICE JOSIE sitting on the porch as she slowly made her way up the steps.

"You look like something the cat dragged in," Josie commented through a puff of smoke.

Lucy glanced down at her damp clothes, felt her bangs still stuck to her forehead. "Thanks," she muttered, for once not worrying about enunciating.

After she'd changed into a dry T-shirt and shorts, she grabbed the quilt off her bed and wrapped it around her like a cape. A sulky mood hung over her. She sat on her bed with her lower lip stuck out as far as it would go and stared at a small spider crawling up the wall next to the dresser. Maybe tomorrow she'd talk to Colin about some stuff. Today she'd chickened out, and then there was the whole meeting with Esther. Tomorrow she'd just do it. Even if he had nothing to say, no opinion, at least it would make her feel better, sharing it—well she hoped it would, anyway. Cocooning herself tighter in the quilt until she resembled an egg roll, she let her body fall sideways, timber, onto the bed.

She must have dozed off, because when she opened her eyes, Josie was standing over her, a concerned look on her face. "Can you breathe under there?"

"Yes," Lucy sighed and flipped the quilt off her head. She saw Josie was holding a wooden spoon. *Uh-oh. She's cooking.*

"Come on," Josie said. "Supper's almost ready."

Lucy looked at the clock, blinked a few times, and held up four fingers. "It's only four o'clock."

"Lawrence Welk is on tonight," Josie said, as if Lucy was an idiot not to know that. "I like to have supper over and everything cleaned up before it starts. That way I can have my Peek Freans and enjoy my show. You can join me. The reception is good today. A lot of the time it's too fuzzy to watch."

Where have I been on all the other Lawrence Welk nights? Probably hiding out in my room, avoiding supper.

"Get the lead out," Josie ordered. "I'll go down and simmer off the rest of the fat."

Lucy waited for Josie to leave then made a gagging face. *Simmer off the rest of the fat? That doesn't sound unappetizing at all.*

Josie was stirring something in a big cast iron pot on the stove. Lucy sniffed the air. It sort of smelled like hamburger. She looked over Josie's shoulder. It sort of *looked* like hamburger, crumbled in some kind of liquid, maybe with some onion too?

"Cut some bread," Josie ordered. "We're having mincie on toast. You probably know it as mince, but we always called it mincie."

Lucy shook her head at Josie's back. *Nope. Don't know it as either.* But she did as she was told, cut two thick slices of bread and popped them in the toaster. While she waited, she watched Josie and nervously chewed on a thumbnail. Josie had a cigarette in her mouth and seemed oblivious to how long the ash was getting. Again. It was dangerously long, dangerously curved. Again. If Lucy tapped her on the shoulder or made any move to alert her, it would only startle her, and game over. All she could do was cross her fingers.

"Pass me an ashtray," Josie said around the cigarette.

How does that ash not fall? Lucy quickly grabbed one off the counter and set it on the stove beside the burner. Josie smoothly transferred the cigarette to the ashtray, intact. Lucy let out a sigh of relief.

Supper turned out to be surprisingly not bad. It tasted better than it looked. Ketchup definitely helped.

It wasn't until they were sitting in the living room in front of the TV with their plate of Peek Frean shortbreads, four each, that it occurred to Lucy that Josie was watching a show about music—music she couldn't hear.

Josie answered her question before she could ask it. "I love watching those Champagne Ladies, with their beautiful hair and fancy dresses. I watch them dance, watch Lawrence move his stick, and I imagine the music. I still have songs in my head. I remember."

For a second Lucy was overcome with a feeling of sadness. What Josie said seemed so bittersweet, though she probably didn't mean it that way. What was it like to lose your hearing? To have it for part of your life, and then have it taken away? She must miss it. Miss the music. Miss the dancing....

Lucy moved closer to Josie on the couch as the Champagne Ladies swirled around the dance floor in their pastel chiffon gowns. "The girl in peach is my favourite," Josie said, smiling and wrapping her arm around Lucy's shoulder. "She's the best dancer. And I think she's in love with that tall fellow who's her partner sometimes."

Lucy nodded in agreement. *She seems so happy to have someone to watch her show with. Actually, she seems pretty happy all the time.*

There was no way Josie had moved that bunny of necklaces because she didn't trust her, or thought she would take them. Josie didn't have a mean or suspicious bone in her body.

There must have been some other reason. Lucy wished she could ask her.

LUCY STOOD AT THE EDGE of the hole watching Colin try to leverage out a large rock with the handle of his shovel. "Hey," she said. "Why don't we skip the digging and hike around the Cape?" She wanted to talk to him, but away from the hole, where he wouldn't get distracted.

Colin shook his head. "Nope. You made me go to the beach yesterday. I missed a whole day."

"That was because it rained! That wasn't my fault!"

Stubbornly, he kept shaking his head.

"Oh, come on," she pleaded. "It'll be fun. Josie said it's kind of like a race. You have to make it all the way around before the tide comes up."

"I'll take a break in the afternoon, but I can't skip another day."

"That won't work; the tide'll be wrong. And I hate to rain on your parade, but I don't think your plan is working. I mean, has your mom ever been out here? Has she even *seen* the hole?"

The shovel handle slipped out from beneath the rock. "No!" Colin snapped.

This was not going the way she'd hoped, but it was now or never. "Listen. I kind of want to talk to you about something." She'd decided to stick with the necklaces, because it was sort of intriguing, like a mystery. He probably wouldn't be much interested in her feelings about her dad. And now her mom.

He looked up and wiped his forehead with his arm. "Okay. Talk."

Since he made no move to get out of the hole, she lowered herself over the side and got in the hole with him. "See, I—well, I found something in Josie's drawer." She was trying to tell him without letting on she'd been snooping.

"You were snooping," he said.

"I wasn't." She quickly shook her head. "I was looking for Noxzema."

"Hi, guys!"

They both whipped around at the same time. There was Kit, looking down on them in full-on Princess Leia regalia, her white bedsheet fluttering in the breeze.

"What is she doing here?" Colin whispered without moving his lips.

"I forgot to tell you. I kind of invited her," Lucy whispered back the same way.

Colin's head slumped forward.

"What are you two doin' down there?" Kit said loudly.

"Nothing." Lucy sighed and hoisted herself up out of the hole. "So, you decided to come."

"Yeah." Kit plunked down on a grassy patch. "Mom wanted me to clean my room, so I thought it would be a good time to pull a disappearing act."

Lucy nodded and sat down beside her.

"Aren't you hot in that thing?" Colin asked, still in the hole.

"No!" Kit snarled. Then she flapped her arms. "The air circulates through perfectly."

Colin rolled his eyes.

"Oh. That's good," Lucy said politely.

"Look." Kit pulled something from beneath the folds of her sheet. "I bought treats." She held up a package.

That seemed to win Colin over. "Red licorice! I love red licorice."

"Well." Kit stuck her nose in the air. "That's a common misnomer. These are actually *strawberry Twizzlers*. Licorice is a distinct flavour, and always black."

Colin pressed his lips together as if to stop words from coming out. He pulled himself up and sat on the edge of the hole. "Okay then, can I have some *strawberry Twizzlers*?"

Kit squinted at him for a second, then held out the package. "Help yourself."

Except for the intermittent crinkling of the plastic when pulling out a fresh Twizzler, they chewed in silence for a while.

"Hey," Colin said to Lucy. "You never finished telling me what you found."

Lucy turned and stared at him.

Colin's eyes got real big. He cringed and mouthed, "Sorry."

Too late. Kit pounced. "You found something? What? What did you find?"

"Nothing." Lucy dragged her hand down her face. "It's nothing."

"Uh-uh." Kit shook her head. "I saw him say sorry. He let the cat out of the bag about something. 'Fess up."

Lucy squeezed her eyes shut and pinched the bridge of her nose.

"Come on," Kit said. "I'm your cousin, for Pete's sake. I can keep a secret. Oooh. *Is* it a secret?"

There was no way out at this point and Lucy knew it. "I, uh, found this ceramic bunny of my mom's in Josie's drawer."

"So you were snooping," Kit said.

"No! I was looking for Noxzema!" How many times was she going to have to explain that?

"Don't get offended," Kit said. "There's nothing I admire more than good snooping skills."

Lucy clenched her jaw. "Anyway. I found this bunny in Josie's pantyhose drawer. It's part of my mom's collection. But this bunny opens up, and inside there were six necklaces. All exactly the same."

"Okay. I'm confused," Colin said. "You want to know if they're real?"

"No," Lucy sighed. "I think they are. But, like, are they my mom's? Are they Josie's? And why were they moved from my room?"

"How do you know they were moved?" Colin asked.

"Well, I'm pretty sure that bunny was on my dresser when I got here. But there are bunch of bunnies on the dresser, so I didn't notice it was gone till I saw it in Josie's room."

Colin nodded thoughtfully. "And you think Josie moved it."

"Yeah. Who else?" Lucy said. She scraped a fingernail against her front tooth, thinking. "What are they for? Why would someone have six of them?"

"Maybe they were on sale," Colin suggested. "Or maybe they really *are* Josie's. The bunnies, too."

"Or maybe," Kit, who had been unusually quiet, said, "they're stolen."

"What?" Lucy exclaimed. "Why would you say something like that?"

"It's like you said. Why would you have six necklaces all the same? What other reason could there be? The only thing you have six the same of is socks and underwear."

"Let me get this straight." Colin tugged on his chin. "Are you saying Josie could be some kind of jewel thief?"

Kit shrugged. "We don't know what she does in her free time."

"That's ridiculous," Lucy said.

"Yeah," Colin said. "I don't think there're many deaf jewellery thieves. Don't you have to listen for noise, so you don't get caught?"

"Yeah," Kit said. "But doesn't being deaf heighten your other senses? Maybe—"

"I think we can safely rule out Josie as a jewel thief," Lucy said firmly.

"Oh, all right," Kit said, but she didn't look happy about it. "Besides, the necklaces are really probably your mom's. Because they were inside *her* bunny."

Lucy narrowed her eyes. "Are you saying my *mom*'s the thief?"

Kit shrugged again.

How dare she. "Well...well, maybe they're *not* hers. Maybe she was just keeping them for somebody."

Kit looked doubtful. "Like who?"

"Like, like...." Lucy's thoughts raced. *Aha!* "Perhaps a sister?"

"Hey!" Kit stood and jammed her hands onto her hips. "Are you saying *my* mom's the thief?"

Lucy crossed her arms and didn't say anything.

Colin put both his hands up. "Let's everybody calm down now. We don't even know if they're actually stolen. You two are acting nuts."

They both glared at him.

"Wait a second," Kit said slowly. "My mom told me"—she pointed at Colin—"that *your* mom was friends with"—she pointed at Lucy—"*your* mom. Maybe she was holding them for, say...a *best friend*?"

"Hey!" Colin frowned. "Are you saying *my* mom's the thief?"

Lucy couldn't help but remember how Esther herself admitted she used to be a little wild.

The three of them stood in a circle, more like a triangle, staring each other down like they were in a standoff.

Lucy blinked first and took a step back. "Okay, guys. This is getting pretty silly."

"You're right," Kit said. "This isn't getting us anywhere."

"Yeah." Colin reached for his shovel. "I'm just gonna go back—"

"You know you're going to have to bring them to us," Kit said.

Lucy jerked her head. "What?"

"The necklaces. We need to see them."

"Why? And no way," Lucy said. "I'm not going back in Josie's drawer and just taking them."

Kit sighed dramatically. "Lucy, it's not like she's going to catch you. You could drag that dresser down the stairs and out to this field and she'd never be the wiser."

Colin scratched his head. "Well, she's not blind. And she'd feel the vibrations...."

"You know what I mean!" Kit shouted at Colin, then to Lucy. "You could easily take them without her noticing. Once we see them, we might be able to figure out where they came from. Then we can decide what to do next."

"Do next?" Lucy echoed.

"Yup. We're going to do our best Nancy Drew impression and solve this mystery." She snapped her fingers in the air. "The Mystery of the Ceramic Bunny. No, no...The Clue in the Ceramic Bunny. Or, I suppose the word 'necklaces' should be in the title, huh?"

Lucy really had no response. She was starting to feel like she was on *Candid Camera*.

"Ugh." Colin made a face. "Can't we be the Hardy Boys instead?"

"No," Kit said flatly. "No, we can't."

Colin turned to Lucy. "Who put her in charge?"

"I think *she* did."

CHAPTER 13

KIT WAS RIGHT. IT HAD BEEN EASY TO SNEAK THE necklaces out of Josie's room. They were safely tucked in the back pocket of Lucy's shorts. She finished up her waffles and carried her plate to the sink, careful to walk sideways, convinced that somehow Josie would see the lump in her pocket and ask what it was. Thankfully Josie was preoccupied flipping through a *Good Housekeeping* magazine. Which Lucy found kind of funny. Basically because the place usually looked like a bomb went off. There were always fabrics and tissue-paper patterns strewn all over the living room, not to mention straight pins scattered everywhere. Thank goodness they had coloured nubs on top that made them easier to spot. And Lucy was pretty sure she hadn't seen a duster or vacuum since she'd arrived.

Shoving the pouch down deeper into her pocket, she tapped Josie on the shoulder. "I'm going to the field."

Josie blew out a cloud of smoke. "Nice to have a chum, isn't it?"

Lucy nodded, inching towards the door. She just wanted to get out of there.

"You know," Josie said. "I noticed something."

Uh-oh. Lucy's heart rate sped up. She kept her hand over her back pocket.

"Your shoulders are peeling awful bad," Josie said.

Lucy's heart rate slowed.

"There's probably a jar of Nivea or Noxzema in the linen closet," Josie continued.

Lucy's heart rate sped up again. "Thanks," she squeaked and backed out of the kitchen, practically falling down the front porch steps.

Noxzema? She knows! She knows I was in her room looking for Noxzema. Lucy shook her head as she walked along the path. *No. How would she know? She'd have to have superpowers. Wait. Didn't Kit saying something about the other senses being heightened?* Lucy shook her head faster. *No. That's insane. Heightened senses don't include mind-reading. It's a coincidence.* She took a deep breath. *Yeah. It's just a coincidence.*

Colin was already hard at work digging when Lucy reached the hole.

He looked up. "Did you get them?"

She nodded.

He dropped his shovel. "Can I see?"

Lucy pointed to a flat rock by a heap of dirt. "Come over here." She pulled the pouch from her back pocket then looked around. "Should we wait for Kit?"

Colin scrunched up his face. "No. Besides, she might not even be coming."

"Are you kidding me? Did you hear her? There's no way she's not sticking her nose in this as far as it'll go."

"We still don't have to wait for her. She's not the boss of us."

"If you say so," Lucy muttered under her breath. She knelt down, unsnapped the velvet envelope, and lined up the six tiny plastic bags in a row on top of the rock.

Colin wiped his hands on his shorts, then opened one of

the bags and slid out the chain. He held it up and let it hang from his finger, studying it like he was some kind of jewellery expert.

"There's a stamp on the clasp," Lucy pointed out. "Ten K. It's ten-karat gold."

Colin studied it for another minute, then put it back in its bag and returned it neatly to the row. "I don't know what to tell you. I've no idea why someone would have six of them."

Lucy tapped her finger against her lips. "You don't think Kit's right, do you? That they're stolen?"

He shrugged. "I suppose anything is possible. But by who? And then that puts us right back to what happened yesterday. Because there's no way *my* mom stole them."

"And there's no way *my* mom stole them." But Lucy noticed her voice wasn't as loud or as firm as Colin's. She really had no idea what her mom had been like, had been capable of in her life before becoming "Lucy's mom."

"And you know Kit's going to say the same thing about *her* mom," Colin said.

Suddenly Kit was there. "Let's see them, then," she demanded, wedging herself between the two of them.

"Jeez!" Lucy slapped a hand to her chest. "How do you keep sneaking up on us?"

"I'm very stealthy," Kit said proudly.

"Yeah, well, you're pushy too," Colin said, rubbing his shoulder.

"Quit being such a baby," Kit said, her eyes zooming in on the lineup of plastic bags. "What do we have here?" She picked up one of the tiny bags and held it about an inch from her eye. "Hmmm... see this little blue stamp? It's from J. B. Jewellers in the village. The same emblem is on their sign."

Lucy sat back on her heels. "What do you think that means?"

"You're not gonna like it," Kit said. "But I still think they're stolen."

"Why do you keep saying that?" Lucy snapped. "As if there could be no other explanation."

"I *told* you you wouldn't like it," Kit said.

"Well, we're pretty sure Josie didn't steal them, and we know our moms didn't, so if there's no thief, how can they be stolen?" Colin said smugly.

"That," Kit said, frowning, "I can't tell you."

The three of them sat in the dirt, staring at the necklaces as if waiting for them to reveal some clue they'd missed.

"Could they have just been found or something?" Lucy offered.

Kit shook her head. "Anyone from around here would know where they came from and would have returned them."

They went back to staring at the necklaces. They seemed to sit there forever—a do-over of their earlier standoff.

"Hey," Colin finally said, turning to Kit. "Where's your sheet?"

Kit glumly looked down at her pink T-shirt and matching pink shorts. "I spilled grape Kool-Aid on it. Mom made me put it in the wash. Plus she says I shouldn't wear it every day. Takes away from the *mystique*."

"Oh." Colin whacked at a mosquito on his leg.

Lucy moved onto her knees. "I should put these back." She began gathering up the packets.

Kit jumped up. "I thought of something."

"What?" Lucy asked suspiciously.

"Hear me out," Kit said. "Let's say they *are* stolen...."

Lucy shook her head.

"But maybe whoever stole them," she continued, "had a really good reason. Like maybe they *had* to."

Colin snorted. "Had to? Nah."

Kit crossed her arms. "You got a better theory, Sherlock?"

"No, but—"

"I think I sort of get what you mean," Lucy said slowly. "Maybe they had been planning to sell them or something. Maybe they needed money."

"Yeah," Kit nodded. "Maybe it was to help someone."

"Like Robin Hood," Lucy whispered to herself. Her eyes shifted to Colin. He was swatting at another mosquito. Didn't his mom used to live with a foster family? With six other kids? She would have been pretty poor. Could her mom have been trying to help her? Or could they have been in on it together?

Colin flicked a dead bug off his arm. "That's kind of a stretch. You guys are coming up with all these crazy ideas and you don't even know if they're actually stolen."

"You're right." Kit bobbed her head. "That's what we need to find out. We're going to that jewellery store."

Lucy gasped. "What? We can't do that."

"Why not?" Kit said. "It's not like we have anything better to do. It'll be fun. An adventure."

"Go the store and do what?" Colin asked sarcastically. "Turn over the goods?"

"No, no," Kit said. "We don't need to take the necklaces. We'll just be doing a bit of investigating, asking a few questions."

Lucy's eyebrows scrunched together. "What *kind* of questions?"

"Don't worry. Leave it to me," Kit said, sounding super-efficient. "I'll have it all planned out."

"I dunno." Colin scratched the back of his head.

"Oh, come on," Kit pleaded. "Don't you want to know one way or another?"

No one said anything.

"Oh, come *on*," Kit repeated. "What's the worst that could happen?"

"Well..." Lucy pulled on her lower lip. "We could find out they *are* stolen. Then what do we do?"

Kit looked thoughtful. After a moment, she shrugged her shoulders. "We'll cross that bridge if we come to it."

Lucy wasn't sure how she felt about Kit's so-called plan. She gathered up the plastic bags, slid them into the velvet envelope, and stuffed it back into her pocket.

"Tomorrow morning." Kit pointed to her watch. "Oh-nine-hundred hours. We all meet right here."

Before anyone could argue, Josie came huffing and puffing down the lane, wisps of smoke trailing behind her. She must have been going somewhere special; she was wearing one of her favourite dresses. Bright red covered with pink and white hearts.

"The fabric was eighty percent off after Valentine's Day," Lucy said, pretending to wipe her nose but really blocking her mouth.

"Hello again, Colin, and hello to you too, Kathleen," Josie said, the cigarette bouncing crazily between her lips. Then she turned to Lucy. "Muriel's taking me to the Co-op. I think you should come pick out some of that fancy milk you want so badly."

Lucy didn't have to think twice. It seemed like a good time to wrap up this get together.

"Oh-nine-hundred hours," Kit called after Lucy as she trailed Josie up the lane.

LUCY SAT ON THE PORCH swing, pushing herself back and forth with her foot. She was on her second glass of real 2-percent milk from a carton. *Yummy.* She leaned her head back on the cushion, closed her eyes, and went over all the talk from the hole this morning. Why had she even opened this can of worms? Why hadn't she just left the necklaces alone?

It was all too late now anyway.

The screen door squeaked open. "You need something to do," Josie said. "Come help me."

Oh no. Lucy's shoulders slumped and her head fell forward. Lucy couldn't begin to imagine what Josie would want her help with. She got off the swing and followed her inside.

In the kitchen, Josie pointed to the table. "Sit."

Lucy sat.

Picking at the curling corner of a laminated Peggys Cove placemat, she watched Josie pull out a bunch of stuff from the cupboard and set it on the table. One thing was a rectangular metal contraption, similar in size to a shoebox lid. It was covered in a kind of rubbery cloth and had knobs on both ends. Beside it, a green tin of Export A tobacco and a flat cardboard box the size of a ruler with paper sticking out like Kleenex. Lastly, Josie added a dish of water, a razor blade, and a small sponge.

"Thought I would teach you how to roll cigarettes," Josie said.

"*Huh*?"

"Just to make it clear, though. Don't ever let me catch you smoking. Your father would kick my arse."

Lucy just stared back, eyes wide.

"Okay now, pay attention."

Oddly fascinated, Lucy watched as Josie laid the strip of paper in the rubbery thing, fitting it into an indent to make a long skinny trough, then she gently stuffed the trough with tobacco. After wiping the edge of the paper with the wet sponge and making it sticky, she turned the knobs on each end, causing the paper to roll around the tobacco, and *voilà*! A foot-long cigarette. Next she took the razor blade and cut the cigarette into four smaller ones. There were little slits in the machine to guide her cuts. She piled them to one side. "Your turn," she said.

Lucy swallowed and pulled her chair in closer to the table.

"Go on," Josie urged. "Give it a try."

A few practice rolls later, Lucy was actually getting the hang of it.

"By the end of the summer, you'll be an expert," Josie said. "Keep going." She picked up one of Lucy's creations, lit it, and took a deep drag. "Excellent," she said as she exhaled.

Lucy kept rolling. Josie did the stacking.

"You met Esther the other day," Josie said. "What did you think?"

"She seemed nice."

Josie nodded. "She's a lovely girl."

They worked in silence for a while, Lucy concentrating on perfecting the width of each cigarette so it was smooth with no bulges.

"What were they like, Esther and Mom?" Lucy asked after completing about a half dozen.

Josie didn't answer. Lucy realized she'd forgotten to look up so Josie could see her mouth. She repeated the question.

"Ha!" Josie butted her cigarette out on the edge of her lunch plate. "They were quite the pair. Bosom buddies."

"But Gran Irene didn't like Esther much, did she?"

"No, she didn't," Josie said.

"Esther said they sort of got into trouble sometimes," Lucy hinted, hoping Josie would offer up some examples, but she just said, "Pfft," and swept some stray tobacco off the table.

"So...they didn't get into trouble?" Lucy took another stab at it.

Josie made a face. "Oh, sure they did. Piddly stuff. There's only so much trouble you can get into around here."

"Then why did Gran Irene dislike Esther so much?"

"Your gran could be a little judgmental," Josie said, standing up some fresh cigarettes in an empty tin. "She wasn't keen on Esther's upbringing and lack of discipline and supervision. Thought your mom should have a higher class of friend or some nonsense." She leaned in closer to Lucy and raised her eyebrows. "I don't know what made her so high-falutin'. It's not like we're Cape John royalty or something. Anyhow, when Esther moved out west with her boyfriend, fresh out of high school *and unmarried*, your gran felt it just proved her point." Josie gathered up another handful of cigarettes. "I know it's not kind to speak ill of the dead, but your gran, my very own sister, had a few rocks in her head if you ask me."

"Mom must have been sad when Esther left." Lucy didn't know what she'd do if Sarah ever moved away.

"Yes, well, she had her own problems to deal with at that

time." Then a strange look passed over Josie's face. "Don't listen to me, dear. I don't know what I'm saying half the time."

Yeah right. Lucy wasn't buying that doddering old lady routine.

Josie quickly pushed back her chair. "You made great progress! Look, you filled a whole tin."

Lucy glanced in the tin at all her neatly rolled cigarettes, her new talent. Her dad would *freak* if he saw her now.

"You're a free woman," Josie announced, adding a long peel of apple skin to the can before snapping the lid on and putting everything away.

Lucy hung back, hovering by the kitchen door. She wanted to ask some more questions about her mom—about what Josie had meant when she said that her mom had had her own problems to deal with. But then she changed her mind. It seemed lately every time she had a conversation about her mom, it left her more anxious and confused.

Adding to that anxious, confused feeling was the fact she still hadn't decided if she was going to meet Kit at "oh-nine-hundred hours" yet. She kept flipping between *what the heck* and *what's the point?* Wanting to think about something else for a while, she wandered into the dining room and pulled a random Harlequin off the bookshelf. She studied the cover. A beautiful girl with long, black hair and violet eyes was in a passionate embrace with a shirtless guy who looked like he had too much suntan lotion on. It was called *Suddenly Love.* Lucy grinned. They always looked so intense on the covers. And they were *always* in a passionate embrace.

She took the book up to her room and flopped onto her bed. The room felt heavy with heat. She was having a hard time keeping her eyes open, but she did manage to make it all the way to chapter five before nodding off.

CHAPTER 14

LUCY'S AFTERNOON NAP LED TO A GOOD TWO HOURS of tossing and turning at her regular bedtime. When she finally did manage to fall asleep, the nightmare seemed to start the second she closed her eyes and didn't stop until she opened them the next morning. She couldn't remember all the details; she just knew it had to do with the necklaces, and that at one point she and her mom were in some unknown jewellery store filled with police. It left her with a breathless, scary feeling down deep in the pit of her stomach that lasted long after she woke up.

She ran a brush through her hair. Maybe the dream was trying to tell her something. Maybe she should just go along with whatever Kit was cooking up, find out about these necklaces one way or another and be done with it.

It took her longer than usual to get herself to the hole. She was late. Secretly she hoped Kit had backed out and Colin was just there digging like usual. *Yeah right. Who am I kidding?* Kit and Colin were both standing there waiting. She wondered if Colin had shown up right at oh-nine-hundred hours like Kit had ordered.

"Told ya she'd show," Kit said to Colin, holding out her hand. "You owe me a quarter."

"You didn't think I'd come?" Lucy said.

Colin shrugged. "I dunno. You didn't seem too keen on the idea."

She didn't say anything. He was right.

If Kit sensed her lack of enthusiasm, she was ignoring it. "Okay, here's what we're going to do," she said in a bossy voice. "I say we head up to the village, hit the jewellery store, and chat up Mrs. Jacobson—she's worked there for a million years. Eventually we get around to asking if the store's ever been robbed. If it has, she'll know. *And* she'll have all the details. How's that sound?"

Colin opened his mouth like he was about to disagree, but then closed it again. "Actually, it's not the *worst* idea in the world."

Then something occurred to Lucy. "If we want to know if there was a robbery, couldn't we just go to the library and look up back issues of the newspaper or something? A robbery would be in the paper, wouldn't it?"

Kit gave her an approving look. "Good thinking, Nancy Drew, but the library's on summer hours, only open part-time. We'd have to wait until next week."

Lucy glanced over at Colin and sighed. "Okay. We'll go with your idea. Like Colin said, it's not the worst in the world."

"Gee, thanks," Kit said sarcastically.

The rest of the morning they spent trying to come up with questions they could use on Mrs. Jacobson to steer the conversation towards robbery, which proved to be not that easy.

"Let's not sweat it," Kit said, standing and brushing some dirt off the butt of her shorts. "We can't sound too rehearsed, she'll get suspicious. We'll decide what to say on the walk."

Kit took the lead, Lucy followed, then Colin, and they made their way down the lane and out to the main road.

Once on the pavement, they spread out and walked in silence. A slight breeze rustled the tall grasses growing in the ditches along both sides of the road, and a farm tractor put-putted from somewhere far off in the distance.

Kit was the first to speak. "I think we should just let the conversation happen naturally, see how far we get."

"Okay," Lucy answered. She had to admit, it wasn't so bad having someone in charge, telling her what to do. It made everything easier.

After about a half hour, the traffic picked up a bit. They were getting closer to the village. Moving to the shoulder, Lucy listened to the gravel crunch loudly beneath her feet. She could feel herself tensing up. Her throat felt dry. But that could have been from the heat or the gravel dust.

The main street came into view and Kit pointed. "There it is, next to the drugstore." The shop was the bottom floor of a pretty house—dark green with cream and black trim.

"Do we have, like, an opening line or something?" Colin asked.

"Don't worry, I got it covered," Kit said.

"What does *that* mean?"

"It means take a chill pill."

Colin gave Lucy a look. She shrugged and followed Kit into the store. A tiny bell attached to the door announced their arrival. It took a few seconds for Lucy's eyes to adjust after the brightness of outside. *What if the store matches the one in my dream? That would be really creepy.* But it didn't. The walls were panelled in a dark wood. The floor as well, and it creaked when they walked on it. The whole place smelled like lemon Pledge. In the back corner, an old lady was polishing a glass display case.

"Just follow my lead," Kit whispered.

"Hey," Colin whispered back, "we're not your backup singers, you know."

The old lady came out from behind the counter and smiled. "Well hello, Kathleen. What a nice surprise. What can I do for you?" Her eyes shifted past Kit. "And your friends."

"Hi, Mrs. Jacobson," Kit said. "This is Colin. He just moved here. His mom's Esther. She used to live here. Maybe you remember her?"

"I do!" Mrs. Jacobson exclaimed. "I remember Esther. Sweet girl."

Colin shifted on his feet, looking uncomfortable. "Um, thanks."

"And this is my cousin, Lucy," Kit added.

"You don't mean Laura's daughter?"

Kit nodded.

"Bless my soul." Mrs. Jacobson's hand flew to her chest and her eyes got all shiny. "She was a sweet girl as well."

"Thanks," Lucy smiled.

Kit went up to the counter and peered down through the glass. "Lucy's looking for...a charm."

Lucy joined her. "I am?" she mumbled under her breath.

"Yes," she hissed, then turned to Mrs. Jacobson. "She needs a souvenir of her summer here."

Mrs. Jacobson pulled a crumpled Kleenex from the sleeve of her sweater and dabbed her eyes. "Well, let's see what we have here." She walked over to the glass display counter, unlocked the door, and lifted out a velvet tray. She set it down and they all gathered around the assortment of charms. Lucy couldn't help but notice the emblem on the tray lining was identical to the ones on the tiny plastic bags back in the ceramic bunny.

"Take your time, see if anything catches your fancy," Mrs. Jacobson said.

Lucy pretended to examine each charm while trying to figure out what she should say or ask next. She needn't have bothered. Kit was way ahead of her.

"Yup. This has been quite the vacation for Lucy," Kit said loudly. "First time she's been back since she was a kid."

Mrs. Jacobson smiled and nodded as she Windexed the other end of the glass counter.

"Being from the big city, country life sure has been an adjustment," Kit went on.

Lucy kept her head bent down over the charms. What the heck was she talking about?

"It's so quiet and unexciting around here compared to the crime-ridden streets she has to endure on a daily basis back home," Kit said.

"I don't endure any crime-ridden streets," Lucy whispered to Colin.

"Like, just before Lucy came here, her neighbour's house was broken into," Kit continued. "During the day! Can you believe that, Mrs. Jacobson?"

Mrs. Jacobson shook her head. "That's such a shame. What gets into people these days? There's a lot to be said for country living."

"I *know*," Kit said. "That's what I told her. I don't think I know of *one* time a house has been broken into around here."

"Nor do I," Mrs. Jacobson agreed.

"Or even a store, for that matter. Because you'd think that would be more likely. You know, more money, more stuff to steal."

"Hmm." Mrs. Jacobson looked thoughtful. "Maybe the Co-op once...but now that I think about it, it was just some shenanigans after a dance at the fire hall next door. *Someone* drove their car through the front window, though."

"So just the Co-op?" Kit said. "Nowhere else? The drugstore? The gas station? Here?"

They all held their breath waiting for Mrs. Jacobson to answer. There were at least a dozen clocks hanging on the back wall. The sound of their unsynchronized ticking was deafening.

"Goodness, no. Not since we opened the doors way back in 1945."

There was a collective exhale.

"Told you country livin' was way better!" Kit slapped her hand on Lucy's back.

"You two sound like the city mouse and country mouse." Mrs. Jacobson chuckled, squirting some Windex where Kit had left new fingerprints.

"Are we ready to head out, then?" Colin asked, edging towards the door.

"What about your charm?" Mrs. Jacobson said to Lucy.

"I forgot my wallet," she said, feeling guilty about wasting the woman's time and letting her think she was going to buy something. "But I think I like the lobster. Could I put it on hold?" She would come back and buy it with her birthday money.

"I'll set it aside for you," Mrs. Jacobson promised. "And I'll even give you the staff discount, too."

"Oh, you don't have to do that," Lucy said.

"Of course I do. Your mother worked here, after all."

Lucy froze. "What?"

"Our Mariah had such a hard time with her first baby. Colic. I had to go up to Barrie, help her out for a few weeks. Your mother filled in for me here, Saturdays and a couple afternoons after school. We ended up keeping her on even after I got back."

"I, uh—" Lucy's words were stuck in her throat.

Colin elbowed Kit.

"Wow. We didn't know that, did we, Lucy?" Kit looped her arm through Lucy's and pulled her in the direction of the door. "Thanks again, Mrs. Jacobson."

After spilling onto the sidewalk, they quickly walked down the street, not stopping until the shop was out of view and they'd reached the Co-op parking lot.

"Now, I know what you're thinking," Colin said in a calm voice. "But just because your mom worked there doesn't mean she took them."

"Yeah," Kit said. "Even though it was the perfect cover."

"Um." Colin made a face at Kit. "You're not really helping." Then to Lucy he said, "Remember what Mrs. Jacobson told us: no robberies."

Lucy shook her head. It was too much of a coincidence. "She could have taken them and they just never realized it."

"Nuh-uh," Colin said. "Did you see the size of that store? It's tiny. There's no way they wouldn't notice six necklaces going missing."

Lucy shook her head again. "Those necklaces are from that store. My mom worked there. She must have taken them. There's no other explanation." She sniffed a couple times. "I don't want that to ever come out. I don't want people to think she was a thief. That she stole from the Jacobsons."

No one said anything for a minute, but Lucy thought she saw Colin and Kit exchange some kind of look.

"I can't believe I'm saying this," Kit said. "I agree with Colin."

"You do?" Lucy frowned. She was right. It didn't sound like something she would say.

"Yup. Someone would definitely notice if all those necklaces went missing."

"You really think so?"

"Yeah," Kit said.

"Yeah," Colin echoed. "Go with what the old lady said."

Lucy gnawed on her fingernail until she drew blood. "But it still doesn't explain why they are where they are."

"Listen," Kit said. "We might just have to accept that it's something we may never have the answer to."

"I suppose." Lucy narrowed her eyes. That didn't sound like something Kit would say either.

Colin swiped at a trickle of sweat dribbling down his forehead. "Can we go now?"

They retraced their steps through the village, and after only a few minutes, someone Kit knew offered them a lift in the back of their pickup truck. Lucy's tailbone would never be the same after bouncing and bumping their way down Cape John Road, but it was totally worth it not to have to walk all that way back in the sun.

"You should have got him to stop, Kit," Lucy said, hopping off the bumper of the truck. "We passed your house."

Lisa Harrington

"Nah. I want to hang out with you guys."

Colin made a face behind Kit's back.

"Oh," Lucy said. "I don't even know if—"

"Guys." Colin sighed loudly. "I'm gonna die if I don't get a drink. You can come if you want." He turned, jumped over the ditch, and started across the field alongside the road.

"Cool!" Kit scrambled down one side of the ditch and up the other. She looked back at Lucy. "Coming?"

Lucy just wanted to go straight to her room, lie down, maybe even call her dad. "Yeah," she sighed. "I'm coming."

The twins were in the front yard of Colin's house building a fort out of the empty moving boxes.

"Colin!" one of them yelled. "Come play with us!"

"Can't."

"You never play with us! I hate you!" the other hollered.

Colin grinned. "Love you, too!"

As they tumbled through the front door and headed down the hall, they passed Esther kneeling on the floor in the den unwrapping picture frames.

"Hello?" she called as they walked past.

Colin stopped, backtracked, pulled Kit with him, and pushed her through the door frame. "Kit. Lucy's cousin. Kit. My mom."

"Oh. Ellen's daughter," Esther said, looking up. "Nice to meet you."

"You too," Kit said.

"We're thirsty," Colin announced.

"There's stuff in the fridge, help yourself."

They marched single file into the kitchen, where Colin poured three glasses of Kool-Aid that they all downed in about a half a second.

"Well, at least we got *some* answers," Kit said, raising her empty glass.

Lucy smiled, hoping she looked sincere, and clinked her glass against Kit's. *Did we, though?*

CHAPTER 15

"HEY, GUYS," KIT SAID. SHE WAS CARRYING A rainbow-striped beach bag. She slid it off her shoulder and plunked down on the grass beside Lucy. "Am I late? Have you been here long? Did I miss anything?"

Lucy lowered her hands. She'd been practicing her duck calls, blowing through a blade of grass pressed between her thumbs. "Nope. Haven't missed a thing."

Colin looked up from his shovelling. "You're coming here pretty often now, huh?"

Kit tilted her head. "You got a problem with that?"

"Noooo, not at all," Colin said, giving Lucy a giant eye roll that he didn't bother to hide.

"Don't mind him," Lucy said to Kit. "I think he's got sunstroke."

"We can only hope, right?"

"Meanie," Lucy said.

A serious look came over Kit's face and she inched herself a little farther back from the hole. She gestured for Lucy to follow. Lucy did.

"I don't mean to be mean," Kit said softly.

"Oh, I know you're only joking."

"Because...well, about the jewellery store."

Lucy frowned. "What about it?"

"I kind of feel bad."

"Why? You weren't mean."

"I could tell you were sort of upset even before we went into the village. I probably should have just minded my own business and not been all bossy about going to Jacobson's."

"That's okay," Lucy said, trying to sound casual.

"Mom says I can be really bossy sometimes."

Lucy smiled, imagining what Colin would have said to that if he'd heard.

"So maybe we should just put the whole necklace thing on the back burner for a while," Kit said.

"Really? You seemed pretty gung-ho to solve the mystery."

"Oh, I still am. But it's when you stop looking for something that you find it." Kit shrugged. "That's another thing Mom says."

"Okay." Lucy didn't feel so sure.

"Look." Kit pulled her bag closer. "I brought all my mags." She started taking them out one by one. "Got *Teen*, *16*, *Tiger Beat*, *Seventeen*...we could look through them while Colin digs."

"Cool," Lucy said, fanning out the stack. "And perfect timing. Josie got some Campbell's Soup recipe book in the mail and she's determined to try out all the recipes. I need to spend as little time at the house as possible."

Kit's eyes got big. "Mom got the same one. Stay away from the Peachy Chicken. Cream of chicken soup and canned peaches do *not* go together. I don't care what anyone says."

"Thanks," Lucy said. "I'll be on the lookout for that one."

"I brought my DoodleArt, too." She dug a cardboard cylinder from her bag. "There's one in here that's all butterflies."

"Oh yeah?"

"Yeah. I noticed your necklace when you came to my house,

and then you had a butterfly T-shirt on yesterday with butterfly barrettes. So, I dunno. I figured you had a thing for butterflies."

Lucy touched a finger to the butterfly hanging from her neck.

Kit pulled a piece of paper out of the tube and held it out. "I haven't started it yet. You can have it if you want."

"Thanks. I do have a thing for butterflies." Lucy unrolled the paper and stared at the black-and-white print. She felt bad for all the times she'd thought Kit was a bit of a nutjob. She wasn't so sure she would have picked up on all the butterfly stuff if she'd been in Kit's place. "Are you sure?"

"Yeah, knock your socks off." Kit turned the tube upside down and shook the markers out onto the grass. "Just so you know, though, the pink one is all dried up."

"What are you guys talking about?" Colin came to the edge of the hole.

"Kit brought stuff to do," Lucy said. She picked a magazine and held it up. "I'll read to you aloud."

"Don't bother," he scoffed. "It's all junk."

"Hey!" Kit said. "There are some great articles in these!"

"Okay, okay." Lucy put up a hand. "I'll only read you something if it's really, *really* interesting."

Colin muttered under his breath and moved to the other side of the hole.

Lucy flipped her magazine open to an article on the dangers of hitchhiking. When she'd finished and vowed to herself to never hitchhike, she leaned over to see what Kit was reading. Kit was poring over a glossy foldout picture. "I just love Shaun Cassidy," she sighed.

Lucy liked the other Hardy Boy, Parker Stevenson, better, even though his eyes were too close together. Roberto's eyes were close together too.

They passed the next half hour flicking through the magazines, discussing the latest fashions and movie star gossip. Colin kept on digging, but every once in a while he'd ask who or what they were talking about.

Then, as Lucy was memorizing a list of pointers on "How to Pick the Right Perm for You," the now-familiar smell of cigarette smoke wafted through the air.

There was a rustle of leaves as Josie came around the corner. "You three have been sitting out here in the sun too long," she said. "You're getting brown as berries. Go down and get yourselves wet."

What? Berries aren't brown. Lucy shook her head. "It's okay. We're fine." She was trying to figure out if she should get a perm.

Josie looked down at her.

"It's okay. We're fine," Lucy repeated, exaggerating her words.

"I know what you said. But it wasn't a question." Josie stubbed out her cigarette. "Get down to the water. Tide's about halfway."

Kit jumped to her feet. "I'm ready." She snapped the strap of her bathing suit underneath her T-shirt and nudged Lucy with her foot. "Got your suit on?"

"Yes." Lucy sighed and got up as well. She couldn't decide who was bossier, Kit or Josie. "Come for a swim, Colin!" she called out.

"Can't," he answered.

Lucy turned to Josie, pointed at Colin, and shook her head.

"Colin!" Josie jammed her hands onto her hips. "Don't make me come over there and kick your arse."

Colin's head whipped up. "Huh? What?"

"She's going to kick your arse if you don't come for a swim," Kit explained.

"Jeez, all right already." He pulled himself up out of the hole and came over to join them.

Kit fanned a hand in front of her nose. "You need a swim more than anyone."

Colin lifted his arm and sniffed his armpit. "Yeah, you're right."

As they followed Josie down the lane Lucy couldn't help notice Colin had an odd look on his face. "You don't smell *that* bad," she assured him.

"No, it's not that. It's Josie's dress."

Josie was sporting a sundress patterned with orange, lemon, and lime slices. It was pretty understated by Josie's standards. "What's wrong with it?"

"I think it's the same as our new kitchen curtains."

"That wouldn't surprise me."

After getting dunked, Lucy stood waist deep in the water. It was so clear she could see right to the bottom. She watched a hermit crab as it scuttled along the side of her foot and across the ripples of the sandbar. She could feel the sand slowly creep over her toes, and the soothing sensation of the waves as they gently tugged her forward then pushed her back. It was like being rocked to sleep.

Kit swam up behind her. "You wanna look for beach glass?"

Colin was doing underwater handstands and Josie was stretched out on the air mattress she always left stuffed under the bottom step. She'd run aground in the shallow water and there was a plume of smoke floating above her. "Sure," Lucy said.

They waded ashore, stooped over, and began to slowly shuffle along the water's edge.

"So you collect beach glass too?" Lucy asked.

"Yup," Kit said. "For Mom. She pays me."

"She *pays* you?"

"She has this giant bowl shaped like a seashell. She thought it would look cool filled with beach glass. I get a nickel for white, a dime for green and brown, and a quarter for blue. It's not glamorous, but it keeps me in candy." She stopped as she spied a piece of white and tucked it in her fist.

"I really want to find blue," Lucy said. Josie had given her a pickle jar. So far she'd managed to cover the bottom. "There's a jar at home on our kitchen windowsill with only blue. It was my mom's. I want to try to fill it."

"Oh, here, then." Kit pressed a triangle of blue glass into Lucy's hand.

"No, no. I didn't mean for you—"

"Relax, cuz. There will always be more glass."

JOSIE PLACED A DISH OF something on the table in front of Lucy.

Lucy eyed the plate warily. *Please don't let it be Peachy Chicken.* She picked up her fork and slowly pushed the mystery food around. *Some kind of bean, chunks of...beef?* "What is it?"

"Mexican Fiesta Beans," Josie announced proudly. "Figured it wouldn't kill us to try something exotic."

Are you sure?

"I think I may have scorched it on the bottom," she continued. "If you come across any bits of black, just pick them out."

Lucy nodded grimly.

"It doesn't look much like the picture in the book." Josie frowned. "Maybe I shouldn't have stirred in all that Cheez Whiz. That was my own personal touch."

Yuck. "I'm not that hungry," Lucy said, glad Josie couldn't hear her stomach growling.

Josie raised a forkful to her mouth, then set it back down. She scrunched up her nose and pushed the dish away. "Maybe exotic isn't all it's cracked up to be. How does cinnamon toast sound?"

Lucy smiled. "Perfect."

IT WAS WHEN SHE WAS fastening her butterfly necklace the next morning that Lucy remembered her dream from the night before. She had been wearing one of the emerald necklaces. Someone had been standing behind her. Even though she couldn't see her face, she was sure it was her mom. She asked Lucy to take it off, but every time she did, another one appeared around her neck. *Spooky.*

She headed outside, the screen door slamming behind her. Colin wasn't going to be at the hole. He had to babysit the twins while his mom went to the Co-op. And because Lucy didn't have anything better to do, she had agreed to help him sort and hang all his photos in his room. His mom had been nagging him and threatened that he wasn't allowed to leave the house again until it was done.

The twins were running around in circles and waving bubble wands through the air when Lucy entered the yard. Their faces were already covered in chocolate and it was only nine thirty.

Colin was waiting for her on the front step. "Oh Henrys," he explained. "Breakfast of champions."

Lucy laughed and followed him into the house and up the stairs. "Don't worry about Kit," she said, knowing full well he hadn't given her a thought. "She went into Truro with her mom."

"What?" He stopped on the stairs and turned. "Oh, right. Kit. Yeah, I was worried."

She gave him a shove.

"Wow," she said, entering his room. "You've got a lot of stuff." Piles of framed pictures lay on the floor and a bunch leaned against the wall. "How do you want to do this?"

"I dunno. Hang them on that wall?" he pointed.

Lucy shook her head. "We can't just hang them willy-nilly. Let's at least map out some kind of arrangement." She knelt down on the floor.

He sighed heavily and crouched beside her. "Can't *you* just do it? Hang them any way you—"

"Hey. Is this you?" Lucy picked up a picture and looked at it closely. It was Colin on a sailboat.

"Yeah. And my boat. We had to sell it before the move," he said wistfully. "Dad promised to put the money towards a new one. Won't be until next summer, though."

"You sort of look like you know what you're doing," she joked.

"I did. I do. I can teach you if you want," he offered. "Like, if you come back next summer."

It hadn't occurred to Lucy that she might come back. "Maybe." She spread out some more of the pictures. "Wait. What's this?"

Colin frowned. "Oh, that one shouldn't be here; it goes in the den."

It was a large black-and-white framed photo of a huge, elegant building. There were a ton of people in assorted uniforms lined up on the sweeping front lawn. "Is it a hotel?" Lucy asked.

"It's the resort my parents worked at out west."

Lucy's eyes scanned the picture, picking out bellboys, maids, cooks, waitresses, even a tennis instructor. "Your mom and dad are in here?"

Colin leaned over her shoulder. "Yeah. There's Mom"—he tapped his finger on the glass—"and there's Dad."

Esther looked younger, but pretty much the same as she did today, except for a different hairstyle and cat-eye glasses. His father looked like a tall gangly kid. "Gosh. How old were they?"

He shrugged. "It was right after high school, I think, so I guess they would have still been teenagers. I'm getting a Popsicle, want one?"

"Sure." Lucy continued to study the picture. *How old are you when you finish high school? Seventeen? Eighteen?* She couldn't imagine picking up and moving so far away from home just a few years from now. There was a bit of silvery writing at the bottom of the photo, but it was partially covered by the frame. She could see the tops of numbers. *Bet it's the date.* Placing her hand on the back of the picture, she slid it up slightly. *Yup. October 1, 1961.* Lucy's mom was born in 1943, so assuming Esther was about the same age, that would make her only eighteen. *That's young!* Lucy set the photo by the door to go back downstairs. *But maybe not in those days.*

"Here." Colin stuck an orange Popsicle in her face.

140

"Thanks." She broke it in half and pulled one stick out of the paper sleeve. "Your dad's a chef, right?"

"Yeah."

"What's he going to do when he gets here?"

"Not sure. Pictou Lodge is the only sort of fancy place around here. Actually, I think he and Mom want to open their own place."

"In River John?"

"That's their big plan."

"You could work there part-time. That would be awesome." Lucy was jealous. "All I'll ever get to do is babysit."

"I'd rather be sailing."

Lucy turned her attention back to the pictures on the floor. "This one's a perfect square," she said, picking it up. "Maybe it should go in the middle." She peeled off a stray piece of packing paper. It was a picture of Colin's family posing on a wharf beside his boat, but there was an extra person in the photo. Lucy kept blinking as if her eyes were playing tricks on her. "Is that...my *mom*?"

"Yeah. I took her out sailing." He said it as if it was the most natural thing in the world.

Lucy leaned back against the bed. "*What?*"

Colin was trying to suck some Popsicle drips off his shirt. "I think she was really keen on learning."

"You *sailed* with my mom?"

"Yeah."

"When?"

"Well...in the summers. First time was in a pram though, so it hardly counts."

Why don't I know this? Where was I that—those—summers?

"Hold on. You said summers, plural."

"She hasn't been for a couple years, but yeah, she visited in the summers."

"How many summers? Since when?"

"I dunno." Colin scratched the back of his head. "Since I was a kid?"

"Since you were a *kid*? Why didn't you ever tell me this?"

"I did."

"No, you didn't!" Lucy said sharply.

"Oh." He looked at her blankly. "Well, didn't you know? It's not like it's a secret or anything."

Lucy racked her brain. Her mom did used to travel a bit. She went to writing workshops, retreats, stuff like that. But she never said anything about visits to Esther, or sailing with Colin. How could there be *another* thing she didn't know about her mom? Was it possible her mom had said something, and Lucy just hadn't paid attention? Lucy hoped so.

Colin balled up his Popsicle wrapper. "Are you okay? You look kind of weird."

"Uh, yeah. She, um, just, I don't think she ever mentioned it. Visiting you guys."

"They were best friends," Colin said, lobbing his wrapper into the garbage can. "Your mom came to visit. No big deal."

"You're right." Lucy swallowed down some orange goo stuck in her throat. "No big deal."

So why hadn't Esther ever come to visit *them*?

CHAPTER 16

LUCY FOUND HERSELF SLUMPED AGAINST THE SAME tree she'd slumped against the last time she'd left Colin's. Maybe she should seriously reconsider any future visits to his home. She didn't know how many more surprises about her mom she could handle.

She stayed there, the bark digging into her back, and thought about what Colin had just told her. She tried taking his view, that it was "no big deal." Was he right? Was she making too much of it? But it almost felt like her mom was living a secret life or something. After her mom died, Lucy had let herself briefly live in a sort of fantasy world where her mom hadn't really died. She was in the witness protection program. Or sometimes she was super-secret spy for the government. She had faked her own death because she had to, and she was alive and well...somewhere. Lucy had never seen a body. The casket had been closed. And who knew what was actually in that urn? Of course, Lucy knew it wasn't true, wasn't possible—but if it were, maybe some of this other stuff would make a bit more sense. Maybe.

Too bad her dad was travelling. She really wished she could talk to him.

JOSIE WAS HUSTLING ACROSS THE front lawn as Lucy came around the bend in the lane.

"I left you a note," Josie said, not slowing down. "I've got to go help Muriel put a rinse in her hair. She's got terrible arthritis. Don't forget supper with Ellen."

"We're having supper with Ellen?" Lucy called after her.

No response.

Lucy sighed, ran up behind Josie, and touched her shoulder. "We're having supper with Ellen?"

"Yes. Didn't I tell you?"

Lucy shook her head.

"Hmph. Well. We're having supper with Ellen." And off Josie went.

Lucy made a list of things to do for the afternoon, mostly to keep her mind off other things. She wrote a letter to Sarah, touched up her toenail polish, finished the latest Harlequin she'd been reading, the one with the shirtless guy on the cover (which pretty much referred to every cover), ploughed through half a sleeve of Ritz crackers, and was working on her butterfly DoodleArt when Josie returned from Muriel's.

"Just let me change," Josie said, jamming her cigarette into an old tobacco can filled with sand that she kept by the front door. There was one at the back door too. And by the garage, the root cellar, and the gardening shed. "Need something a little more snazzy for a dinner out." She gave Lucy a good once-over. "Wouldn't kill ya to snazz yourself up a bit, either."

LUCY SMILED WHEN SHE SAW Kit standing at the front door. She was back in her Princess Leia outfit. *Wish I'd worn a bedsheet instead of this itchy blouse.* It was new, and the elastic on the puffed sleeves was a bit too tight.

"I decided to dress for dinner," Kit explained.

"You're not the only one," Lucy said, gesturing over her shoulder at Josie.

"Wow. Not everyone can pull off that shade of blue eyeshadow with an orange dress." Kit nodded approvingly. "And a matching hat, no less."

"Don't bother offering to take it from her," Lucy said. "There's about six cigarettes stuck in behind the plastic flowers."

In the kitchen, Gordon, Kit's dad, was standing at the stove. "Lucy! Hope you like lobster!" he boomed, dangling a giant greenish-brown crustacean over a boiling pot of water. "Fresh off the boat today!"

Lucy's eyes widened and she sucked in her breath. It was still moving as Gordon plopped it in.

Ellen looked over at her and said, "Honey, would you like me to throw some extra knackwurst on the barbecue? That's what Kathleen's having."

Lucy blinked a few times. It still caught her off guard how much Ellen reminded her of her mom. After a second, Lucy said, "Sure," even though she didn't have clue what knackwurst was.

Knackwurst turned out to be like super-fat hotdogs. Lucy smothered them with ketchup and Ellen's homemade bread-and-butter pickles. The pickles must have been a family recipe; they tasted exactly like Lucy's mom's. It was like being reunited with an old friend.

"Good, huh?" Kit said.

Lucy didn't know if she was referring to the knackwurst or the pickles. It didn't matter anyway. "*Delicious!*" she answered with her mouth full.

"They're from the Sausage House."

Lucy remembered the drive up, how when she and her dad passed that place with the "Homemade Sausages" sign, she'd thought it was gross. She couldn't have been more wrong. "Does anyone want the last one?" she asked, her fork hovering over the platter.

It didn't take long for Lucy to figure out where Kit got her offbeat sense of humour and her passion for *Star Wars*. Through the whole meal, Gordon acted out scenes from the film using the cooked lobsters. When he picked up one lobster and made it say to the remaining pile of lobsters, "These aren't the droids you're looking for," Lucy laughed so hard she choked on her potato salad. By the time she finished her strawberry shortcake, her face hurt from smiling.

When it was time to go, Ellen put her arms around Lucy and gave her a tight hug. "We'll do this again," she promised.

"We can't let you starve to death," Kit joked as she slapped Lucy on the back.

"May the Force be with you!" Gordon hollered from the porch.

When they got back to Josie's, Lucy sprawled out on the porch swing like a beached whale. She'd forgotten what it felt like to be full. She'd hoped the walk home would help. But it hadn't. Not a bit.

She stared up at the peeling paint on the porch ceiling and smiled. She may be in pain right now, but it was worth it. Everyone around the table, the food, Gordon's lobster skits...they all kept her from thinking about the things that were bothering her. The things about her mom.

LUCY COULD SEE THE GIANT frown on Colin's face even before she got to the hole. He was standing there, arms folded, like he was waiting for her.

"You're late," he said.

"I am? I didn't know there was an official schedule."

He shrugged. "I was sort of thinking you were still mad about yesterday."

"Oh." She sat on the edge of the hole and let her feet hang over the side. "No. I just wish you'd told me that you knew my mom."

"I figured you knew. How was I supposed to know you didn't?"

Lucy stared straight ahead and didn't answer.

"And, like, how well do you know your mom's friends, anyway?" he added.

"Couldn't you tell how surprised I was when you said you were at the funeral?"

"No," he said simply.

Lucy rolled her eyes. "Plus you made it sound like you didn't know why you were there. Obviously you were there because you *knew* her. You made it sound like you were dragged against your will."

"I *was*! No offence, but funerals, even your mom's, are not my idea of a good time."

Lucy loudly flipped her flip-flops against her heels and didn't say anything.

"Look," he sighed. "Like I said the other day. Our moms were friends. She came to visit. I don't get why you're so cranky about it."

She kept flipping. "Why didn't your mom ever come to visit *us*?"

"I dunno. Maybe she didn't like you guys."

"What?"

"I'm *joking*."

"Ha ha," Lucy said, folding her arms. "Well, didn't you think that was weird? Like, how you knew my mom, but I didn't know yours?"

"Guess I never really thought about it." He sat down beside her. "You know, my mom had a couple little kids at home, maybe it was just easier for your mom to visit my mom. And it's not like we had a ton of money for travelling."

Lucy fell quiet again, thinking. That made a bit of sense. After a minute, she said, "It's hard to explain. You'd think being here, I'd feel closer to my mom. But I don't. It's the exact opposite."

He opened his mouth, looked like he was forming a word, then clamped it shut. She wondered what he was going to say.

Was he trying to think of something helpful, but couldn't come up with anything? Suddenly, his face brightened. "I bought jujubes."

Jujubes are helpful in their own way, I guess. "Can I have all the green?"

"Sure." He got up and rooted for a bag he had stashed under a tree.

"Whatcha got there?" Kit said, appearing from nowhere.

Colin straightened too quickly and whacked his head on a branch. "Stop sneaking up on us!"

"I didn't. You're just completely unaware of what's going on around you."

Colin snatched up his bag of jujubes, holding them close to his chest so Kit couldn't see. He turned his back to her and tossed the bag to Lucy. "Don't eat any red."

Kit craned her neck. "Oh. Jujubes. It's okay. I don't like them."

"Goody for us," Colin muttered under his breath as he jumped into the hole and picked up his shovel.

Kit dropped her beach bag onto the grass next to Lucy. "I brought my mags again."

"Cool," Lucy said, pulling out the stack.

Colin looked up. "Aw. Not those again."

"Wait." Lucy quickly thumbed through the pages of one. "I saw something last time. Here. Horoscopes. That's not junk. When were you born?"

"October thirty-first," he replied grumpily.

"Halloween? No way! Lucky bum!" Kit exclaimed. "What year? How old are you, anyway?"

"Nineteen sixty-one."

"Wow. Almost sixteen," Kit said sideways. "You'd never know it. He acts about ten."

"Shush," Lucy said to Kit, then called out to Colin, "Scorpio. Okay, listen to this. Your horoscope says, 'Your popularity will increase over the next month, but don't let it go to your head. Keep an open mind and accept advice from close friends. Also remember it is important to take breaks.'" She turned to Kit and whispered, "I made that last part up. I want to go for a swim later."

Kit choked back a laugh. "Hey, Colin. That's a pretty good one. At least it's not saying there's anything *bad* in your future."

"Yup," he said popping the *p*. "Made *my* day."

LUCY DECIDED TO PASS ON Josie's latest concoction from the Campbell's Soup recipe book. It had canned tomatoes in it, and she hated canned tomatoes. Thankfully, Ellen had sent them home with all the leftovers. Lucy had been living on them for a couple days. Luckily there was still strawberry shortcake left. Lucy got down a big plate, built herself two giant shortcakes, and squirted on a giant mountain of whipped cream. *That's a perfectly fine supper. There's even fruit in there, so that makes it healthy, right?*

If her dad were here, he'd be having a cow about right now.

As she struggled to finish the last few bites, she began to question her choice. But then she saw Josie tear open a packet of Alka-Seltzer and knew she had chosen wisely. She was pretty full, at least. That made four nights in a row. All she wanted to do was grab a book and lie flat somewhere. Bed sounded good, even though it was only seven-thirty.

She went to the bookcase in the dining room and pulled a Harlequin out of the middle of the row. *The Reluctant Bride.* She was pretty sure she'd already read it—it was getting hard to keep track. Probably a good idea to choose a couple more for backup. As she set *The Reluctant Bride* on top of the cabinet, she accidentally knocked over a silver picture frame. Crossing her fingers, she bent to pick it up. *Please let it not be broken.* She inspected it for damage. All good. It was a wedding picture, black and white. The bride was wearing one of those fringy flapper dresses. *Wait. Is that Josie?* Lucy squinted. *It is Josie. Amazing!* She was beautiful. So elegant. *Wait. Are those birds on her headpiece?* Lucy held the frame closer to her face. *Yup. Definitely birds.* Her eyes moved to the bridesmaids. There were five. She was pretty sure Gran Irene was the maid of honour. The bridesmaid dresses were pretty, a shorter version of Josie's. But the picture was in black and white, so it was hard to tell what colour they were. Knowing Josie, they were probably bright green or bubble-gum pink. Lucy was just about to put the picture back when something caught her eye. All the bridesmaids were wearing the exact same necklace, a chain with a small oval locket.

Lucy stared at the picture for a long time, her eyebrows knitted together. She traced her finger along the neckline of every bridesmaid, mentally replacing each locket with an emerald necklace. *No, that can't be it, can it?*

The necklaces had been pushed to the back of Lucy's mind. She'd done it on purpose, too worried about what the actual truth might turn out to be. It'd been fairly easy, especially as she stewed over her mom's mysterious visits to Esther and sailing excursions with Colin.

Lucy stood the silver frame back up on top of the cabinet.

So Kit had been right after all. When you stop looking for something, that's when you find it.

CHAPTER 17

"**D**UH! IT'S SO OBVIOUS!" KIT EXCLAIMED, SMACK-
ing her forehead with the palm of her hand. "Bridesmaid
gifts. I can't believe we didn't think of that!"

"It's only a guess," Lucy said.

"*Hello*! It makes perfect sense."

Colin pulled himself out of the hole. "It does seem to make
sense."

Lucy had debated whether or not to share her theory. No
one had mentioned the necklaces in a while, and she was perfectly happy to keep it that way. But if she was right about this,
it proved her mom was innocent, didn't it? She wanted Kit and
Colin to know that.

"You know what this means, don't you?" Kit wagged her finger at Lucy. "One, that your mom didn't steal anything. And two,
she maybe almost got married." Kit paused. "But then didn't?"

Lucy nodded and chewed thoughtfully on Colin's leftover
jujubes. She'd already thought of that, the idea that her mom may
have almost gotten married before. But wouldn't she have said

something to Lucy? Isn't that something a mother would share with her daughter? *Apparently not*, she thought to herself. *Not my mom, anyway.*

As if reading her mind, Colin said, "Didn't you say your mom didn't talk much about her past?"

"Yeah, but still."

"Well, it *is* possible," Kit said, "that she got the necklaces for when she married your dad. And then she just changed her mind or something. Picked another type of gift."

Lucy rooted around in the bag for a green jujube. "Yeah. Maybe."

"Well." Colin scratched his head. "If you want to know for sure, we could always ask *my* mom."

Kit clapped her hands together. "Yes! Let's do that!"

Lucy couldn't think of a reason not to. She wanted to know, didn't she? "Okay."

"Let's go," Kit said, standing up and brushing off her shorts.

"What, *now*?"

"Yeah. You got other plans?"

"I, I—"

"And you should go get the necklaces," Kit said bossily, and then turned to Colin. "We should take them to show them to your mom, right? In case we have to jog her memory."

"I dunno." Colin frowned. "It's not like she'd forget Lucy's mom was going to get married."

"Well, she could deny it if she doesn't want to tell us. She could say something like, 'I don't know what you're talking about,' or, 'That never happened,' but then we could whip out the necklaces and say, 'Oh yeah? Explain these then!'"

"Um." Colin's frown deepened. "She's not on trial for murder, you know."

Kit ignored Colin's remark and said to Lucy, "We should take them. Go on." She jerked her head in the direction of Josie's. "We'll wait for you."

Lucy looked over at Colin. He just shrugged.

"Give me ten," Lucy sighed. She reluctantly got to her feet and headed back to the house. Josie was snoring, asleep on the porch swing, an open Harlequin on her stomach. Lucy tiptoed past. Upstairs, she yanked open Josie's dresser drawer, reached under the pantyhose, and grabbed the bunny. Tilting back the head, she scooped out the velvet pouch and slipped it into her pocket. She hurried back down the stairs and out the door. Josie was still snoring.

ESTHER WAS AT THE COUNTER slicing a loaf of bread when the three of them barrelled into the kitchen. She looked up when she heard them. "Hi guys," she said. "I was just making sandwiches for the twins, but help yourself if you're hungry."

"Mom," Colin began, "Lucy—"

"Josie dropped the bread off this morning. Apparently she gave up on the welcome muffin basket. She was out of wheat germ." Esther shuddered. "Probably for the best, don't you think?"

"Great, Mom, but—"

"And your dad called," Esther said. "He hopes to be here real soon."

"Mom!" Colin shouted impatiently. "Lucy has something she wants to ask you."

"Oh." Esther took in their serious faces and put down the knife. "I'm all ears."

"Just cut to the chase!" Kit was jumping up and down like she had ants in her pants. "Show her the necklaces!"

Lucy spun around. "Do you want do it?"

"No, no." Kit shook her head. "This is your thing."

Esther gently placed a hand on Lucy's shoulder. "Do you have something to show me, hon?"

For a moment Lucy didn't move. Then she said, "Yeah. I found these." She pulled the velvet pouch from her pocket. Her hands were sweaty as she took out each necklace, slid them from their packets, and laid them in a row on the counter.

Esther stood behind her, watching quietly.

Stepping aside to let Esther see, Lucy watched her as she leaned in to get a better look. She could tell Esther recognized them.

"Well?" Kit said impatiently.

"I forgot all about those," Esther whispered, seemingly to herself.

"You've seen them before," Lucy said. "You know what they are."

"They're your mom's," Esther said. "She bought them a lifetime ago. At least, that's what it feels like now."

"Are they bridesmaid gifts?" Kit blurted.

Esther nodded. "They were supposed to be."

"I *knew* we were right!" Kit pounded the counter with her fist.

"What are you talking about, *we*?" Colin piped up. "Lucy. Lucy figured it out."

"We *helped*," Kit shot back.

"On what planet?" Colin said.

Lucy clenched her teeth. "Could you two please?"

"Sorry," Colin said.

"Sorry," Kit said, but in a lower voice, and to the floor.

Lucy edged closer to Esther. "There must be a story that goes with them. Can you tell me?"

"Well, I..." Esther began picking at her fingernail polish. She stopped and glanced over her shoulder as if maybe she was hoping someone would show up and interrupt them.

"Please?" Lucy said.

Esther drew in a deep breath. "Your mom, she, uh, she was engaged before, when she was really young. Things didn't go as planned, and the wedding never happened."

Lucy digested the information. She had figured it was something like that. It felt different now, though, hearing someone say it out loud, confirm it. "And then what?"

"That's it, pretty much."

"Oh." Lucy had hoped for more. "Why didn't she ever tell me?"

"I'm sure she would have. She was probably waiting until you were older."

Kit picked up one of the necklaces. "Why did she keep them? Why didn't she return them?"

"She couldn't." Esther flipped over the necklace in Kit's hand and pointed to the circle of gold behind the emerald, the back of the setting. "If you look real close, you can see they're engraved with each bridesmaid's initials."

"What?" Lucy took it from Kit. She was right. How did she not notice? There they were. "E. M.?"

"That one would be Ellen's," Esther said.

"Is yours here?" Lucy asked.

"No." Esther shook her head. "I was maid of honour. I asked her not to get me a gift. Figured as a newlywed, she could use the money."

Lucy checked the others. They all had tiny letters. "I wonder whether if I'd seen the letters I would have guessed they were gifts."

"Maybe," Esther smiled. "I'm not sure I would have. I don't have great detective skills, though."

Lucy passed one to Colin so he could see too. He waved it away. He seemed to be studying his mom. "Why didn't it work out?" he asked.

Esther didn't answer right away. "I'm not sure if it's my place to say," she finally said. "Lucy, I think maybe you should talk to your dad, and maybe he should be the one—"

"My dad knows, and he didn't tell me either?"

Esther sort of winced.

"You should just go ahead and tell me, because if he didn't want me to find out from someone else, he should have told me himself." Lucy stuck out her chin. "So should my mom have, for that matter."

"It's not always that easy," Esther sighed. "When you have to tell someone something, and you're worried about what they'll think, worried that it might change things." Her eyes darted around the kitchen like she was trying to avoid looking at anyone. "There always seems to be an excuse to put it off."

"Mom." Collin rolled his eyes. "What are you even talking about? Just tell her, would ya?"

"Look, I—"

"Mom!"

She stared up at the ceiling for a moment. "Fine," she said shortly and pulled out a stool.

Lucy leaned against the counter, Kit on one side of her, Colin on the other.

"Laura started going out with Dean at the start of high school," Esther began quietly. "Dean Clark. Great guy, popular, good at everything. They were still together in grade twelve, and on Valentine's Day they got engaged. They planned to get married right after graduation and move to Halifax. Dean was going to Dalhousie on an engineering scholarship, and Laura had found a job at a nursery school near the university. Seemed like they had it all figured out."

"And then what?" Kit asked, her eyes getting bigger by the second.

"As the wedding got closer, I think Dean kind of got scared, got cold feet. The thought of university, studying, working, a new wife, was starting to sink in. A few weeks before the wedding, he called it off. He stayed to graduate, then he packed his stuff and moved to the city alone. Laura was left behind, broken-hearted and humiliated."

Lucy pressed a hand to her chest. "Oh, no."

"And you can only guess what it was like living in a small town. The gossip was non-stop. And let me tell you, people are not always kind. They grabbed onto this, came up with ridiculous stories, and beat it to death, just because nothing ever happens here. Hard to find anything better than a good scandal."

"Poor mom," Lucy said. "What happened? Did she ever see him again?"

"No, she didn't." Esther lowered her eyes and went back to scraping her nail polish. "Dean died shortly after all that mess."

"What?"

"In Halifax. Hit by a car when he was walking home late one night. I couldn't believe it when I got the letter from your mom. Dan and I were out in Banff, working by then. I always felt bad I missed the funeral."

"It all just sounds so awful," Kit said.

"It was pretty rough. After a while I finally convinced her to come out and stay with me. She really needed a break. I thought a change of scenery would do her good." Esther reached over and tousled Colin's hair. "She helped me out when you were born."

"Stop." Colin flinched under her hand.

Esther rolled her eyes and picked up one of the necklaces again. "I think I remember Laura once mentioning removing the stones and making them into a ring or something—to remember him by. I guess she forgot."

"Or never got around to it," Lucy said.

The kitchen was quiet.

"That's the whole story?" Lucy finally asked.

Esther swallowed. "That's the whole story."

At that moment, the twins came slamming into the house.

"There you are!" Esther jumped off the stool. "I was wondering when you two would finally show your faces!"

"We're starving!" they cried in unison. "We need food!"

"Let's go wash up first," Esther said. She tried to manoeuvre them towards the hallway.

"Mom!" Teddy said, jumping out of her reach. "We can wash our hands ourselves."

"I know. Just, uh, you look extra dirty." Esther herded them out of the kitchen.

Lucy gathered up the necklaces.

"Let's get out of here before they all come back." Colin held the back door open and they filed out onto the deck.

A second later, there was a bunch of racket from inside. A clink, then a splat, then, "Hannah!"

"She knocked over her milk," Colin said. "Hannah always knocks over her milk."

Then, "I'm not eating squares. Triangles! I only eat triangles!"

"It's true," Colin said. "Teddy only eats triangle sandwiches. You'd think Mom would catch on." He started down the steps. "I'm going to the hole for some peace and quiet. Coming?"

They crossed Colin's lawn.

Lucy felt Colin looking at her. "You okay?" he asked. "You have a funny look on your face."

"Oh. That's just my 'Wow, I can't believe my mom never told me any of this' look. You must be getting used to seeing it by now," Lucy said sarcastically. "Maybe you just don't recognize it because now my dad's part of it too."

The corner of Colin's mouth twitched. "So *are* you okay?"

"I guess. I don't know. I'm not sure how I'm supposed to feel—besides in the dark, I mean. I think I said it before, but I guess she was allowed to have a life, right?"

"Yeah," Kit said. "But that's *some* life. I can't believe all that happened to your mom and you never knew a thing!"

"You're not helping," Colin said.

Kit shot him the evil eye. "Sor-*ree*. I'm just sayin', it's pretty amazing. I think it should be made into a movie, or a book, or something."

Lucy glanced over at Colin. "What's wrong? You have a funny look on your face too." She leaned closer to him so she could whisper. "You know Kit's only being Kit."

"It's not that."

"Then what?"

"It's my mom."

"What do you mean?"

"I've just been going over it all in my head. When she said that was the whole story?" A muscle twitched in his jaw. "I kind of got the feeling that it wasn't."

CHAPTER 18

LUCY KEPT HER FINGERS CROSSED ON ONE HAND AS she dialled the phone with the other. She was pretty sure her dad was getting back from wherever he'd been today. *Please be home, please be home.*

The ringing stopped, but before Lucy could open her mouth to say hi, she heard, "Look. What's done is done. I just wish you'd—"

"Dad?"

She heard him suck in his breath. "Lucy?"

"Yeah, it's me."

"Gosh, pumpkin. I'm sorry."

"Who did you think it was?"

"Oh. I, uh, we, we have this new intern in the office, and he, uh...."

Dead air.

"Yeah?" Lucy prodded. "What did he do?"

"Motion," her dad said. "He filed the wrong motion."

"Geez. You sounded so mad."

"He keeps calling to apologize. I thought it was him again, but it was you. What a nice surprise!"

"Dad. Everyone makes mistakes. Promise you'll accept his apology. You don't want everyone at work to think of you as the cranky guy."

"Okay, pumpkin. Don't worry about it."

"Dad, promise."

He sighed. "I promise. So hey, how are things up there?"

"I talked to Esther."

"Oh yeah?"

"She told me about Mom and how she almost got married to her boyfriend from high school."

More dead air.

"And I know you already know," Lucy added.

"Yes, I do."

"Don't you think Mom should have told me? Or you should have told me?"

"Why?"

His answer caught her off guard. "Um, because." It was the only reply she could think of.

"She was going to tell you."

"Yeah, right."

"And as for me telling you, well, I guess I just didn't see the point."

"The point is so I could know my mom better."

"You *do* know your mom. You lived with her every day for fourteen years."

"Thirteen," Lucy said flatly. "And a quarter."

Her dad sighed again. "Your mom was a very private person. She had lots—"

"Of secrets? Is that what you were going to say? Because, no kidding. I seem to be finding out a new one every day."

"Pumpkin."

"And are they only secrets to me? Am I the only one? Do you and everybody else know everything about everything?"

"That's not how it is at all. Like I said, she was planning to tell you all this. That was what last summer was going to be all about, and then—"

"Yes, I know, and then she got sick. But why was it something she needed to plan? And why would it take a whole summer? What was the big deal? Was it about Dean? Ellen? Or something else?" Lucy was practically out of breath.

"Look," he said. "I'm coming up."

"What?" Once again, he caught her off guard.

"I'm coming up."

"Why? Are you going to take me home?" An odd feeling started to churn in her stomach. "But the summer's not over yet." *Do I actually not want to leave?*

"Why don't we just play it by ear?"

"You don't have to come up. I'm fine." She backpedalled, afraid she had come off too angry when she was mostly frustrated. "Really, I'm fine."

"I know. I just feel like seeing you. Is that okay?"

"You mean for a visit?"

"Sure. A visit."

"Oh." Lucy relaxed a little.

"I'm still up to my eyeballs with this case, but as soon as I can tie up some loose ends, I'll be on my way."

"Honestly, you don't need to." She couldn't explain it, but for some reason she just didn't feel like rehashing all this face to face. "Everything's okay here."

Again a few seconds of dead air. "Well, if you change your mind let me know and I'll come. Deal?"

"Deal."

"Love you."

"Love you, too. Bye," she said and slowly replaced the receiver.

LUCY SAT DOWN BESIDE COLIN at the edge of the hole. He was swearing under his breath as he tried to pick a splinter out of his dirt-encrusted hand.

"That's gonna get infected, you know," she said.

"Nah. It's fine." He stuck his finger in his mouth.

"*Ew.* That's really going to help."

She slid herself back onto the grass and, using Colin's knapsack as a pillow, she stretched out, closed her eyes, and let the sun beat down on her face. "I called my dad last night."

"Yeah?"

"You know how you said you didn't think your mom was telling us the whole story?"

"Yeah."

"I got that same feeling from my dad."

"Yeah?"

"Wow, Colin," Kit said, kicking off her flip-flops. "Has anyone ever told you you have a real way with words?"

"When did you get here?" Lucy said, lifting herself up on her elbows.

"Would you quit sneaking up on us?" Colin said.

"Only a few seconds ago," Kit said to Lucy. Then to Colin, "I didn't."

"Don't mind him," Lucy said. "He has a splinter."

"Don't worry, I won't." Kit fished through her bag and pulled out a bottle of Coppertone. "So you both think your parents are lying to you, huh?"

"I'm not sure if they're straight-out lying," Lucy clarified. "Just not telling us everything." She looked over at Colin. "Right?"

Colin nodded.

"Interesting." Kit pinched her lips together. "You have to remember, though, parents are weird. They act weird, they say weird things."

"No. This isn't the usual weirdness."

"Well." Kit squirted a huge splorch of lotion onto her arm. "If you *both* feel it, then they probably are." She held the bottle out to Lucy. "You know, you could talk to Josie about it now. I mean, now that you know your mom was supposed to get married and everything. The cat's out of the bag. And really, it's not like it can be *that* much of a secret. There must be people around here that know."

"There probably are. Apparently, it's just a secret to me."

"If it makes you feel any better, I didn't know about it," Kit said.

Colin shrugged. "Me neither."

"Anyhow," Kit said, "Josie might be able to tell you more of the story. Like, fill in whatever you think is missing."

"But how do I ask her without telling her I found the necklaces snooping around in her drawer?"

"Just tell her you were talking to Esther about your mom and it all came out. You don't even have to mention the necklaces." Kit spread her giant splorch of lotion up her arm to her shoulder. "Though I *am* dying to know why she moved them from your room. I mean, you have to wonder, right?"

"Probably she didn't want me to find them and start asking questions. I once tried asking her about what happened between my mom and your mom and she said something like it's not her story or whatever."

"Yeah, that's possible," Kit said.

"And Esther sort of said the same thing," Lucy went on. "But I don't know who they think is going to tell me if it's not them. My mom can't. And my dad sure hasn't told me anything."

Colin held up his finger. "This is looking pretty grody. Anyone want to go down to the beach? I should soak this in salt water."

"Sure," Lucy said.

"Sure," Kit said. "Salt water fixes everything."

AFTER GETTING THEMSELVES DUNKED, COLIN flopped on Josie's air mattress, keeping his injured finger submerged in the water. Lucy decided to do a sweep for beach glass while the tide was low. Kit followed and they walked, bent over, along the water's edge, watching for a flash of colour.

When they'd made it to the point, they turned back and met up with Colin, who was stuffing the air mattress under the bottom step. "You guys find anything?" he asked.

"Yeah, come see," Lucy said as she and Kit knelt down and emptied their pockets. Kit had accumulated a good-sized pile. Lucy had three pieces of blue, two of them courtesy of Kit, and one piece of solid white, probably from a broken dish.

Lucy picked up the piece of china and rubbed her thumb against the smooth edges. Even though it technically wasn't blue, it had a faded blue flower pattern on the top. She could feel the texture of the design under her finger. "This reminds me of a candy bowl Mom had. She'd fill it with Quality Street every Christmas."

"Do you think about her a lot?" Kit asked.

Colin frowned and shot Kit a look.

Kit frowned back at him but with her nose scrunched up.

"It's fine," Lucy said to Colin. Then, "Sometimes it seems like I think about her a lot, and other times I'll suddenly realize that it's been a whole day and I haven't thought about her once. Then I feel guilty. I feel guilty because life keeps going on without her."

"You shouldn't feel guilty," Kit said, dividing her pieces into piles according to colour. "It's not like you're ever going to forget her for real."

"I know. But I worry she's going to start to fade. Sometimes when I try to remember what she looks like, it's sort of cloudy."

"You have pictures, right?" Kit said.

Colin rolled his eyes, then said to Lucy, "That's probably pretty normal, you know, that she's...cloudy sometimes."

"It was so gradual, I hardly noticed. When she first died, I saw her everywhere, all the time. On the street, at the grocery store. At least I'd think it was her for a minute, anyway."

Kit and Colin stayed quiet.

"We went to the hospital right after we found out, like right after Mrs. Gardiner came and told us," Lucy continued. "But her bed was already empty, the room bare and cleaned out. Just like that." She still remembered the smell of disinfectant and how her shoes echoed on the floor when she walked into the stripped-down room. The nurses had packed all her mom's things into a box and sat it on a chair by the door. The mobile, wrapped in tissue paper, was on top. One yellow butterfly had escaped and dangled over the side. "See, I never saw her," Lucy said, feeling the need to explain. "Never saw her dead. So how could I be sure? For a long time, I wouldn't go anywhere except to school, not to friends' or anything. I was afraid she'd come home and no one would be there."

Lucy went back to rubbing the piece of china, afraid to make eye contact in case they were both wearing horrified expressions. "I know that must all sound really crazy. I never told anyone that before." She swallowed nervously. "You guys must think I'm nuts."

"You *are* nuts," Colin said. "I mean, not *actually* nuts. I just mean you're nuts to think we would *think* you were nuts." He coughed to clear his throat. "You know what I mean."

Kit scratched her forehead. "Like I said before, Colin, a real way with words."

Lucy laughed. She couldn't help herself.

"And just so you know," Kit said, adding another piece of blue to Lucy's pile, "I would think all those exact same things, so you're not nuts at all."

CROSSING THE LAWN, LUCY COULD see Josie sitting on the top porch step. She was eating something from a bowl with her fingers. Lucy sat beside her, and hoping it was something normal, leaned sideways to see. *Phew. Blueberries.*

Josie shook the bowl in her direction.

Lucy scooped out a handful, and they both ate in silence.

"I'd better get off my arse and refill this bowl," Josie said. "Muriel brought over some mustard pickles. I told her I'd return the favour with a pint of berries."

Lucy touched her arm. "Wait." She turned and made sure Josie could see her mouth clearly. "I found out about my mom, that she almost got married before."

"Oh?" Josie said, but she didn't seem surprised. "How'd that all come about?"

Lucy could feel her cheeks warming at the thought of explaining the snooping, and actually taking the necklaces—*twice*.

Josie was watching her, waiting.

"I was talking to Esther about my mom, and it just sort of came out."

Josie nodded.

"She told me about how the guy, Dean, died, and how Mom was heartbroken, and how she came out to visit her to kind of recover from it all."

"Well, it's good that you know."

Lucy tried to figure how to ask if that was the whole story without really asking. "Is that how you remember it?"

Josie frowned and stared at her thoughtfully for a moment. "Finally, we're making some progress," she said, then got up and went down the steps and around to the blueberry patch behind the house.

"AND YOU'RE SURE THAT'S WHAT she said." Kit dumped her bag out on the grass and passed Lucy the newest issue of *Tiger Beat*. "She said, 'Finally, we're making some progress.'"

"Yup," Lucy said.

"And that's it?"

"That's it. She could have read my lips wrong," Lucy offered. "Misunderstood the question."

"Even if she did, what was she talking about? Who's *we*?"

Lucy shrugged.

"And doesn't *some* progress mean there's *more* progress to be made, *more* story to tell?"

"I don't know. Maybe?" Lucy squinted at her. "I can't tell

anymore. I might just be paranoid."

Kit tapped a finger against her lips. "I think it's time to talk to *my* mom."

"No." Lucy flipped through the magazine. "I don't want to do that."

"But your mom and my mom must've still been on speaking terms when this Dean guy was around," she pointed out. "She was even a bridesmaid, remember?"

Lucy didn't answer. She folded down the corner of a page that had a picture of exactly how she wanted her hair.

"We're running out of options here," Kit huffed. "What's the worst that can happen?"

"Um." Lucy didn't know.

Like a giant gopher, Colin's head popped up out of the hole. "The worst that can happen is that her story is the same as everybody else's and she doesn't tell you anything new."

"Yeah, I suppose."

"And aren't sisters supposed to have a special bond or something?" he added.

Not these sisters. But Lucy had to admit, Kit and Colin made some good points. Laura and Ellen were sisters. They'd lived in the same house. They *may* have had a special bond, been good friends before they weren't.

"Okay," Lucy sighed. "Let's talk to your mom."

"Yay." Kit shot a fist into the air. "The only glitch is she's gone to Truro today to get her hair done, so come over tomorrow after breakfast. Mom's always in a good mood and chatty in the morning. I usually haven't gotten in trouble yet."

"YOU DON'T THINK WE'RE TOO early, do you?" Lucy asked. "Kit never said when she eats breakfast."

Colin didn't have a chance to answer before Kit pushed open the door and almost knocked him over. "Okay!" she shouted back over her shoulder. "They're here! We're leaving!"

"Wait." Lucy was confused. "I thought we were supposed to talk to your mom."

Kit nudged her down the steps. "Change of plans. Just go."

"But—"

"Just *go*!" she hissed.

Colin shook his head. "I guess we're going," he said to no one in particular.

They followed Kit down the driveway and up the road till they reached a little grassy clearing off to the side.

Lucy spun around. "What's going on?!"

"You're not going to *believe* what I found." Kit fumbled around in her back pocket. "Letters!" She held them up.

Lucy recognized the handwriting right away—her mom's. "Where did you get those?"

"Digging through my mom's bureau."

"You were digging through your mom's bureau?" Colin asked.

"Yeah. I do it all the time. Don't you?"

"Uh. *No*."

"What about your dad's, then?"

"My dad doesn't have a bureau."

"Oh. Well, this time I was actually looking for something. My 'first day of school' outfit that I know for a *fact* arrived yesterday. My granny in Ottawa sends me one every year."

"I'm sure that makes it A-okay then," Colin said dryly.

Kit waved her hand dismissively. "Might be more of a girl thing." Then she turned to Lucy. "These letters weren't there the last time I was poking around; there's no way I would have missed them. I think Mom just got them out, like maybe you being here made her remember them or something." She shuffled around the envelopes. "I'll put them in order."

"You *read* them?" Colin asked.

"Of course I read them." Kit sighed.

"It's fine, it's fine," Lucy said impatiently. "What do they say?"

Kit looked like the cat that swallowed the canary. "Let me

just say, I think a lot of your questions will be answered, that's for sure. Do you want me to read out loud?"

"Sure. Just hurry up."

They sat on the grass in a circle. Kit cleared her throat dramatically. "Okay, this first one is dated August first, nineteen sixty-one. But there's no stamp or address, just my mom's name on the envelope. 'Dear Ellen, By the time you read this letter I'll be gone. Esther is not doing well. I have to go help her and stay until the baby is born. But more than that, I have to get out of this place. Since Dean died, I just don't feel like myself. Every day gets harder. I know the agreement was for me to stay and look after Mom when she got sick, once it was clear I was no longer going to Halifax. I thought I could do it, but I can't. I know this isn't fair to you. I know you were planning to leave the end of this month for nursing school. I know how hard you worked to save, and how much you wanted to go. I'm sure if you explain the situation, they will hold a spot for you. I pray Mom's recovery is fast so you can eventually get there. Please give her my love. I won't blame you if you never forgive me. I deserve it. But I hope one day you'll understand and know that I did what I had to do. Love, Laura.'"

Kit passed the letter to Lucy. "Do you want to look at it?"

Lucy's eyes scanned the page. "My mom just took off?"

"Bolted," Kit said, nodding. "The rest of the letters are all postmarked Banff, Alberta." She opened the next one. "This one is dated September sixteenth. 'Dear Ellen, How is Mom? Josie wrote and told me that you couldn't get her to leave the farm. I know Josie offered to move out there instead. Do you think maybe you can get Mom to go along with that? I know how stubborn she can be. Tell her it's for you, that you need the help.' Then she goes on about getting Muriel and Jerry to pitch in, wanting them to talk to your gran, stuff about the town in Banff where she's staying, and she ends with, 'Again, I'm so sorry. Love, Laura.'" She passed the page to Lucy.

Lucy didn't take it this time. "What's the next one say?"

"The next one wasn't until November fourth. 'Dear Ellen, Esther had a boy. She named him Colin.'" Kit paused. She and Lucy glanced over at Colin.

"That's me," he said.

Kit continued: "'There were some complications, so I will stay to help out. I hope to be home by the end of November. You haven't answered my letter. I really didn't expect you to. Josie's letter said that Mom finally agreed to let her move to the farm and that they are managing pretty well. I hear she is doing better. Maybe it's not too late for you to go. You could register for the second term. Fingers crossed. Love, Laura.'"

"I don't suppose Ellen's a nurse," Lucy said.

Kit shook her head, "Nope," then opened the last envelope. "This one is November twelfth. 'Dear Ellen, I will be arriving in Truro the evening of the thirtieth. Josie has made arrangements for Jerry to come in and get me. I look forward to seeing you, Mom, and Josie again. I've missed you all very much. I will do whatever I can to make this up to you. Love, Laura.'"

Seconds passed. Kit slapping at a mosquito broke the silence.

"How could she leave?" Lucy said. "When her mother's sick, and her sister's supposed to go away for school? She dumped everything on Ellen."

"I dunno," Colin said. "She was in kind of a tough situation. Her best friend, my mom, was far away from home with no one. Maybe she really thought my mom needed her more."

"She had your dad," Kit pointed out. "*My* mom was trying to live out her life's dream."

"Like I said," Colin muttered, "tough situation."

It was what Lucy had been too afraid to even let herself think about. The whole mess with Ellen was her mom's fault. Her mom was in the wrong, the bad guy.

"Look on the bright side," Kit said, plucking the first letter from Lucy's hand and folding it up. "At least you were right. The fight wasn't about a desk."

CHAPTER 19

LUCY AND COLIN PARTED WAYS AT THE TOP OF JOSIE'S driveway.

"See you tomorrow?" Colin said.

"Sure." It was the first word Lucy had spoken since they'd left Kit's. Colin had kept quiet as well. It was like he knew she didn't feel like talking.

Walking past Josie's house, she made a beeline for the lane that led to the beach. Once down the stairs, she didn't look for beach glass, she didn't wade out into the water; she just sat on the bottom step with her chin resting in her hands, thinking. *I don't blame Ellen for not speaking to my mom. I'm not sure I would have either.*

Lucy gave a little snort. And how convenient it was for Esther to leave all that stuff out of her story, all the stuff about *her*. Maybe it was to save Lucy's feelings. Or maybe it was because Esther felt guilty Lucy's mom left home to help her. Lucy shrugged to herself. Her brain was all jumbled—she didn't know what to think.

She stayed and watched a dark green fishing boat *putt-putt* across the horizon and dock at the wharf, then she got up and slowly made her way back to the house. Josie was nowhere in sight. That was good. Lucy still didn't feel like talking to anyone. Hiding out in her room was the logical choice, but it was so hot, she knew it would be like an oven up there. She lay down on the porch swing and shut her eyes. A minute later, her eyes opened. There was a faint popping sound, like faraway fireworks, but something told her it was coming from inside the house.

Lucy cautiously opened the front screen door and listened. The popping had stopped.

"Would you look at that?" Lucy heard Josie say from upstairs.

"Uh-oh," Lucy said and ran up to find her.

Josie was standing outside her sewing room, head tilted back, looking up at the ceiling. Lucy looked up too. She felt her eyebrows scrunch together. There was a brownish liquid dripping rather steadily from the attic trap door. Drips were joining with other drips and making their way around the entire perimeter of the door, starting to fall in giant plops onto the red rug.

What is that? Lucy ducked into the bathroom, pulled a towel off the hook, and spread it over the floor.

"Well, I'll be," Josie said, still looking up, her hands on her hips. "I forgot all about those."

The whole upstairs smelled sweet, like candy. Lucy stuck out a hand to catch a drip and hesitantly held it to her nose. Familiar. She rubbed her fingers together. Sticky. She tugged on Josie's sleeve till she turned and made eye contact. "Forgot about what?" Then pointed at the ceiling. "What *is* that?"

"Root beer. It was supposed to be a surprise. So, surprise," she said grimly.

"Root beer?"

"Homemade. You have to keep it someplace warm." She made a face. "But I guess it got *too* warm up there. The tops must have popped off."

"Should we go up and see?" Lucy reached for the string hanging from the door.

"Nah." Josie made another face. "Too much mess. Let the squirrels and racoons take care of it for us."

Lucy's jaw dropped. The thought of small animals scurrying around, licking up the root beer, especially at night, gave her the heebie-jeebies.

"Run down and get a cloth and some paper towel and we'll clean up the stuff we can see," Josie ordered.

It didn't take Lucy long to figure out that when Josie said, "we'll clean," she really meant Lucy. Josie sat on her sewing bench, puffing away on a cigarette, directing Lucy and pointing out spots that she'd missed on the ceiling, while Lucy balanced precariously on a stool with a soapy cloth and the roll of paper towel. It took forever, the mixture was super syrupy. She had to admit she was a little disappointed that it hadn't worked. The goo smelled really good, just like A&W root beer, her favourite.

That night when Lucy went to bed, she tossed and turned for a long time. Should she talk to Josie about Ellen's letters? Josie was around when it all happened. Maybe she could explain it from another point of view. Maybe there was another side to the story. Lucy got up to go see if Josie was still awake. She only made it halfway across the room. Who was she kidding? There was no other point of view, no other side to the story. The letters weren't Ellen's version of what happened. The letters were in her mom's own words. That was what happened. Plain and simple.

As she was about to finally fall asleep, she thought she heard the *pitter-patter* of tiny feet on the ceiling above her. *Please let that be my imagination.* She pulled the pillow over her head, jamming the corners in tight against her ears like giant earplugs.

"THE CRAZY THING WAS," LUCY told Colin and Kit the next day, "she didn't seem that bothered by any of it. She didn't even seem to care that there'd be raccoons and squirrels running around her attic."

Lucy had started with the root beer story right away. She wanted to distract them from mentioning Ellen's letters. She didn't want to talk about them. She didn't know how to defend her mom. It worked. Kit and Colin were both doubled over, their hands pressing on their stomachs.

"I'm serious, guys," Lucy said. "Sometimes I really worry about her. Doesn't she know the damage raccoons can do? We had one at home and it ripped all the air vents off our roof!"

"Don't worry about it," Kit said. "Here in the country, nobody cares about sharing their house with a few raccoons."

"Not to mention," Lucy continued, "she totally made me do all the cleanup. My neck is so stiff I can barely turn my head. See?" She grimaced as she slowly tried to look behind her. "And I can only raise my arms up this far." She grimaced again as she tried to lift her arms, but they wouldn't go past her shoulders.

"Man, I wish I could have been there." Colin grinned.

"Me too. I could have used the help," Lucy said as she massaged her neck. "Sometimes I wonder what would have happened if I hadn't been here. Would she have stood on a chair and tried to clean it up herself? I almost lost my balance—twice. What if she fell? Should she even be living alone?"

"Uh." Kit raised her eyebrows. "You might not want to share those thoughts with Josie. She doesn't strike me as the type that would take kindly to being told she can't look after herself."

"I wasn't saying that, exactly."

"Don't worry, we'll check in on her after you leave," Colin offered.

"Okay, I guess." Lucy sighed. "Thanks."

Colin looked at his watch. "Listen. I have to go back home for a bit. Mom needs me to babysit. You guys wanna come?"

Lucy and Kit looked at each other and shrugged. "Sure."

Esther was waiting at the front door. "Hi everyone, bye

everyone," she said as she hurried to the car. "Should be less than an hour. Post office, a couple quick errands. The twins are playing in the backyard."

Kicking a path through a sea of scattered toys and Lego, Colin led them down the hall into the den. There was a giant smear of what looked to be strawberry jam on the door frame that Lucy carefully avoided. Kit crouched down and picked up a crushed plastic Spiderman cup and a baby doll with all her hair cut off. "Now I understand why Esther basically peeled out of the driveway," Kit whispered to Lucy.

"Should we check on the twins?" Lucy asked.

"Why?" Colin turned on the TV and restlessly flipped back and forth between the two channels. "Trust me. If there's a problem we'll hear about it."

Lucy readjusted the rabbit ears to get a clearer picture.

"So, I sort of think I should say sorry," Kit said.

Colin looked up. "It's all right. Apology accepted."

"Not to you, idiot. Lucy."

Lucy moved the rabbit ears to another position. "Me? Why?"

"The letters. I was so excited to get some answers and solve the mystery, I forgot that, well, that it might not have made your mom look so great."

"Oh. Um, it's okay. Not your fault."

"Yeah. But still," Kit said.

"Really, it's fine. It was your mystery too. And at least now you know that your mom was totally in the right. You know, about not talking to *my* mom."

"Well, I wouldn't say *that*. She could have forgiven her—her own sister. Plus, it was like a bazillion years ago."

Colin sighed and turned off the TV. "Is it really that big a deal? I mean, so your mom made a bad decision when she was a teenager. Is it going to change the way you think about her?"

"I'm not sure," Lucy answered honestly.

"But wasn't she a great mom and all that?"

"Yeah."

"And didn't you think she was a good person and stuff?"

"Of course."

"Then what difference does it make what she did in her past, way back whenever? You didn't even exist then. Why should you even care?"

Lucy opened her mouth to argue, then closed it.

"Everyone deserves a second chance, right?" he said simply.

"Yeah, but," Kit piped up, "don't people always say that actions have consequences?"

"*Who* says?" Colin said. "What people?"

Kit glared at him. "*People.*"

Colin shook his head and sighed.

"Looks like your mom's finished unpacking," Lucy said, attempting to change the subject.

Colin looked around like he was seeing the room for the first time. "Uh. I guess."

"Your dad must be coming soon."

He picked up two yo-yos that were tangled together. "Fingers crossed. Sometimes it's like living at a circus."

Kit drifted over to examine the photos on the wall. "What's this ginormous place?"

"It's where my parents worked out west."

Kit leaned in closer. "Are your mom and dad in here?"

It was the photo Lucy had seen before, up in Colin's room. She got up and pointed them out to Kit. "There. And there."

"Look at your mom's awesome cat-eye glasses!" Kit cried out. "When *was* this?"

"Colin," Lucy said. "Can I look at the date again?"

"Yeah, whatever." He was still busy with the two yo-yos.

Lucy pulled the bottom edge of the frame away from the wall and shoved her hand up behind, sliding the photo under the glass and revealing the tiny silvery writing: *October 1, 1961.*

"Wow!" Kit exclaimed. "I need to get me a pair of those glasses!"

Colin turned the TV back on and they ended up watching *Sesame Street* because they pretty much had no other options.

"You know," Kit said, "my head almost explodes every time they don't believe Big Bird about Snuffleupagus."

Colin and Lucy looked at each other. "Yeah, me too," they said in unison.

TRUE TO HER WORD, ESTHER returned in under an hour. Lucy and Kit left for home to grab some lunch.

In Josie's kitchen, Lucy made two peanut butter and jelly fold-overs and carried them out to the porch swing. She picked off pieces of crust and thought about what Colin had said, how he'd said he didn't see what the big deal was. He seemed to think a lot of things weren't a big deal.

Was he right? Maybe it wasn't a big deal. Why did she care so much about what her mom did in the past? Her dad would probably agree with Colin. He'd probably say the same thing he'd said to her before. Something like, "Your mom is the person you've known for fourteen years"—thirteen and a quarter—"and that's what matters," blah, blah, blah. Assuming he even knew about all this. *God. Does he?* Lucy rubbed a chunk of crust between her fingers until it was nothing but crumbs. *But isn't your past part of you? Doesn't it make you who you are? And what if something you did in the past hurt other people? Like Ellen. There needs to be consequences.* Kit was kind of right too.

Argh. Too much in my head.

She placed her uneaten fold-overs on the table. One of Josie's Harlequins was lying there, and she picked it up and glanced at the cover. *Shades of Autumn.* She snuggled down deeper into the cushions and began to read: *October was Diane's favourite month. When she was little, it was because of Halloween.*

Huh, Lucy thought and smiled. *Colin's birthday.*

But all that changed. Now it was because it was the month she would marry Luke, the man of her dreams. In only a few hours, Diane was going to be Luke's wife. This one was going to be good. Diane was obviously headed for disaster; you can't have a happy ending at the beginning of a book.

But as she read along, she was having a hard time focusing. She wasn't able to get past page one. Her eyes kept drifting back to the first paragraph. *Have I read this before?* She took another look at the cover. *No.* She started again, from the beginning. *October was Diane's favourite month. When she was little, it was because of Halloween.* Suddenly Lucy froze, and she stayed that way for what seemed like a long time. Then she slammed the book shut, tore down the stairs, and raced across the lawn.

When Lucy reached Kit's house, she was bent over, gasping for breath, and digging a fist into the stitch in her side. She pounded impatiently on the screen door, praying it would be Kit who answered.

Kit appeared, a surprised look on her face. "Hi!"

Lucy reached out an arm and pulled her onto the porch.

"Whoa. What the heck?"

"I just need to ask you a couple questions," Lucy said quickly, still bent over. "Make sure I'm not losing my mind."

"Okay."

"Remember when we were sitting around the hole with your magazines and talking about our birthdays and horoscopes and stuff like that?"

"Yup."

"When did Colin say his birthday was?"

"October thirty-first. Halloween. I'm so jealous."

"And he told us the year, too. What was it?"

"Nineteen sixty-one."

"Are you sure?"

"Yup. I'm the one who asked him. I wanted to know for sure how old he was to see if he might be in junior high with me, but he'll be at the high school."

"That's what I thought too," Lucy whispered.

"Why? You're freakin' me out."

Lucy took a deep breath. "You know that picture of Colin's parents? The one in the den with them standing in front of the hotel? The one we were just looking at?"

"Yeah."

"You asked the date it was taken. Do you remember what it was? What was written on the bottom?"

"October. October something?"

"It was October first, nineteen sixty-one. It was in tiny silver writing. You could hardly see it." Lucy could hear herself speaking faster and faster.

Kit scrunched her eyebrows together. "So?"

"Colin was born on October thirty-first, nineteen sixty-one. That picture was taken on October first, nineteen sixty-one. Notice anything *unusual* about Esther in the picture?" Lucy held her breath and waited for Kit to put it together.

Slowly Kit's face began to clear and her eyes got big. "She should be pregnant!"

"And she's not."

"Holy crap," Kit said. "Maybe the date on the picture is wrong."

Lucy thought for a second. "I don't think that's very likely."

"Maybe Colin's wrong about his birthday."

"I think he probably knows when he was born, and how old he is."

"You're right," Kit sighed. Then perked up. "*Or.* What if his parents lied to him about his birthday? I've heard of that before. Maybe they weren't married when he was born and they were worried people would be all judgey."

"I suppose...." Lucy let the idea roll around in her head. "It could be something like that."

"And you're *sure* Esther's not pregnant in that picture?" Kit asked. "Maybe we missed it, or it's just the angle or something."

Lucy squished up her nose. "Pretty sure. She's standing sideways at the end of a row."

They both fell silent, thinking hard.

"What now?" Kit said.

"Well, first we should probably just double-check that photo. Her stomach might be blocked by a head or something."

Kit raised her eyebrows. "You said she was standing sideways at the end of a row."

"We still need to double-check." Lucy's tone was firm. "And maybe we just didn't *read* the date right," she added. "Like, the numbers could be smudged or worn."

"We *both* read the date wrong?"

"Anything's possible." Lucy crossed her fingers. On both hands.

CHAPTER 20

JOSIE SLID THE BOTTLE OF SYRUP ACROSS THE TABLE to Lucy. "I believe I could rent you out to haunt a house," she said.

Lucy poked at her waffles with a fork. "I don't feel that great," she mumbled. She was really just exhausted. Between Ellen's letters and the fact that there was now some kind of mystery around Colin's birthday, she hadn't gotten a lot of sleep.

Reaching over, Josie lifted Lucy's chin. "Say it again."

"Don't feel great," she repeated and went back to poking at her waffles.

Josie lit a cigarette and looked at her thoughtfully through a haze of smoke. "Are you fighting with your chums?"

Lucy shook her head.

"You're probably constipated." Josie set her cigarette in the ashtray. "Let me get you some bran and marshmallows."

Lucy's back snapped straight. "No!" But Josie was already getting up. Lucy grabbed her arm. "I'm fine!"

"Are you sure?"

Lisa Harrington

"Yes, yes! I'm sure." She pointed to Josie's chair. "Really. I'm fine."

Josie sat back down and took a drag off her cigarette. "Could it be you're a little sad because you missed out on the root beer?"

"Yup." Lucy nodded quickly. "The root beer. That's what it is."

"So sorry, honey." Josie squeezed her hand. "I'll make it up to you."

Oh no. "You don't have to," Lucy said. "You've done...enough." Thankfully, at that moment there was a loud knocking. She pointed towards the door. "Door. I'll get it." And she ran from the table to the front door.

It was Kit. She had both hands cupped against the screen as she peered into the house.

"Hey." Lucy frowned and opened the door. "What are you doing here?"

"Ha! You look like me." Kit pointed to Lucy's scary bedhead, then her own.

"Thanks a bunch," Lucy said, combing her fingers through her hair.

"I couldn't sleep a wink," Kit said, all dramatic. "We need to go look at that picture again."

Lucy leaned against the door frame. "Well, we can't right now."

"Yes, we can. Let's go to Colin's and pick him up."

"We can't pick him up. We always all meet at the hole. We can't just show up at his house. That would be weird."

"I showed up at *your* house."

"Yeah. And it's weird."

Kit rolled her eyes. "Wow. Didn't know you were such a stickler for rules."

"Change is bad," Lucy said. "Let me just tell Josie I'm leaving and we'll head over to the hole. Like *normal.*"

Lucy returned a moment later and led the way down the

184

porch steps. "Come on," she said to Kit. "And relax. We'll figure out some way to get back to see that picture."

Colin was already there, digging. He gave them a quick nod when he saw them.

"We wouldn't have been able to pick him up anyway," Lucy said out of the corner of her mouth. "He's always here first."

Kit nodded, then she gasped. "Isn't he going to think it's suspicious we showed up together? We never do that." Before Lucy could answer, Kit yelled out extra loudly, "I, uh, had to drop off something to Josie from my mom! Um, that's why we came together!"

"Great!" Colin was busy trying to turn over a rock and didn't even look up.

"I think he bought it," Kit whispered, sitting down on a grassy spot.

"Bought what?" Lucy asked. "You need to cool it. He would never notice us arriving together, but he might notice if you're acting like a lunatic."

"You're right, you're right." Kit took a deep breath. "Calm and cool, that's me."

To counterbalance Kit, Lucy was determined to act *super* normal. She pulled out the bag of magazines Kit kept tucked away under a nearby bush and tossed her a couple. The morning passed like any other. Lucy and Kit read aloud some articles about back-to-school fashions, hairstyles, and celebrity gossip. Then they tortured Colin by explaining in great detail how to "Tame Frizz Forever," as well as how to "Double Your Summer Fun with 27 Easy Beauty Tips." They even made him take an "Are You Fit to Babysit?" quiz while he sporadically swore under his breath whenever the odd rock halted his digging. His quiz results were iffy at best.

Lucy felt Kit nudge her. She glanced up to see Josie coming towards them, huffing and puffing, a cloud of smoke floating above her head. "Good day, everybody."

They all raised their hands and waved.

"I was feeling so bad about the root beer disaster," Josie said to Lucy.

Lucy saw Colin and Kit smirk at each other.

"I made you an extra special treat to make up for it," she continued.

Uh-oh. Lucy closed her magazine.

"I've just finished frosting the most beautiful chocolate cake." She looked very pleased with herself.

Lucy's eyes narrowed.

"Why don't you all come up for a piece and a cold drink? I had to improvise with the icing, but I think in the end it all worked out," Josie said with a wink.

Lucy turned away so Josie couldn't see her lips. "If you know what's good for you, you'll say no," she warned them.

But they ignored her. "Sure," Colin and Kit told Josie in unison.

Lucy closed her eyes and let her chin drop to her chest. *Don't say I didn't warn you.* She followed behind them as they walked up the lane.

After they were settled on the front porch with their drinks, Josie came out carrying what looked like a chocolate cake.

"Ta-da!" she said proudly as she placed it on the table.

Suspicious, Lucy pulled her chair closer and leaned in for an inspection. There was something not quite right. It was the icing. There was definitely something wrong with the icing.

Colin and Kit watched Lucy first touch the cake with her finger, then tap it lightly with her knuckle. The icing was solid. There was a group intake of breath.

Looking up at Josie, Lucy asked, "What did you put in the icing?"

Josie puckered her lips. "Well, I was out of icing sugar, but I had a box of Pot of Gold someone gave me at Christmas, so I melted it down and spread it over the cake." She shook her head. "I added some butter. I didn't think it would set up so hard. Probably shouldn't have put it in the fridge, but it's so damn hot out."

Lucy couldn't help notice Josie had the same expression on her face as she had when she'd stared up at the root beer dripping from the ceiling. Like she just couldn't understand how this could have happened.

Josie picked up the knife and tried to cut the cake. It wouldn't go through. Next she tried stabbing tiny holes, scoring a line across the cake. That didn't work either. "Just a second. I'll be right back." She disappeared inside.

"You guys should have just said no," Lucy sighed.

"No way," Colin said. "I wouldn't have missed this for anything."

"Yeah, I'm sure it will be fine, uh, once we get it cracked open," Kit said, trying not to laugh.

"Don't hold your breath," Lucy said.

Josie returned, carrying a meat tenderizer. She wedged the tip of the knife into the cake, then gently hammered the top of the handle with the tenderizer until a spiderweb of hairline fractures were created. "Dig in!"

Using a couple of extra knives, they were able to pry the cake open. It wasn't so bad, really. The cake was slightly undercooked in the very centre, but it tasted fine, and once the cake was peeled away, a delicious chocolate shell was left behind to munch on.

"Yum," Kit said, licking her fingers after her second chunk.

"I guess it could have been worse," Lucy admitted. "It *has* been worse," she added.

"You have to wonder, though," Colin said, frowning at the cake. "What happened to all the fillings? Like the nuts and cherries and stuff?"

Lucy and Kit frowned at the cake too. "I think we're better off not knowing," Kit said.

After they made a pretty decent dent in the cake, everyone sat back in their chairs with their hands on their stomachs.

"We should swim this off after lunch," Kit suggested.

"I can't even think about lunch," Lucy said. "But definitely after a bit. I've some chores to do for Josie." Josie had asked her to roll up batch of cigarettes, but Lucy didn't really feel like telling them that. She wasn't quite sure what people would think about her new-found skill.

Colin stood and dusted some shards of chocolate off his T-shirt. "Actually, my dad's due home this afternoon. I kind of wanna be there," he admitted sheepishly. "You guys could hang with me and wait if you want."

Lucy and Kit looked at each other. *The picture.* "Sounds good," they answered.

"Call me when you're finished earning your room and board," Kit said to Lucy. "I'll pick you up on the way."

LUCY CLEARED OFF THE KITCHEN table and quickly got out all the supplies. This was her third go, and she was pretty accomplished by now. She could easily roll a batch in less than thirty minutes. When she finished, she dropped a long curl of apple peel into the tobacco can, put everything away, and phoned Kit.

It seemed like Lucy had barely hung up the phone when Kit arrived on the doorstep.

"You must be captain of the track team," Lucy commented.

"No. Patrol leader. Girl Guides," she wheezed, out of breath. "Be prepared."

"Lead the way then, patrol leader."

"I thought of something else on the way over," Kit said between breaths. "Maybe Colin's adopted."

Lucy stopped in her tracks. "Huh?"

"Well. Esther lived in a foster home. Maybe, you know, she wanted to adopt someone who needed a home, to like, give back or something."

"I never thought of that." Lucy started walking again. "You could be right. That would explain the picture." But then she stopped again. "No. That doesn't work. That first letter said Mom went to help Esther because she was having a bad pregnancy."

"Um...maybe Esther just *told* her that to get her there."

"Why?" Lucy said incredulously. "Why would she trick her? And why would she need help with an adoption?"

Kit closed her eyes and pinched the bridge of her nose. "I got it! Maybe she didn't want anyone to know Colin was adopted. Maybe she wanted everyone to think she was pregnant and she needed your mom to be part of the plan. She needed your mom to come and help her with her pretend pregnancy and then go back spread the word here at home."

Lucy let out a giant sigh. "That makes absolutely zero sense."

"Hey!"

"Why would Esther care about what they thought of her back here? She had no family to worry about. Also, why would she want to hide adopting a kid? Adoption is a *good* thing."

"Yeah, I guess." Kit nodded, looking deflated. "And if he *was* adopted, he probably would have said something by now." Her eyes widened. "Unless he doesn't know!"

"Oh, calm down, would you?"

"Well, how about my theory that they told him the wrong birthday on purpose?" Kit asked. "Because it didn't match up with when they got married or whatever."

"Yeah...." Lucy rubbed her forehead. "If it was such a big deal, I think they would just lie about when they got married instead of his birthday."

Kit dragged her hands down her face. "My brain hurts."

"We still have to double-check the picture. This could be all for nothing."

Kit didn't say anything.

"And even if it isn't, like if we're right about Esther not being pregnant...." She turned and looked at Kit. "What are we supposed to do with that information?"

"What do you mean?"

"Well, do we tell Colin? I can't picture us doing that." She paused. "I can't picture us going to Esther, either."

"So you want us to just keep it to ourselves?" Kit's voice was all squeaky.

"Yeah, I guess. I mean, it's not really any of our business."

"I know I said before that I could keep a secret, but I think I should tell you, that's a lie. I'm not that great at keeping secrets."

"I'm sure you could use the Force or something if you had to," Lucy said.

"It's easy for *you* to say. You're leaving for home in a while. I'm going to see Colin all the time."

"Kit!" Lucy said impatiently. "I'm sure we'll figure something out later if we have to."

"Okay, *fine*. I won't say a word for now. But I kind of wish I didn't know whatever it is we know. I think it's going to cause me a lot of stress."

COLIN PASSED OUT POPSICLES. "SORRY. The twins don't like orange, so that's all that's left."

"That's okay! We *love* orange!" Kit exclaimed.

Lucy shot her a warning look.

"Do you want to watch TV or something?" Colin said.

"You bet!" Kit cried.

Lucy shot her another look.

Colin didn't seem to notice anything unusual and turned the TV on. He flicked the channels a couple times. "*Spiderman* it is."

After a few minutes, Lucy casually wandered across the room to the photo on the wall. She searched out Esther. Third row, on the end. She was turned slightly inwards, facing the centre, and definitely not pregnant. Lucy's eyes shifted to the bottom corner. Miraculously, the photo hadn't slid back down into the frame from the last time she'd shoved it up. The photographer's signature and the date were clearly visible: *October 1, 1961*. No matter how much she squinted, how closely she leaned in and examined it, the date didn't change. She felt a hard ball form in her stomach. Could one of their theories really be right? Even the wacky adoption one?

The front door slammed, making her jump.

"Hello! Scotty? Kids? Anybody? I'm home!" a voice shouted.

Lucy felt an odd sensation, like something pinged against the side of her brain. She gave her head a little shake.

Colin leapt out of his seat. "Dad!" Then as if remembering Lucy and Kit were there, tried to play it cool. "Dad," he said in a deeper tone.

A tall man in a golf shirt and shorts stood in the den doorway. "The king of the castle has finally arrived!" he bellowed with his arms in the air. "Bring me my loyal subjects!"

Colin went over and gave him a loose hug.

Suddenly there was a ton of noise, kids running, suitcases toppling over—total chaos. Lucy and Kit shuffled off to one side, to observe from a safe distance.

Eventually Colin motioned them over with his hand. "Dad, this is Lucy and Kit. Guys, this is my dad."

Colin's dad shook both their hands. "Nice to meet you girls. I guess I should thank you for saving my son from dying of boredom. I heard through the grapevine that he was pretty miserable to live with before you took pity on him."

"Dad," Colin groaned.

There was more commotion as the twins tried to drag a large suitcase down the hall, cherry Popsicle melting and leaving a trail behind them. "Did you bring us anything?" Teddy shouted.

They were ignored as Esther stepped over them and gave Colin's dad a kiss on the cheek. "Dan, come have a cold drink," she said. "You must by dying after that drive."

Colin, Lucy, and Kit sat back down in the den. They could hear Esther yelling at the twins. "Would you get away from that suitcase? You're breaking the zipper!"

"We're looking for presents!"

"He wasn't away! He didn't go anywhere! Now *get*!"

They stomped off down the hall and outside to the deck, grumbling the whole way.

"Sorry about all the racket," Esther said as she stuck her head in the doorway of the den. "Colin, could you take those suitcases upstairs?"

"Sure."

"I mean now, not later."

"Yes, Mom," Colin sighed.

"Scotty! Come take a look at these papers from the bank!" Dan called out from the kitchen.

Lucy's head swung towards the direction of Dan's voice. *Wait. What?*

"Coming!" Esther shouted down the hall, then looked at Colin. "*Now*, Colin."

Colin got up from the sofa. "I'm doing it! *Jeez.*" He waited until Esther left the room, then sat down again.

Kit scrunched up her nose. "Who's Scotty?"

"My mom. Everyone called her that when she was a kid."

"Why?"

"She hated her name or something. Her last name was Scott, and I guess she was sort of a tomboy." Colin shrugged. "So she says."

Lucy touched a finger to her temple. That pinging sensation was back, but worse—like a swarm of bees trapped in her head, trying to get out.

"Oh, that's so cool. Having a name where everyone thinks you're a boy and then *voilà*! You're a girl." Kit fluttered her eyelashes dramatically. "Wish I could do it with mine, but Gibbons definitely doesn't work. Gibbs? Gibby? Bon? Bonbon?" She shook her head. "Nah. And I don't think Tapper works either, Lucy. Tap? Tappy? Appy? Nope. Not lookin' good."

But Lucy wasn't listening. She could only stare back at Kit while the pinging continued loudly in her ears. She shook her head again, hoping it would go away, but it didn't.

Colin noticed and asked, "You okay?"

"Yeah. I just...I feel kind of hot," Lucy said softly. A sweaty, clammy feeling was beginning to creep over her, starting at her toes and working its way out to her fingertips.

"I'm going to start to think it's my family or something. Not that I blame you," Colin tried to joke. "You want a glass of water?"

"No. I just need some fresh air."

"It's probably the cake," Kit chimed in. "I'll go with her. I was heading out anyway."

"Yeah," Lucy said. "You should spend some time with your dad."

Lucy ducked out the front door and walked quickly away from Colin's house.

Kit caught up and touched her arm. "Did you check? Did you see the date? Were we right?"

"Um, yeah. Yeah," Lucy said distractedly. "We were right."

"Hey. Are you really sick or something? Because I thought it was just an excuse, like to tell me about the picture."

"No. It wasn't an excuse."

"Oh gosh, sorry. Can I do—"

"I'll be fine. Don't worry." All she wanted was to get home to Josie's. When they got to the end of the lane, she said a quick goodbye to Kit and ran across the lawn. Once on the porch, Lucy glanced back over her shoulder. Kit was still standing there, staring after her and scratching her head.

CHAPTER 21

LUCY SAT ON THE FLOOR AND LEANED AGAINST THE side of her bed. She needed time to think, time to figure this all out. She hadn't really caught it the first time Colin's dad had yelled the name. But her brain had. It had tried to send her a message—she just hadn't let it through. It wasn't till she heard it again, and Kit had asked who Scotty was, that Lucy felt her memory kick into overdrive. The word *Scotty*. It was back. She'd heard it before. A couple times.

The first was when she'd eavesdropped on her dad's phone call. He'd been talking to a Scotty. Then there was that note from the box in her closet, the one her mom had written. The name had been written on that as well. She'd already connected those two Scottys, assumed they were the same person; how many Scottys could there be out there? They had to be the same one: Esther.

She thought back to that phone call, tried as hard as she could to remember it. What did her dad say?

"Part of me wants to forget the whole thing...How do you think she's going to react...How do you think he's going to react?... No, we'll do it together."

Forget what? And who is *she*? And *he*, for that matter? Did Dad even know Esther? Well enough to do something together? Do what?

And the note from her mom:

Talk to Scotty...figure out what to do together...please forgive me.

Again with the *together*. What could they possibly have to do *together*?

Lucy's head was starting to throb. What did it all mean? And why did she have such a sick feeling about it all? If she was living in a soap opera, she would think they were having an affair. No way. Not possible. She must be spending too much time with Kit. Or reading too many Harlequins.

She got up to stretch and walked over to the window. On the way, her eyes landed on the ceramic bunnies on the dresser. The big one was still in Josie's drawer under her pantyhose. She hadn't thought about the necklaces in a while—there'd been so much other stuff going on.

She leaned her forehead against the glass and stared out over the front lawn. Had her mom stood here and done the same thing? Did she use to hide out in this room to be alone and try to figure things out? Especially after Dean broke it off and abandoned her? Was this where she decided to leave home and ruin Ellen's life? How could she have chosen Esther when her family needed her here? And all to help with—well, there was no pregnancy, so an adoption? Could Kit be right? It made no sense. She was missing something.

The glass was getting warm. Lucy straightened and stepped away from the window. Her eyes swung back to the collection of bunnies. She got that pinging sensation again. Snippets of things Esther had said about her mom and Dean seemed to echo in her head. Things like how he called off the wedding because he got cold feet, and how devastated her mom had been, and how Esther had persuaded her to come help with her pregnancy, that the change of scenery would do her good. Mom had talked about Esther's pregnancy in her letters home to Ellen. If there was no pregnancy, that meant she was lying.

"No," Lucy said out loud. "Mom's not a liar." Esther *had* to have been pregnant. There was no way her mom would have left for anything less. There was no way she would have left without a good reason. "Not—" Lucy's brain paused, like it was shifting things around, putting them in order till they fit. Almost like a puzzle. Click. "Unless she had to."

What if her mom hadn't lied about the pregnancy? What if she just lied about who was pregnant? What if *she* was the one who was pregnant?

Her heart felt like it was skipping every other beat. Or maybe it was doubling up; she couldn't tell anymore. Lucy sank into the worn, velvet armchair. Even though she wasn't standing, she felt dizzy. She drew a deep breath in through her nose and let it slowly out through her mouth. Back in grade six, her mom had told her to do that when Lucy had been waiting in line to audition for the honour choir and she'd thought she was going to faint.

Kit's words sounded in her head: *Maybe they weren't married. People can be all judgey about that sort of thing.* She was right. People could be all judgey. Would her mom have been worried about what other people thought? Maybe. Maybe she was more worried about what her family thought. What her mother thought.

Her mom and grandmother weren't close, not from what Lucy ever saw. But had they been at one time? Would Mom have been ashamed to tell her? Afraid? Did she think Gran Irene would never forgive her? That she would disown her?

Kit's words sounded in her head again, this time from the Co-op parking lot: *We might just have to accept that it's something we may never have the answer to.*

She lifted her hair off her sweaty neck. Maybe she had read too much Nancy Drew, or watched too much *Columbo*. Or she was just exhausted and her mind was going all out of control. Closing her eyes, she could actually feel the thoughts zooming around in her head, like they were shooting across her brain and bouncing off the sides of her skull. Her eyes flew open. Colin.

She thought of the first time she'd met Colin and had a conversation with him. There had been something familiar about him. She had thought he reminded her of Jean Pierre from clarinet class, but perhaps it hadn't been that at all.

It was time to talk to somebody, but who? Her dad, for whatever reason, had lied to her. Esther? She figured she was lying too. Josie. It was time to talk to Josie.

After a few more deep breaths—in through the nose, out through the mouth—Lucy left her room to go search for Josie. She found her in the side garden. Lucy tapped her on the shoulder. "Can I talk to you?" she mouthed.

Josie nodded, took off her gardening gloves, and pointed to the bottom porch step. They both sat, and Lucy waited while Josie pulled a cigarette from under the ribbon on her sunhat and lit it.

Only wanting to tell this story once, Lucy reminded herself to speak slowly and carefully enunciate her words. An afterthought, she ran up and grabbed the notepad and pencil off the table, just in case, for backup.

She took a final deep breath and began. "Kit showed me some letters Mom wrote to Ellen."

Josie nodded and took a drag.

"She said she was sorry for leaving, but she was going to help Esther through her bad pregnancy," Lucy continued, then waited for a reaction. Josie didn't seem to have one. Worried she hadn't understood, Lucy wrote, *"Esther had a bad pregnancy."* Something changed in Josie's expression but she still didn't say anything, so Lucy added a question mark after the word *pregnancy.*

Josie's head was making little shakes. "I'm not the one who should be talking to you about this."

You're all I've got at the moment. "Esther wasn't pregnant, was she?" This time she didn't wait for a reaction. She put a big X through *pregnant*.

After a pause, Josie finally said, "No, she wasn't."

Lucy's stomach dropped like an elevator. *I was right.* Part of her had hoped that Josie would cut her off at some point, tell her she was crazy, off her rocker, nuttier than a fruitcake. And then Lucy would tell her about the phone call, and the note, and the date on the photo. But none of that happened.

Her mouth felt dry and she had to swallow a couple times before continuing. "Esther's not Colin's mother," Lucy said. "My mom is. Was." Josie wouldn't have been able to tell, but her voice had cracked on almost every word.

A look passed across Josie face, more a cringe, like she was in pain. She nodded.

"That means..." Lucy's back went rigid and her breathing turned shallow. "Colin's my brother. Stepbrother. No, half. Half-brother."

Josie frowned and lifted Lucy's chin. "Say it again."

Her hand shaking slightly, Lucy wrote, "*Colin's my brother.*"

It seemed to take Josie a long time to respond. She sucked on her cigarette and exhaled a giant billow of smoke. "I really wish your father was here."

It was Lucy's turn to take a long time to respond. "Why?" she asked, her tone flat. She was pretty sure her dad must know all this. He'd kept it from her, and she didn't how she felt about that yet.

"They wanted to tell you together," Josie said. "That was their plan, anyway."

Lucy closed her eyes. The phone call. Now it made sense. That's what they were going to do together—break the news. "Dad. How long has he known? Forever?"

Josie looked puzzled. Probably because Lucy's brain was working a mile a minute—she knew she wasn't speaking clearly. She wrote, "*Dad. How long?*"

"Not long," Josie said gently. "Just before your mom passed."

The note. Was that part of her deathbed confession? *How dramatic.* She knew that was a bratty way to think about it, but she didn't care at the moment.

"Did *you* know?" Lucy asked.

"No." Josie flicked her ash. "Shortly after your Gran Irene passed, Esther wrote me a letter explaining everything. Then your father came to see me, told me how he and Esther had been trying to figure out what to do. They hatched this fairy-tale plan to bring you here, let you meet Colin, let you guys get to know each other so that when they finally spilled the beans you two would"—she paused and shrugged—"maybe be all happy about it."

Lucy's eyebrows shot up. "That's a pretty stupid plan. What if we hated each other? Then what? They weren't going to tell us?"

Josie just sighed heavily.

"Or even worse," Lucy went on. "What if we liked each other. Like, *liked* liked? Ew!"

A look of confusion settled on Josie's face. Lucy started to write out what she meant but then stopped. She didn't feel like explaining it. "Never mind," she said.

"I told them they were livin' in a dream world," Josie said. "But they weren't listening to some batty old woman. In the end, all I could do was offer to help any way I could."

Off in the distance, the horn from a fishing boat sounded. Lucy leaned back and rested her elbows on the step behind her. There was something, a piece of wood or a chunk of peeling paint, digging into her arm. She pushed down harder until she could feel it almost breaking the skin. "I think it was selfish," Lucy said.

Josie reached over and turned Lucy's head. "Say it again."

"My mom. I think she was being selfish," Lucy said clearly. "She wrecked everybody's life then left us to put it all back together."

"She probably thought she was doing the right thing."

"The right thing would have been to take the secret with her," Lucy said.

"You don't really think that, do you?" Josie gently patted Lucy's knee. "And if your mother hadn't told your father, Esther would have."

"How do you know?" Lucy couldn't imagine that Esther would want to do that. Reveal to everyone, *including* Colin, that he's not her son? "With Mom gone, it was really only her secret to keep."

"Well, there was Dan. But in her letter she said it was time to deal with everything," Josie said. "That's why she moved back."

Lucy pressed her lips together to stop them from trembling. Everything was such a giant mess.

"I think we should call your dad," Josie announced.

Dad. She was mad at him for keeping this from her. She wondered how he was going to wiggle his way out of this one.

"Shall we?" Josie butted out her cigarette and stood.

Lucy nodded and pulled herself up from the step. She felt so tired. Then she stopped and turned. "So you didn't invite me here for the summer. That was their idea."

"True." Josie licked her thumb and rubbed some orange Popsicle off Lucy's jaw. "But I never dreamed I would have you, Laura's daughter, for a whole summer." Josie put her arm around her shoulders and nestled her snug against her chest. "I felt like I'd won the purse at Bingo."

Lucy buried her face in Josie's bumblebee-patterned gardening smock. The weird mentholly smell didn't bother her anymore.

LUCY'S HANDS WERE SWEATY AS she dialled. She could feel her finger slip when she stuck it in the hole. As soon as her dad said hello, she melted into tears.

"Lucy? What's wrong? Are you okay?"

"Yeah." She grabbed some Kleenex off the top of the fridge and noisily blew her nose.

He waited until she finished. "Pumpkin?"

"I'm okay, I'm okay," she hiccupped.

"You don't sound okay."

Silence. Then, "I know about Colin," she said.

Silence again. "How?"

"There was this photo, and then I—" She stopped. "Does it matter?"

"No, I guess not," he sighed. "I'm so sorry you found out—well, that you found out…not from me. It wasn't supposed to happen this way."

"Yeah. So I heard."

"You must be pretty angry."

"I'm more angry I didn't find out from Mom."

"Look. I can be there in two hours."

"No," Lucy sniffed. "It's fine." She wasn't sure if she even wanted to see him.

"It's *not* fine. We should talk about this," he said softly. "We *need* to talk about this."

"I'm kind of talked out right now."

"How about if I come up tomorrow? I have to be in court first thing in the morning, but I should be able to be there by lunchtime."

She opened her mouth to say no again, but then the tears came back. She unravelled the balled-up Kleenex. "Okay."

"And don't worry, pumpkin. Everything's going to be fine." He paused. "Is there, uh, anything I can help with now? Anything you want to ask?"

Lucy didn't answer.

"Okay then. You just sit tight until I get there."

"Dad?"

"Yes?"

"Aren't you mad at Mom? Aren't you mad she lied to you? To us?"

After a few seconds he said, "I'm not sure how to answer that."

After another few seconds, Lucy said, "Is there a difference between lying and not telling someone something?"

"There could be."

"Dad?"

"Yes?"

"Why did she keep it a secret? Why didn't she tell us?"

Lucy listened to him breathing. "She probably had what she felt were important reasons at the time," he said.

"Do you think she thought we wouldn't understand?"

"I don't know."

"I'm sad she never gave us the chance to find out."

"Me too. See ya tomorrow?"

Lucy nodded into the phone. "Okay. Oh, and wait, Dad?"

"Yeah?"

"Yours and Esther's plan? It was the worst plan ever."

He paused again. "You're probably right. Unfortunately, they don't write any how-to books covering this kind of thing. Trust me. I checked."

She knew he was trying to make a joke, but she didn't bite. "Like did you and Esther actually think we would be like, 'Awesome. We're brother and sister. Your mom is my mom. My mom is your mom. How great is that?'"

"That would definitely make things easier."

"Dad. That's not funny."

"I know, I know," he sighed. "Forgive me. Love you, pumpkin."

"Love you back," she mumbled, almost against her will.

THAT EVENING, LUCY STAYED IN her room and didn't go down for supper. "I'm not hungry," she said when Josie stuck her head around the door.

She lay on her bed staring at the ceiling for what felt like hours. *How could Mom have a baby and then just leave it? Give it away. How could Esther keep someone else's baby and tell everyone it was hers?*

Rolling over, Lucy reached her arm under the bed and felt for the corner of her suitcase. She slid it out just enough to dig into the side pocket and pull out her mom's passport. Shortly after her mom died, Lucy found it in the kitchen drawer. She kept it with her because it was the most recent picture, snapped only a few weeks before she'd gone into the hospital. Her parents had been planning a trip to Portugal that fall. She flipped it open and stared at the photo. Sometimes people told her she looked like her mom. Ellen did. Esther did too, said she had her mouth. Lucy wasn't so sure. Actually, the more she studied the photo, the more she could see Colin. The shape of the eyes, and they had the same nose. But maybe she was just imagining it.

A burning feeling began to inch its way up the back of her throat and she flung the passport across the room. She heard it hit the wall and fall to the floor. After a second, she jumped from the bed and scooped it up, checking for any damage. Frantically, she smoothed out the bent page as a tear dripped down her face and splashed onto the laminated photo. She crawled into bed clutching the passport to her chest and finally fell asleep.

When Lucy woke the next morning, she snuck out while Josie was standing at the counter eating her bran-coated marshmallows. She took the road instead of the lane to avoid Colin and Kit, who would probably already be at the hole.

She found Esther in the kitchen, washing dishes. Lucy raised her hand to knock on the screen door, but Esther happened to look up right at that moment. "Hi, honey," she said. "Colin's not here."

"That's okay. I came to see you."

Esther raised her eyebrows. "Oh?" She turned off the tap.

Lucy felt her heart thumping in her chest. She could hear it in her head and wondered if Esther could hear it too.

"Here." Esther pulled out a stool. "Do you want to sit down?"

Lucy shook her head. "I, uh, I'm not really sure how to start." She nervously pulled at a loose thread on the hem of her T-shirt.

It was like she wanted to give Esther time to figure it out so she wouldn't have to say it.

Esther gave her a strange look but didn't answer.

"I just thought you should know," Lucy whispered, "that I know."

It was quiet except for the hum of the refrigerator. Esther finally spoke. "How? Josie? Your dad?"

"No. It was a bunch of things." That's all she felt like giving as an explanation. "But that doesn't matter right now. You should tell Colin."

"I know." Esther touched her fingers to her lips and nodded. "I know I should."

Lucy hadn't moved from the doorway. She stood there awkwardly, trying to think of what to say next.

Esther sat down on the pulled-out stool. "Can I ask you something?"

Lucy nodded.

"How did you feel? Like, when you found out."

The question seemed to come out of nowhere. "How did I feel?" Lucy repeated. Were there words that could express how she felt? Did she even *know* how she felt? "Well, not *great*. I mean, this was a secret you and my mom kept for years. How do you think I feel? How would *you* feel?"

Esther lowered her eyes and stared at her hands.

Lucy leaned back against the door frame. "Actually, I don't think it's *my* feelings you should be worried about right now."

"Is your dad here?" It was like Esther sort of zoned out and hadn't heard her.

"This afternoon."

"Will you guys come?"

"Come where? What do you mean?"

Esther looked up. "Could you be here when I tell him?"

Lucy started shaking her head. "I—I don't think that would—"

"Please?"

All Lucy wanted to do was turn and run. Then she saw the raw desperation on Esther's face. "Uh. Okay. I guess." As soon as she said it, she regretted it. But she kept her mouth shut. Her being there might make it easier for Colin.

She certainly wasn't doing it to make it easier for Esther.

"ARE YOU SURE ABOUT THIS?" Lucy's dad asked.

"No. But it's too late now."

Lucy's dad stared apprehensively at the bowl Josie had just placed in front of him. "What's this supposed to be?" he whispered.

"Dad, she can't hear you, remember? You can talk normal. And it's *supposed* to be stew."

He glanced behind him at Josie ladling out a bowl for Lucy, then back down at his own bowl. "Are you sure?" he whispered again.

Lucy rolled her eyes. "Am I sure that it's stew? Or am I sure about being there when Esther tells Colin?"

"Both, I guess," he said, putting down his fork.

"Try the carrots. They're from the garden and usually pretty good."

He turned up his nose and pushed the bowl away. "Shall we get this over with, then?"

"You mean eating our stew?" Lucy stabbed her fork into a carrot. "Or going to Esther's?"

He smiled grimly. "I think I'll pass on the stew. I'm not that hungry." Then he stood and held out his hand. "Let's do this."

Lucy chewed her carrot and looked thoughtfully at her dad's extended hand. "I have to have a few bites first so she knows I made an effort. I'll meet you outside."

He nodded, and let his arm drop. "Okay. Take your time. I'll wait for you on the porch."

A chunk of undercooked carrot lodged in Lucy's throat as she watched him leave.

CHAPTER 22

COLIN DRAPED HIMSELF OVER THE ARMCHAIR. "What's up?"

Lucy looked at him from across the room. She couldn't understand it. He didn't seem suspicious at all. Wasn't he wondering why his mom called him downstairs? Why Lucy and this strange man were here?

"Colin," Esther said, smiling nervously. "This is Lucy's father, Mr. Tapper."

Colin gave a quick nod. "Hey."

"Uh, hey." Lucy's dad mirrored Esther's nervous smile.

"We," Esther started, then stopped. "I mean *I. I* have something to talk to you about." Her voice trembled slightly and Colin's dad reached over and squeezed her shoulder.

Lucy's insides felt all twisted and knotted up. *Oh, no. This is really happening.*

As if picking up on Esther's serious tone, Colin sat up a little straighter in his chair. "Like what?"

"Um. Something I should have told you a long time ago." She

kept clasping and unclasping her hands. "Something I hope you'll be able to forgive me for."

Lucy's heart was ricocheting around inside her chest. She wished she was anywhere but here and had to stop herself from hiding behind the nearby curtain.

"Just start at the beginning, Scotty," Colin's dad coaxed. "I'll be beside you the whole way."

She reached up, covered his hand with hers, and took a deep breath. "Remember when I told Lucy about her mom being engaged before? To Dean?"

"Yeah," he said slowly.

"Well. I said he called off the wedding because he got cold feet. But there was a bit more to it than that. Laura was pregnant. That was the real reason."

There were a few seconds of silence, then Esther continued. "You'd think that would make Dean want to marry her more. But I guess he wasn't ready to be a father. He took off."

Lucy looked around the room to see if anyone had a reaction. There was nothing.

"Laura didn't have a clue what was she going to do," Esther went on, "and she was too terrified to tell her mother." She shook her head. "God, Irene would have had a heart attack."

Lucy thought of something and she said it out loud without thinking. "Did Gran Irene find out? Is that what made her sick? Made her have a stroke?"

"That would sort of make sense, wouldn't it? But no. She had her stroke right after the wedding was cancelled. And of course, that made the idea of Laura telling the truth even more out of the question. She was too worried Irene wouldn't be able to take it, that it would affect her recovery."

Colin looked confused. "But Mom. What does—"

Esther put up her hand. "Please. Let me get this all out." She took another deep breath. "Then to top it all off, Dean died. I was out west and had just started a new job. I couldn't come back. Laura was in a bad way, at the end of her rope, and there was nothing I could do to help. I knew that she was running out of time—there was only so long she'd be able to keep the secret. I still can't figure out how she managed to hide it for as long as she did." Esther went over and sat in the chair next to Colin. "Then finally I had an idea."

Lucy watched the confusion on Colin's face deepen.

"I got Laura to start telling everyone that *I* was pregnant," Esther told Colin. "The expectations for me here were already pretty low, running off with my boyfriend and all that, so no harm done." Esther smiled weakly. "Dan and I were married at City Hall as soon as we got to Banff, but no one knew or cared except Laura. Anyhow, I made her spread the word that I was having a really hard time and that I was begging her to come. It was my idea to pawn her engagement ring and buy a train ticket. I knew if I just got her out there with me, it would all be okay. She arrived in August and stayed with me and your dad until she had her baby. Three weeks early. On Halloween."

Everything stopped. Silence enveloped the room like a heavy wool blanket. Then someone cleared their throat. Lucy didn't know who because she was staring at her feet. She didn't want to look at Colin; it would be too brutal, like an invasion of privacy or something. Finally she got up the nerve to glance sideways. She could tell he was processing. A second later it happened. He'd put it together.

"You're not my mom," he said hoarsely. "Lucy's mom is." He kept blinking over and over, like he couldn't make sense of the words he was saying.

"I'm so sorry," Esther said and buried her face in her hands.

There were a bunch of different expressions flickering across his face. They kept changing. At one point, Lucy saw him mouth the word no.

Colin's dad, Dan, took a step towards him. "Son—"

"You're not my dad. Don't call me that!"

Dan looked stung.

Lucy felt her own dad's hand encircle hers and give it a squeeze. But her hand just lay there limp. She sort of felt numb, like all this was her fault and she wanted to take everything back.

"Colin," Esther pleaded. "We really thought we were doing what was best. Laura couldn't raise you. Your dad and I could. It all made sense. Back then."

Dan knelt down beside Colin's chair. "Colin. I can't imagine what you're feeling." He put a hand on his arm. "But just remember we love you. We couldn't love you any more if you were our own."

Colin yanked his arm away and stared back at his dad like he didn't recognize him.

"You *are* our own," Dan added, his voice breaking with emotion.

Then, as if all of a sudden remembering she was there, Colin swung his head towards Lucy. "Did you know? Were you in on this?"

Lucy's lips parted in a gasp.

"No," Esther said quickly, answering for her. "She didn't know a thing. We, me and your dad, *and* Mike"—she gestured to Lucy's dad—"we were going to tell you both together this summer."

"Oh. Well I guess that makes everything okay then," Colin mocked. "Since you were going to tell us this summer anyway."

Esther shoved her hair back off her forehead. "You probably won't believe me, but it wasn't supposed to be a forever thing. It was only supposed to be until Laura figured out what she wanted to do."

"You mean until she figured out if she wanted me!"

"You don't understand. After Laura came home, Ellen wasn't speaking to her. Irene wouldn't even look at her. They both felt betrayed and angry that she just up and left them when they needed her most. Laura couldn't bring herself to tell them the real reason she left."

"They may have understood," Lucy said softly.

Esther frowned. "Ellen, perhaps. But your gran?" She stood and wiped her palms on her shorts. "Who knows. I've been wrong about pretty much everything. Maybe it would have been all hearts and flowers."

"So you guys did nothing?!" Colin exclaimed. "You kept me, and she let you?"

"We were waiting for the right time. It just never came."

"That's your excuse?"

"You were happy with us!" Esther's eyes were wet with tears. "Laura knew that, knew you had a good home. Like your dad said. You are our son. In every sense of the word."

"Stop calling me that!"

"But you are. Time kept passing. The twins were born. You are part of the family, *our* family."

Colin's eyes narrowed. "I'm not part of any family. I'm an orphan," he spat. "Both my parents are dead."

Esther's hand flew to her stomach like she'd been punched. Then she lifted her chin. "Yes, Laura was your biological mother, but I am your mother in all the ways that matter. You are my son and I love you. You don't know what it was like waiting for the day to come when she'd ask for you back, how terrifying it was."

"*That* obviously never happened," Colin said sarcastically.

"It's easy to look back now and say what we *should* have done, but sometimes doing the right thing is hard," she said, sweeping her fingers across her cheeks.

"Well, we wouldn't want you to do anything *hard,* now would we?" Colin's eyes darted around the room. "I gotta get out of here."

Esther stepped sideways and tried to block his way.

"Let him go," Dan said gently.

She moved aside.

Lucy watched Colin storm out, heard the screen door bang shut.

Esther sank back down onto the chair.

"He'll need some time," Lucy's dad said to Esther.

"Promise me, Mike, that you'll stick to what we discussed," Esther whispered. "That you won't take him."

"Of course."

"Because you have more claim to him than I do," Esther pointed out.

"I told you," Lucy's dad said, "I would never dream of taking him from you."

Esther leaned her head back and closed her eyes. A tear trickled out of the corner of one eye. "I don't want him to think Laura didn't want him. She did."

"He'll come to understand that. In time," he said.

"I feel guilty I kept him. I feel guilty I didn't make more of an effort to have them spend time together, get to know each other." She twisted up her mouth. "Maybe I should have encouraged her to come clean, tell Colin she was his mother, take him and make him part of her life, her family." She let out a high-pitched laugh. "Who am I kidding? There's no way I would have ever been able to do that. What kind of person does that make me?"

"I'm not defending anybody," Lucy's dad said, "but it's not all on you, Scotty. For whatever reason, Laura never asked to take him back. Not that I would have wanted her to, but she could have at any time—and she didn't."

The room fell quiet again. Her dad's words could be taken in more than one way. There was an uncomfortable awkwardness that went along with that, and Lucy felt it.

"I can only assume it was because she couldn't bring herself to tear apart our family," Esther said softly. "How does one go about doing something like that without destroying everyone's lives? In the end, we were both just giant cowards."

Lucy found her voice. "Is that why you took Colin to Mom's funeral? Because you felt guilty?"

"Partly, maybe. I knew it was only a matter of time till he found out the truth. I wanted at least to be able to tell him he got a chance to say goodbye to his mom, even if he didn't know it at the time." A fresh tear leaked out and dribbled down Esther's cheek.

Lucy was conflicted. Should she feel grateful to Esther for everything she did to help and protect her mom? For some reason Lucy couldn't quite get there. "If Mom had never gotten sick, would you guys have ever told?"

Esther opened her eyes. "It doesn't matter. She did get sick. And she told. She told your father."

"That's not what I asked, though."

"Secrets like this rarely stay secret." She shrugged her shoulders. "But honestly? I don't know. I certainly never pushed for it. Laura wanted me to move closer to home so at least she could see Colin more often. I was afraid, though. Partly because I didn't want to see them bond. That would hurt too much. And also because I didn't want to come back here. I had this strange—I dunno, this strange feeling that if Irene ever laid eyes on him, she'd know right away. He does look a lot like her, you know. I managed to convince Laura of that too. I think it sort of scared her and she stopped asking." She raked her hands through her hair. "But I was probably just looking for an excuse."

"Oh." It was all Lucy could think of to say. Esther still hadn't really answered her question. Something dawned on her. "Gran Irene died without knowing she had a grandson."

"Not to sound cruel, but I can't help but think that it was for the best."

Lucy wasn't so sure. It did sound cruel to her. But then she thought about all those trips to the nursing home, how Gran Irene barely knew who they were. Throwing Colin into the mix wouldn't have helped anything.

A concrete weight seemed to be pushing down on Lucy's chest. Feeling the need to escape, she let go of her dad's hand and slipped out the back door. Colin was nowhere to be seen.

"He headed for the path," a voice said.

It was Kit. She was dangling off the tire swing in the yard.

"What are you doing here?" Lucy sputtered.

"You didn't come to the hole this morning," Kit said. "After lunch I went to Josie's to see if you were okay. I thought you might still be sick. She told me your dad was here and that you were at Colin's, and then she told me I should just go home and wait to hear from you."

"So you came here."

"Well, my Spidey senses were tingling."

Lucy glanced towards the open window. "You heard everything?"

"I got the gist. I don't even know what to say."

"That's good, because I don't want to talk about it."

"So it's true? Your mom is Colin's mom? You guys are like... brother and sister?"

"I thought you said you didn't know what to say."

"Sorry," Kit mumbled.

The screen door swung shut and Lucy's dad hurried down the back steps. "Are you ready?" he said to Lucy. Then he looked at Kit. "Hi. You must be Kit. I'm Lucy's dad."

"Nice to meet you. What's your first name, though?"

He raised his eyebrows. "Uh, Mike."

"You're my uncle. I'm going to call you Uncle Mike."

"Sounds like a plan," he said, then turned to Lucy. "Can I talk to you for a second?"

"It's okay, I'm leaving," Kit piped up. "I'm gonna go find Colin."

"I'll catch up," Lucy said as Kit took off towards the path.

"Well." Lucy's dad scratched at his stubble. "All that with Colin. That went, uh...."

"Not so great," Lucy finished.

"You hit the nail on the head," he said. "How much time do you need?"

"For what?"

"To pack your stuff."

"Pack my stuff?"

"You didn't think I was just going to leave you here, did you?"

"I hadn't really thought about it."

"I assumed you'd be happy. Going home early. You didn't want to come in the first place, remember?"

"Yeah, I know, but—"

"Listen, pumpkin." He sighed and rubbed his eyes. "I think you should come home. We need time, just the two of us, to figure this out, get our heads around it. We need to decide how all this is going to fit into our lives, how we *want* it to fit into our lives. And I don't think we, or you, can do that here." He paused and looked over his shoulder at Colin's house. "Not with it all around you every day."

There was something about his tone that made Lucy frown and tilt her head. There was an edge to it.

Suddenly an imagined mental image swam before her eyes. Her dad standing at her mom's bedside while she wrote him notes explaining everything—explaining Colin. Was that really how she did it? Lucy had only found that one note. Were there others? Hopefully her mom had told him when she could still talk. What was it like for him when he found out? Like her, he probably would have been just fine with this staying a secret forever. He must have felt awful—to be blindsided when it was really too late to do anything about it.

"Okay, Dad," she said quietly.

"Good." His face filled with relief.

"It's just that I can't go right now, like today." The thought of rushing through a goodbye to Josie and possibly not even being able to say goodbye to Colin and Kit....

"Can I have a week, maybe?"

"A *week*?"

"Yeah."

He gave her a tired smile and placed a hand on her hair. "To get your affairs in order?"

She nodded. She knew Colin was going to have a hard time adjusting to what he had just found out, harder than her. But like it or not, he was part of her family now, and she might be the only one who could help. She had no idea how, but some tiny voice was telling her she should stay and at least try. Maybe the voice was her mom's.

"I guess you could call it that."

"Should we head back to Josie's?"

"You go. I'm going to track down Kit. Who hopefully tracked down Colin."

"Okay. Good luck." He hugged her tight. "See you in one week."

"Love you, Dad."

"Love you, too."

LUCY COULD SEE A FLASH of pink through the trees—Kit's T-shirt. She was crouched down behind a bush a little way away from the hole. Lucy ducked down and joined her.

"I just got here," Kit said. "I checked the beach first. Thought he'd go there to contemplate life and stuff. But then I found him here. Digging. I didn't know what to do, so I'm spying."

Lucy spied too for a moment. "He's not digging. He's putting the dirt back in the hole."

"That's what I thought he was doing, but I told myself I was probably just hallucinating." She looked over at Lucy. "Why would he do that? He spent *forever* digging that hole."

"I'm not sure," Lucy said slowly. Then she backed up into the trees and stood. "Come on."

"Where?"

"To get some shovels."

"Why?"

"We're going to help him fill in that hole."

Kit's jaw dropped. "How many times have I told you, I have very delicate hands."

"Exactly zero times," Lucy said folding her arms.

"*Fine.*" Kit hung her head in defeat. "Let's go get some shovels. And gloves," she added.

CHAPTER 23

LUCY AND KIT MADE THEIR WAY ACROSS THE FIELD to the hole, dragging behind them two shovels they'd found in Colin's barn. He didn't look up; he didn't say a word; he just kept shovelling. The girls joined in, and for hours they worked in silence. The only sound was of dirt and rock as it slid onto and then off the metal shovels.

The sun was beginning to set and they still weren't even close to being finished. Lucy's shirt was plastered to her back and she could feel the sweat running down her arms and dripping off her elbows. She glanced over at Kit and wondered if she was thinking the same thing as her. Was Colin ever going to stop shovelling? Or speak, for that matter?

Dusk streaked oranges, pinks, and reds across the sky, which was beautiful but also brought the bugs out in full force. Lucy and Kit started swatting at mosquitoes like they were doing a dance.

It was as if the slapping sounds made Colin realize they were still there. He looked up. "Thanks," he said.

Kit let out a huge breath. "Finally! I don't think I've been quiet for this long in my whole life!"

Colin ignored her and rested his chin on the handle of his shovel. "Guess I'm not going to finish this tonight."

Lucy chewed on her lip for a second. "We can get a fresh start tomorrow morning. That'll give us the whole day. The three of us should be able to get it done." She didn't have to look to know Kit was glaring at her.

"Sure," Kit said half-heartedly.

"You should go home. Get some rest," Lucy said to Colin.

"Home," he scoffed. "Yeah, right." He stabbed his shovel into the nearby pile of dirt and started walking off in the direction of the beach.

"Wait." Lucy ran up behind him. "Do you want some, I dunno, company?"

He shook his head. "No. No thanks," and continued on his way.

Lucy watched him until his outline was swallowed up by the darkness.

Kit came and stood beside her. "Don't worry about him," she said. "The beach is good place to think about things. He needs a place like that right now."

JOSIE'S TUNA NOODLE BAKE SAT like a brick in Lucy's stomach—even more than most of her cooking.

"Don't bother finishing that," Josie said, taking away Lucy's plate. "Let's have strawberries and ice cream out on the porch. I got a new Harlequin. I'll let you read it first."

Lucy nodded. She couldn't believe it, but she couldn't imagine anything she'd rather do at the moment.

Josie hadn't mentioned Colin or asked about what happened at Esther's. Lucy assumed her dad had filled her in on everything before he left and that she was probably waiting to see if Lucy would bring it up first. She wasn't going to.

Later, as Lucy was getting ready for bed, there was a light knock. "Come in," she called, then winced. *How do I keep forgetting?* She went over and pulled open her door.

Josie was standing there holding the missing ceramic bunny from her pantyhose drawer. She tilted back the head and took out the velvet pouch. "These are for you," she said. "I came across them a while back when I was housecleaning."

Housecleaning? Really?

"I was sneaky and took them out of your room," Josie continued. "I'd forgotten they were there. I didn't want you to find them and start asking questions." She made a face as she stared down at the pouch. "I probably didn't even need to, though. Most likely you would never have found them. You don't seem like the snooping type."

Lucy dropped her eyes to the swirly roses on the rug. *No point bursting her bubble now.*

"These were your mother's. She bought them as bridesmaid gifts for her wedding to Colin's father," Josie said, placing the pouch in Lucy's hand.

About to close her fingers around the pouch and say thanks, Lucy realized that she should be acting curious, like she didn't have a clue what this was. She plastered on a puzzled frown and asked, "What are they?"

"Open it."

Lucy unsnapped the pouch and slid out the necklaces. "Ooooh. Pretty," she said, pretending to be all surprised.

"They're emeralds. Emerald was always your mother's favourite."

It was? Suddenly she remembered her mom's dinner ring. It was a square emerald surrounded by little diamonds. Her dad had given it to Lucy after her mom died, but it didn't fit and was a bit too fancy for a fourteen-year-old. She'd just tucked in the back of her jewellery box and forgotten all about it until just now.

"Maybe you can think of something creative to do with them," Josie said. "Something your mother would have approved of."

"Okay," Lucy said, nodding. "I will. I promise."

KIT WAS SITTING ON THE grass, scraping the yellow middle out of a daisy with her fingernail. "Do you think he'll show?"

"Yup." Lucy sounded more sure than she felt.

"I wonder how his night was."

"Not good, I'm guessing."

"Do you think he talked to them or anything?"

"He probably went straight to his room."

Kit wound the daisy stem around her finger. "Same as my mom. I told her the whole story, like everything I heard at Esther's. She got this look like she was melting. I thought she was going to faint."

"It's a lot to take in."

"She went to her room and stayed there for hours," Kit said, leaning back on her elbows. "I gave up waiting and went to bed."

Lucy didn't say anything. She kept watching the break in the trees where Colin usually appeared.

"I bet she spent some of that time rereading those letters," Kit added after a moment.

"You're right. I bet she did. They have a whole different meaning now."

"I have a confession," Lucy started. "In the beginning I was convinced the fight had to be your mom's fault, that there was no way it could have been *my* mom's fault. I was wrong, and I'm really sorry."

"Don't be. I thought your mom ripped us off by taking that desk, and robbed me of my inheritance. Call it even?"

Lucy smiled weakly. "Thanks."

"Though you probably kind of wish that was how it had really gone down," Kit said.

"No kidding."

Minutes later, Colin did appear. There was no "Hey" this morning, only a nod in their direction as he yanked his shovel from the pile.

Kit pulled a pair of pink mittens from her knapsack and slipped them on. Lucy rolled her eyes and handed her one of the shovels.

They worked in relative quiet except for some scattered bursts from Kit.

"It's way easier filling it in than digging it out, huh, Colin?"

Colin shrugged.

"I may sign up for softball. After this my arm muscles will be massive."

Colin shot her a doubtful look.

"Try this bulldozer move I invented." Kit demonstrated how she pushed the dirt over to the hole instead of lifting and flinging. Lucy actually did start doing it like that.

"Hey, Colin! Guess you can start calling me *cuz* now."

Lucy held her breath.

Colin made a face.

Josie brought them a pitcher of Kool-Aid with a stack of plastic glasses. Colin mouthed the word *thanks*. Lucy didn't think that counted as speaking.

THEY DIDN'T FINISH FILLING IN the hole that day. But by suppertime the next day, they were done.

Colin stared at the large patch of fresh, dark dirt. "It looks like a giant grave."

Lucy kept quiet and waited. She was hoping Colin would say something else. He'd literally uttered fewer than a half-dozen words in the last three days.

"Nice symbolism," Kit said, nodding her head in approval. "Like we were burying something, don't you think?"

Lucy sighed. Sometimes she wished Kit would just stop talking.

"Yeah. My life," he said dully.

Exhausted, Lucy dropped her shovel and sat down on the grass. She tried to think of something to say, something to make him feel better, but there was only one phrase that kept repeating over and over in her brain. "I'm really sorry, Colin."

He frowned. "Why are *you* sorry?"

"Because I started digging around," she said, then motioned towards the hole. "Not *your* kind of digging. The other kind."

"Neither kind of digging mattered," Kit inserted. "Yours." She looked at Colin. "Because, well, we've just spent the last few days, you know, *un*digging." She turned to Lucy. "And yours, because they said they were going to tell you guys anyway. It would have come out, whether you'd been digging around or not."

Lucy had to admit, Kit sort of had a point. "What happens now?" she asked Colin. "What are you going to do?"

"Well, it's not like I'm going to pack my bags and set off to find my real parents. They're both dead." His voice was cold and flat.

There was an uncomfortable stretch of quiet.

Until Kit broke it. "But you're not going to do anything silly, right? You're not going to run away just to run away."

"Nope," Colin said. "Nowhere to go."

"Okay." Kit seemed reassured. "I'm outta here. Big Cove Camp next week. Mom's taking me shopping. I need a new sleeping bag."

"Good luck," Lucy said.

Lucy and Colin sat quietly and listened to the drone from the fishing boats as they returned to the wharf after their day out on the water.

Colin laid back on the grass and covered his eyes with his arm. "I woke up in the middle of the night thinking, what was the point? Like what was the point of telling us? It could have just gone on and on. We didn't need to ever know."

"I'm not going to lie. I thought that too."

"I think they're more concerned with making themselves feel better than us. Well, my mom—I mean, *Esther*, anyway. I can't speak for your dad."

She didn't necessarily agree, but she knew he was in no mood to hear that. "What's it like at home? Are you guys speaking or anything?"

"Not if I can help it. Though last night when I woke up, I did go in and ask M—Esther why they bothered."

"What she say?"

"She said it would have to come out sooner or later. She said my birth certificate has my last name as Mosher."

Mosher. Mom's maiden name.

"She said so far she'd been lucky. When she registered me for school, she told them she'd been widowed but had recently remarried. That she wanted me to go by Conway, not Mosher. They bought it. But she knew her luck wouldn't last forever."

Lucy nodded thoughtfully. "I don't think luck ever does."

THE NEXT MORNING, WHEN LUCY crossed the field to what used to be the hole, Colin was already there. Something had told her he would be, even though the hole was no more. She stood beside him and surveyed the vast circle of lumpy dirt. "Hey."

"Hey."

Kit came up behind them. "I wondered if you guys would be here," she said. "I almost didn't come. My arms are killin' me. I had to soak in the tub for an hour."

"I'd rather not stay in that house," Colin said, picking up a rock and whipping it into the trees. Lucy heard his elbow crack with the force of his throw.

"You're still mad, huh," Kit said.

Colin looked at her. "You don't think I should be?"

"I didn't say that. But I mean really, you can be mad all you want—that's not going to get you anywhere, though. It's not like you're going to be able to go the rest of your life never speaking to them again."

Lucy raised her eyebrows. It always surprised her how reasonable Kit sometimes sounded.

Colin didn't answer and picked up another rock.

"Do you remember that time you told me everyone deserves a second chance?" Lucy said.

He looked at her sideways. "That doesn't sound like something I'd say."

Kit whispered to Lucy, "*I* remember. He did say that."

"I know," Lucy whispered. "Let it go, though."

"So, what do you guys wanna do now?" Kit said.

No one said anything.

"I think we should do something with Colin's hole." Kit put her hands on her hips and looked around. "Maybe get some big rocks and put them around the border."

"You guys do what you want," Colin said. "It's not *my* hole anymore."

"Come on, Lucy," Kit said, prying up a nearby rock. "Help me."

Lucy couldn't think of a reason not to, so she started lugging rocks over to the border of the hole with Kit.

Colin watched them for a while, and then, either out of guilt or boredom, started to lug rocks over too. It went faster then. They had almost the entire circle completed. "You only need about a dozen more," he said, stepping back and wiping his hands on his T-shirt.

"You giving up?" Lucy said.

"No. I gotta go. Dad—Dan—is taking me to look at boats."

"Cool," Lucy said, trying not to look surprised.

After he left, Kit said, "Do you think they're trying to bribe him?"

"He had to sell his boat for the move. A new one was always part of the plan, though not till next summer." Lucy bent down to adjust the position of her last rock. "So yeah. It's probably a bribe."

"Take it if you can get it," Kit said cheerfully.

THE NEXT COUPLE DAYS PASSED and Lucy could see subtle changes in Colin. Things were certainly not back to normal, but there were fewer prickly silences, fewer strained conversations, between *them*, anyway. She had no idea what was going on at home.

Josie kept a constant eye on her, always shoving food at her. Her dad called every night to ask how she was doing. She insisted to everyone she was fine. And for the most part, she was. There were times she felt sad, and mad, but then she would just turn her focus to Colin—it was way worse for him. For some reason that made it easier to act like she was okay. Though sometimes she wished she could be more like him. He didn't act for anybody.

"Well, I think that looks great!" Kit exclaimed, standing back to admire her handiwork. She had been constantly bringing baskets of assorted flowers that she'd stolen from her mom's garden and transplanting them into the "anti-hole," which is what they called it now. Lucy wondered how long it was going to take Ellen to notice all her flowers were missing. She was going to freak.

"It does look good," Lucy said, pressing down on the dirt around the newest clump of flowers.

Kit looked around. "Where's Colin?"

"He's at the beach. He's checking to see if there's anywhere to maybe build a wharf for a boat."

"That's actually a good sign. Like he's thinking ahead."

"Yeah, I guess."

Kit rooted around in her knapsack and pulled out a pink-and-yellow pinwheel. "This is to mark your first summer here." She stuck it amongst the flowers. "I still can't believe you're leaving tomorrow."

"I know." Lucy looked at her watch. "I really should go," she said reluctantly. "I've got to pack."

"Okay, we'll save our final goodbyes for tomorrow," Kit said. "Josie's invited everyone for lunch."

"Uh-oh."

"Don't worry. It's a potluck. Just bulk up on the potato salad, that's what my mom's bringing."

Lucy walked back to Josie's. She took her time, taking in the details, storing them in her memory. In one way, it felt like she just got here; in another, it felt like she'd lived an entire lifetime in less than six weeks.

She dragged her feet up the stairs to her room, much like she had on her very first day. The room was a mess, not cleaned once since she'd arrived—probably nothing to brag about. She pulled her suitcase into the middle of the floor and started throwing things in. There didn't seem to be much point in folding, or separating clean from dirty; she just gathered everything up and tossed it in. The familiar smell of smoke made her turn around.

Josie appeared in the doorway, puffing on a cigarette, sporting a new creation. A dress covered in Canadian flags. *Must have been on sale after Dominion Day.* "You should think about coming back next summer," Josie said, squinting through the haze.

"Really?"

"I'm going to miss having you around," she said gruffly.

Lucy nodded. "I'll think about it."

"Oh yes. The boat. Apparently Colin's getting one."

"No. I said I'll think about—" Lucy stopped and smiled. "Never mind."

Josie left the room, a cloud of smoke hanging in the air behind her.

Lucy stood up and flapped her arms. That was one thing she wasn't going to miss. She picked up her jar of beach glass off the windowsill. *I didn't fill you to the top, but maybe I will next summer. Next summer I won't get sidetracked.* She carefully rolled it up in her beach towel and placed it in the suitcase. Next, she collected all her stuff off the dresser. Many of the items left behind a perfect outline in the dust.

With her finger she wrote, *Lucy was here.*

Guess I'm one of those people now, too, she thought.

CHAPTER 24

"IT HAS A FISH IN ITS MOUTH," LUCY SAID, POINTING to a heron as it gracefully swooped in and landed on the sandbar. It was her last morning, and she and Colin were sitting at the top of the beach stairs.

"Not for long," Colin said.

They watched the heron tilt its head back and swallow the fish whole.

Lucy made a face. "Yuck."

"What time's your dad coming?" Colin asked.

"Any minute now." She rested her chin in her hands and stared out over the ocean. The tide was dead low, as low as she'd ever seen it. And the water was so flat and still, it perfectly mirrored the blue of the sky.

"Don't you want to be at the house when he gets there?" Colin asked.

"No. I want to sit here for a while." Her eyes returned to the heron and she followed it along the length of the sandbar. But then it suddenly flew away, startled by a bright yellow fishing boat as it pulled away from the wharf piled high with lobster traps.

"Josie says that I'm more upset about all this than I think I am." The words seemed to tumble out of Lucy's mouth all on their own. "She says it'll hit me after the dust settles, like later, when I'm back home. What if she's right? Makes me kind of afraid to go."

"Yeah," was all Colin said, but she wasn't sure if that meant he agreed or not.

There remained a bit of a strangeness between them. Neither one of them had talked about the obvious—that they were brother and sister. But maybe that was okay for now.

She lost track of how long they sat there, gazing at the water, saying nothing, breathing in the salty smell of low tide. The sound of whistling floated through the air. *Star Wars*. Lucy hadn't heard that for a while. She glanced over her shoulder to see Kit coming towards them in her full Princess Leia getup. Lucy smiled widely. She was glad to see her. Conversation seemed to flow more easily when Kit was around—she filled in any breaks or pauses, even if it wasn't always with the right words.

"Lucy!" Kit called. "Your dad's here!"

"Okay, thanks."

"Nice outfit," Colin said, rolling his eyes.

Kit fake smiled. "I wore it for Lucy. For her last day."

"I feel honoured," Lucy said.

"Well, they're *all* up there," Kit said dramatically. "In *deep* conversation."

"About what?" Colin asked.

Kit put her hands on her hips. "What do you *think*? About you guys, of course. About doing stuff to bring the family together, blah, blah, blah, that kind of thing. And oh yeah, prepare yourselves, Josie will be cooking Thanksgiving dinner."

"Yikes." Lucy couldn't even begin to imagine all the ways Josie could massacre a turkey dinner. It was a disaster waiting to happen.

As if reading her mind, Colin said, "Isn't turkey one of

those things you have to cook right? So we don't all die of food poisoning?"

Lucy nodded. "Yup."

"It'll be fine. I'll suggest Mom be supervisor. Anyway," Kit turned to Colin. "I can't believe I forgot the most important part. I heard your mom—" She frowned. "Um, I mean *Esther*, tell Lucy's dad that the offer she and Dan made on the old diner in the village was accepted. They just got the call before they came."

"Oh." He turned back to stare at the ocean. "Good for them, I guess."

"Show a little enthusiasm, would ya? Don't you know what this means?" Kit asked him.

"Not a clue."

"*Hello*? You, me. Summer jobs for life!"

He didn't respond.

Lucy nudged him. "I know you said you'd rather sail, but it might be nice to have some cash too."

He just shrugged.

"He'll come around." Kit bent over and gave Lucy a hug. "It's going to be awesome. You can come back every summer and we can all work together."

Lucy smiled and nodded, because she didn't know what to say to that.

"Let's go, guys," Kit ordered. "They sent me to find you. They're gonna wonder what's taking so long."

Lucy glanced sideways at Colin. He didn't look like he was going anywhere soon. "Tell them we'll be up in a minute," she said.

"Okay, but don't take forever. I'm starving." Kit spun around, hiked up her bedsheet, and ran up the lane.

Lucy watched her go. "I'm going to miss her."

"For about five minutes."

"Be nice. Or you don't get your present." She reached into her pocket and pulled out the velvet pouch. "Here. I think you should have these."

He leaned away from her like they were poisonous. "Why?"

"Because they were for your parents' wedding, and—" She was still having a hard time getting used to the idea that one of those parents was hers too. "And, well, I sort of had an idea."

"Like?"

"If I were you, I'd sell them and put the money towards your new boat."

"I can't sell them. They have initials on them, remember?"

"I thought of that, but then I remembered Esther saying that my mom—I mean your—I mean our..." Lucy stopped and licked her lips. "Esther said that *Mom* was planning on having the stones taken out and made into something else. I bet if you took them back to Jacobson's they could do that. They could sell them and give you the money or whatever."

"Nah." He shook his head. "I don't want them."

"I really think." She stopped again. "She would have liked that idea."

He kept shaking his head.

"Just take them," Lucy insisted. "You don't have to do anything right away."

Colin stared at her outstretched hand. Finally, he said, "Okay." And he took the pouch and jammed it into his pocket. "Believe it or not, I got you something too."

"You did?"

She watched Colin pull out a wad of tissue paper from his other pocket. He passed it to her and she quickly unwrapped it. Her lips parted in tiny gasp when she realized what it was. "Ha." She held up the silver lobster charm. "This was the one I wanted, but I never made it back."

"I thought, what with everything that's been going on, you probably forgot about it."

"I *did* forget about it. I can't believe you didn't."

"Well. I really only remembered because we drove by the

jewellery store. We were on the way back from looking at boats. I made Dad—Dan—stop."

Lucy closed her fingers around the charm. "Thanks."

The tide had finally turned and a tiny breeze rippled across the water and up the stairs, just enough to catch the loose piece of tissue paper. Colin reached out and grabbed it as it was about to float over the bank. "Tell me something about her that I don't know."

It took Lucy a second to figure out what he meant. "Oh." He meant his mom. *Their* mom. "Um. Let me think. When she ate corn on the cob, she ate it one row at a time. She was like a tiny vacuum cleaner. The cob was spotless every time. It was bizarre."

"Hey!" He sat up straighter. "*I* do that! I do that too."

"I always knew you were a weirdo."

He gave her a shove. "What else?"

"Okay. Well, even though she grew up on this beach, she didn't like the water much. Some boy held her head under when she was, like, ten. She was always afraid of drowning after that. She must have really loved you to let you take her sailing. Me and Dad could barely get her on the harbour ferry." As Lucy said the words, she experienced a twinge of something. Jealousy? She jumped to her feet. "We should go."

They didn't rush, the heat making their steps leaden and slow. When Josie's house came into view, they stopped. Everyone was gathered on the front porch talking and sipping drinks. Lucy searched for her dad's face. When she found it, she was immediately filled with relief. But she also felt the burn of tears following right behind. It was because she was torn. Part of her was sad to leave Cape John, Josie, Kit, and Colin. The other part couldn't wait to get away. She needed to not think about things for a while. Though being home wasn't going to actually stop her from thinking. Josie's words were still crystal clear in her mind, what she'd said about it hitting her later, but at least if she wasn't here, she could be by herself and deal with it instead of having to pretend and put on a brave face and worry about everybody else. Did that make her selfish?

"What the heck does Josie have on? She's all in black." Colin craned his neck. "And is that a veil?"

"Oh, yeah. That. It's actually mosquito netting she stapled to her hat."

"Seems kind of depressing for a family lunch. Or is she just really sad to see you go?"

It didn't go unnoticed, Colin's use of the word *family*, but Lucy made no comment and just said, "No. It's for Elvis."

"Huh?"

She jerked her head around. "Elvis Presley. He died yesterday."

"What?"

"You didn't know?"

"No. I've sort of been in, you know, solitary confinement—self-inflicted," he added. "Guess I'm out of touch with world events."

"Muriel came over and told us last night. Apparently, they found him on the bathroom floor."

"Wow," Colin said slowly. "But it's a bit strange, isn't it? He's a singer. She's deaf."

Lucy laughed. "I thought the same thing. Josie said he was such a good-looking fellow when he was young and she loved to watch him dance. Something to do with his, uh, pelvis. What was the word? Gyrate. Oh, and also she felt they shared the same eye for fashion."

"Wow," Colin said again.

Someone on the porch must have noticed them standing at the edge of the yard. The news spread through the crowd, and one by one, everyone turned and began to wave. All of them waving and smiling, smiling and waving.

"Why are they acting all weird like that?" Colin said.

"They're probably not sure how they're supposed to act."

Neither Colin nor Lucy seemed to be able make their feet move off the lane and onto the grass. It was like there was some kind of invisible wall blocking their way.

Lucy lifted her chin and took a deep breath. "Well, you know what they say. You can pick your friends...."

"And you can pick your nose. But you can't pick your friend's nose," Colin finished.

"Gross, no! You can pick your friends, but you can't pick your *family*."

Colin raised an eyebrow. "Are you sure that's how it goes?"

"Yes," Lucy said, stepping onto the grass and pulling Colin behind her. "I'm sure that's how it goes."

WILLIAM HARRINGTON

L ISA HARRINGTON'S NOVELS INCLUDE *The Goodbye Girls* (2018), *Twisted*, short-listed for the Canadian Library Association's YA Book of the year, *Live to Tell*, winner of the White Pine, Ann Connor Brimer, and SYRCA Snow Willow Awards, and *Rattled*, published in 2010 to critical praise. Her work has also appeared in *A Maritime Christmas*. Lisa lives in Halifax with her family and puppy, Hermione. Visit Lisa online at lisaharrington.ca.